BOX OF SECRETS

SUSAN JANE WRIGHT

Crime Writers of Canada Awards of Excellence Finalist

Box of Secrets

Susan Jane Wright
Box of Secrets ISBN 978-1-9990-6842-4 (Paperback Edition)

Manufactured in Canada

Editor: Pip Wallace
Front cover photograph: Max Saeling
Book Design by JCVArtstudio

First Printing September 2021

Susan Jane Wright: susanjanewright.ca

To my darlings,

Roy, Kelly, and Eden

Prologue

Secrets come in all shapes and sizes. Some are silly little things, embarrassing once revealed but harmless; others are complex, dark, and deadly with a venomous sting. Only a fool tampers with another person's secrets without knowing their contours.

Julianna Westerberg was no fool. She'd discovered a secret that, if, handled carefully, would yield a remarkable opportunity.

Julianna was on the fast track at Gates, Case and White, one of the biggest law firms in the city. She would make partner in two years, three years tops. It was rare for lawyers at her level to be offered partnerships, but it had happened once before. Phil Dennison, the lead lawyer on Julianna's file, made partner in four years. Julianna worked harder and was smarter than Dennison, why should she have to wait any longer than he did?

Today Julianna was meeting with a very rich client, ostensibly to explore his options now that his latest business venture had run aground. The banks refused to lend him a penny (let alone the mega millions he required) unless he put everything he owned, including his mansion—the one that looked like a wedding cake—and his Bugatti, up as collateral.

The client was livid when she called to give him the bad news, then fell silent when she outlined what she'd discovered in her painstaking review of his corporate structure. By the end of the phone call it was clear to her client that the purpose of today's meeting was not to address his failed business strategy, but to advance Julianna's career. Today she would persuade the client to transfer all his legal work from Phil Dennison to her. Dennison would object, of course, but the golden rule at the firm was 'you eat what you kill.' If she became the lead lawyer responsible for all the client's legal needs, Dennison's reputation would be in tatters and hers would shine. In a few short months she'd become the youngest female partner in the firm's history. She was certain of it.

Julianna squared her shoulders as she entered the elevator and rode down to the main lobby. Normally she'd meet her client upstairs in the elegantly appointed lobby of Gates, Case and White, but today was Sunday, the elevators were locked down to visitors.

The elevator doors whispered open. She crossed the marble lobby and was surprised to see he'd brought someone with him, a lean wiry man who acknowledged her with a curt nod when they were introduced.

The three of them returned to the elevator bank and she waved her plastic cardkey in front of the sensor before pressing the button for the forty-fifth floor.

Her client made small talk as they ascended. Wasn't it a lovely day? Perfect weather for the long weekend, he said. Yes, she said, noting with wry humour that all the lawyers in the banking group were 'working from home' this weekend, the implication being she was the only one *really* working.

Julianna eyed her client's associate as they stepped off the elevator and entered Gates' reception area, a dizzying mix of reds, greys, and blacks. The wiry man was nothing like her client. Silent, bordering on surly, not the least bit convivial. She thought he was creepy and was glad she'd set up the meeting in the large boardroom that opened out onto the patio (Dennison called it the 'loggia') instead of the claustrophobic little conference room across from her office.

She waved her cardkey at the sensor on the double doors to the big boardroom and invited them to make themselves comfortable while she went back to her office to retrieve her file. Did they want coffee, tea, water? No, they were fine.

Upon her return she found the client and his associate standing outside in the afternoon sunshine, admiring the view. The concrete patio was protected by a guardrail, a waist-high sheet of plexiglass. She knew it was solid but its transparency made her queasy. She called to them. They didn't hear her, so she joined them outside, her hair lifting in the breeze which was surprisingly cooler up here than at street level.

Once again she invited them inside. Oh no, the client said, it would be a shame to waste such a glorious afternoon. Fine, she didn't need her notes to outline her position. The client narrowed his eyes after she finished speaking. "Have you talked to Dennison about this?"

"Why would I? You're the client, all you have to do is call him and tell him you're replacing him with me."

The client compressed his lips in a thin smile.

She'd made a mistake.

He shot a hard look at his associate. There was

movement. She felt unbalanced, for a moment she thought it was vertigo, and then she screamed as she hurtled down forty-five floors to the pavement.

The client returned to the conference room and picked up Julianna's file, taking care not to touch the surface of the polished rosewood conference table. His accomplice scanned the conference room; when they were satisfied everything was as it should be, they entered the elevator and descended ever so quietly to the main lobby.

They left by a side door, avoiding the crowd that had gathered in horror around the crumpled body of a young woman, once a rising star at Gates, Case and White.

1

EARLY AUGUST – 8 weeks to Election Day

I didn't see them at first when I entered The Bakehouse. I was dawdling at the bakery counter, eyeing the rainbow array of macarons when the sound of crashing crockery dragged my attention to three well-dressed patrons tucked into a quiet corner. Michiel Van Dijk, the most popular mayor the city had ever had, Nick Silva, his chief of staff, and Lisbeth Muller, his head of government relations, frozen for a moment in echoing silence before a server magically appeared with a broom.

"Lovely," Michiel said, as a cloud of icing sugar settled back onto the Paris Brest lying in the lap of his perfectly creased trousers.

"Michiel, Michiel," Lisbeth said, as she handed her boss a napkin. "We really can't take you anywhere, can we." He laughed. "Don't smear it," she said, "use a brush or something," as if most people walk around with a clothes brush tucked into their pocket.

Nick leaned back in his chair, an amused smile on his face. People rave about Michiel's charm and continental good looks, but in my opinion, it's Nick with his rich brown eyes, long straight nose and a smile that looks like it's hiding a secret, who stands out in a crowd.

"Evie Valentine," Nick waved an elegant hand. "We were just talking about you." All eyes swivelled in my direction. I paid for my macarons—it's Friday, I splurged on a dozen—and squeezed in beside them at the tiny marble-topped table.

"How are you, Nick?" I had forgotten for a moment that Nick goes by Nicholas now. His dark eyes became even darker but he let my *faux pas* pass. I've known Nicholas for eight years. We were in the same year at law school and articled together at Gates, Case and White. Michiel was two years ahead of us. We were no longer close but some relationships, particularly those forged in the bowels of a mega law firm, endure.

"You remember Michiel and Lisbeth," he said. I smiled hello. "We were just talking about Michiel's re-election campaign."

Before Nicholas could go any further Michiel interrupted him. He leaned across the cramped table and said, "My campaign kicks off in earnest in two weeks. Evie, I need your help." The tiny lines that appeared around his eyes made him look rugged, like a wrangler, but I doubt he's been astride a horse more than a couple of times in his thirty-nine years.

His request surprised me. "Why? You're a slam dunk." The election was in October, more than two months away, everyone knew Michiel would win, the only question was by how much.

Four years ago, Michiel Van Dijk was just an unknown lawyer with an unpronounceable name who, along with the Chicken Man (a nut who promised to change the city's bylaws so everyone could raise chickens in their backyards) stood no chance of winning in a race that included two high profile city councillors and a television personality.

Being a nobody, Michiel lacked donors with deep pockets so Nicholas, as Michiel's campaign manager, did something ingenious. He combined the guerrilla marketing techniques of a small start-up firm with traditional fundraisers like coffee parties and rallies. He turned Michiel into a magnet for enthusiastic young supporters who spread the word through social media. Everything Michiel said or did, no matter how trivial, appeared on Twitter, Instagram, and Facebook (his unfortunate encounter with the cream puff would be trending by now). Within a week of filing his nomination papers everyone was asking, 'Who is this Michiel guy?'

Michiel capitalized on the buzz by pitching himself headlong into an acrimonious battle with the City over the closure of three inner city swimming pools. His slogan, *Every Kid Deserves a Summer*, evoked images of squealing children plunging into chlorine-scented pools and set him apart from the other candidates who were oblivious to the impact of budget cuts on kids too poor to pay for summer camp.

If Michiel could generate enough momentum to rank in the top three in the Labour Day poll he'd be a contender. By some miracle he came in third and the election morphed into a three-way race between Michiel, a long-term city councillor and a TV personality who turned out to be more flash than substance.

The youth vote turned out in droves on election day. Michiel throttled the competition and became the youngest mayor in the country.

Four years later, Michiel wanted to recreate the magic in an election everyone knew he'd win hands down. His biggest fear was that come election day no one would show up and he'd win with the lowest voter turnout on record.

"Right," I said, after Michiel laid out his thoughts. "I'd love to help but I know nothing, zip, nada, about campaign strategy."

Nicholas glanced at Michiel. In addition to being Michiel's chief of staff, he was once again Michiel's campaign manager; this was the opening Nicholas had been waiting for. I recognized the intense expression I'd seen on Nicholas' face when we worked together at Gates. It was a little harder to carry off at The Bakehouse with the evening sun slanting through the wooden blinds directly into his eyes.

"We're not looking for campaign strategists," he said, "what we really need are smart people who aren't afraid to work hard and get their hands dirty."

"What about The Brat Pack?" I asked. The Brat Pack was a hyperactive bunch of young political activists who'd met on Michiel's first campaign and honed their skills to the point where they could join any campaign, be it for school trustee or prime minister, and deliver the votes.

"Oh, they're with us," Nicholas said, "but too many of them think they're the only reason Michiel won. I can't risk a colossal clash of egos." That made sense. Michiel had a way of making whoever he was talking to feel like they're the most important person in the room.

"What do you have in mind?" I asked.

"How about working with Lisbeth?" Nicholas said.

"What, like an office manager?" I glanced at Lisbeth. She had luminous blue eyes and shiny black hair that framed her face like raven's wings. She fixed me with an appraising stare. I couldn't tell whether she wanted my help or not.

I continued, "I've never managed an office in my life. I can't even put paper in the copier without it getting shredded." The best thing about working at a big law firm is there are plenty of legal assistants around to deal with the administrative side of things. Your job is to bill eighty-plus hours a week. You don't have time for breakfast? They'll get you a Danish. You're too drunk to get home from a closing dinner? They've pre-ordered cabs.

"I'll show you," Lisbeth said, her voice as smooth and cool as ice. "Unlike our last campaign where we had to do everything ourselves, this time we have so many volunteers I can't keep track of them all. That's where you'd come in, Evie. I have overall responsibility for the campaign office, you'd be my assistant. There's nothing to it."

If Lisbeth handled her campaign duties as efficiently as her responsibilities as the head of Michiel's government relations group, there really would be nothing to it.

"You'd set up volunteer schedules, keep the coffee on, order swag and campaign literature, oh, and put Domino's on speed dial." She pinned me with those eyes, then smiled. "I'm sure you'd enjoy it."

Satisfied with her pitch, Lisbeth picked up her espresso with one perfectly manicured hand and waited for me to agree.

"I am interested." I said cautiously. "I may be able to give you a third of my time, but I want to run it by my partner." Keith Lawson was a couple of years ahead of me at Gates when I suggested we start our own law firm. After a couple of months of sneaking around behind the firm's back we announced the creation of Lawson Valentine, the city's first law firm to focus on green energy. We'd been in business for four years and never regretted our decision.

Michiel and Nicholas exchanged glances. They knew they had me.

Two days later Julianna Westerberg fell to her death from the forty-fifth floor of Gates, Case and White. She was the first to die; she wouldn't be the last.

2

Mornings are chaotic at our house. Louisa was on night shift which made Quincy my responsibility. I don't know if all bull terriers are this fussy, but Quincy has to eat by 7 a.m. or all hell breaks loose. This means we have to be out the door for our morning run by 5:30. Every morning Quincy and I have the same conversation. Do we want to do the nature run along the river or the urban run through the Mission District where we can check out the breakfast specials at the coffee shops?

Quincy felt like terrorizing the fauna today so we picked the nature run. As usual, the jog back to the house, and food, was much faster than the jog away from it.

I dodged Quincy as he barrelled past me into the pantry. Holding him back with one hand I dug around in the dog food bag with a plastic cup. "Quincy, you little pig, you've eaten the whole thing." Quincy bounced up like a brindle rubber ball, sending me and the food dish flying. "Okay, okay, settle down. There's got to be another bag in here somewhere." There wasn't. Quincy had Shreddies and yoghurt for breakfast. He didn't seem to mind.

Quincy is Louisa's dog. My little sister is a nurse. She's brilliant at her job but lousy at picking husbands and made the classic mistake: she married her boss, a pediatrician. He loves kids—provided they belong to someone else. Too bad he waited five years to tell Louisa.

The divorce went relatively smoothly until they had to decide who got Quincy. I'm convinced he didn't really want the dog but used Quincy as leverage to get more than his fair share from the sale of the house and division of assets.

It seemed natural for me to invite her and Quincy to stay with me until she got back on her feet. That was three years ago and she shows no signs of leaving, which is fine by me. We were close as children and became even closer after our parents died. We compare notes on potential boyfriends, visit art galleries and farmers' markets and hunker down in front of Netflix. I complain to Louisa about my unrealistic clients and she vents about the neuro ward and the bureaucracy that threatens to push the hospital into the abyss. It's a very satisfactory arrangement for all concerned.

Quincy flopped down on his bed in the TV room while I had a shower. I wanted to catch Keith first thing to tell him about my plan to work two-thirds time from now until election day, October 6.

~

Keith and I have complementary work habits. I get in around 8 a.m. and stay late. He arrives at the crack of dawn and leaves by five o'clock so he can get home in time for dinner with his wife and young daughter and still squeeze in a couple of hours for splitting rails or building retaining walls or whatever it is he does out there on his country acreage. I found him at his desk poring over the newspaper.

"Did you see this?" He pointed to a story above the fold in the second section. "'City Police Investigating Suspicious Death'." He has a soothing voice; if he weren't a lawyer he could be a radio announcer.

I plopped down in his visitor's chair and placed two fresh lattes on his desk, pushing one closer to him.

He gave an appreciative nod and continued reading. "'About 1:30 p.m. officers responded to a report of a disturbance at 400-3rd Avenue SW. Upon arrival they found a woman on the pavement. Emergency responders pronounced the woman dead at the scene.'"

I caught my breath. "That's—"

"—Yep, on the sidewalk right outside Gates, Case and White. Apparently, the dead woman is Julianna Westerberg, a lawyer with Gates. She fell from the forty-fifth floor." He glanced up. "Did you know her? I don't remember her."

I shook my head. I didn't remember her either. Not that that meant anything. Junior associates were little more than cannon fodder at Gates, worked to exhaustion and tossed out if they complained.

He continued reading. "'The homicide division has taken over the investigation and an autopsy is scheduled for later this week. Investigators are asking anyone who may have spoken with Westerberg in the days leading up to her death, or anyone with information about the case, to contact police.'"

Two photos accompanied the story. One showed a couple of burly police officers cordoning off the sidewalk with yellow caution tape. The other was a close-up of Julianna and her partner Paul laughing into the camera. They were an attractive couple.

"I wonder how Dennison is handling it," Keith said. Phil Dennison is Gates' managing partner and top biller. In a law firm, like most large corporations, money and power go hand in hand. Dennison's leadership style, if one could call it that, left a lot to be desired. He was a former football player who thinks a law firm is like a football team, just with more players on the field.

I snorted. "Based on personal experience, Dennison's number one priority will be to keep the firm's name out of the papers. Julianna's family and coworkers? Not his problem."

There was an awkward silence as we flashed back to the events that triggered my decision to leave the firm.

Keith coughed, then changed the topic. "So, what's on your mind? You're not running off to the Island, are you?"

"Hah!" I love Vancouver Island but had no intention of ditching Keith and our partnership. I told him I'd bumped into Michiel, Nicholas and Lisbeth at The Bakehouse and they'd asked me to volunteer on Michiel's re-election campaign.

"I could give them a third of my time, things slow down here in the summer so it shouldn't be a strain on the firm's resources." Given that there were only three of us, this may have been an overstatement. Nevertheless, I pressed on. "It's not as crazy as it sounds at first blush." *First blush?* Now I sounded like Rumpole of the Bailey. "The Pegasus application is going to the regulator in mid November; AJ can keep the paper moving through September and I'll be back full time to do witness prep in October. I've got a few smaller applications on the go, but they won't be filed until November or early December. It's doable. Besides, I'm only a phone call away and the campaign office is just a few blocks south if AJ needs me." Alexander James Braxton, or AJ as he's known to everyone but his mother, is 32 and whip smart. He joined us three years ago. Keith still calls him *young* AJ, which is kind of funny given that AJ is only two years younger than I am. We're going to offer him a partnership next spring.

"I can be here in a heartbeat if things go pear-shaped."

Pear-shaped?

Keith nodded thoughtfully. "It's not the time commitment I was wondering about, it's whether our firm wants to be identified with a particular mayoral candidate."

"Look at it this way," I said, "every major law firm in town is going to donate to one or more candidates. Lawson Valentine has always been innovative, on the forefront of change; we're just donating my time, not our money." I wiggled an eyebrow at him.

He laughed. Lawson Valentine may be a creative, forward-looking law firm but Keith is a cautious, thoughtful lawyer who takes his time making decisions. Given my tendency to dive into situations headlong, this was probably a good thing.

"You know," he said, "making deeper connections with the mayor's office could be good for business."

That was a valid point. We had a solid roster of clients in renewables and alternative energy, but the extra cash flow from real estate and municipal law helps top up our billables.

I stood up and smiled at him, resisting the urge to give him a hug. I grew up in a Hungarian household, we were touchy-feely that way, but spontaneous bursts of affection were no longer appropriate in the workplace. "Right, well

I'd better get back to work. We've got a busy two months ahead of us."

Neither of us realized it at the time, but the events of the next two months would push us and our firm to its limits.

3

A few days later I was standing in the Grabba Java line waiting to place my coffee order when the bozo in front of me started yakking on his cell. This bozo was better dressed than most bozos, probably a lawyer or investment banker or something, working on the deal of the century.

The barista tried to catch Mr. Bozo's eye to take his order. He ignored her. He was too busy yelling instructions at Steve. *Poor Steve*. Mr. Bozo's face was very red. It was only eight-thirty in the morning but clearly things were already going sideways.

The barista stared hard at him and yelled, "Next?" No reaction.

I tapped him on the shoulder. "You're holding up the line." He placed his hand over the phone and glared at me.

"I beg your pardon?"

"Wrap it up," I said. "You're holding up the line."

He glowered. "Do you know who I am?"

"Do you know who *I* am?" I countered. He paused. The wheels were turning. Was I *somebody*?

He gave up, shook his head.

"I'm nobody, just like you, now get off the phone and place your order."

His mouth opened, then closed, the wheels in his tiny brain ground to a halt. He huffed at the barista that he wanted a latte frappa something and stormed off into the corner. The woman behind me chuckled.

I paid for my drink and went out into the morning sun. The air was still and unusually warm which didn't bode well for the campaign office. Campaign HQ, as we like to call it, is eight blocks from my house which is good, I love walking; but it's on the fourth floor of a six-storey building still under construction, which is bad, the workmen prop the lobby doors open and this wreaks havoc with the air conditioning.

How Michiel sweet-talked the owner into giving us a short-term lease on this space was a mystery. You took your life in your hands trying to get into the place, weaving around beeping Bobcats and construction detritus to get to the front door. It was much easier if you drove down the alley behind the building and came up from the underground parkade.

The campaign office occupied the entire fourth floor, a cavernous space of unfinished concrete and floor-to-ceiling windows with a three-car elevator bank running right through the middle. It was brightly lit and sparsely furnished with my desk, Lisbeth's desk, some filing cabinets, a work area, and a coffee area stuffed with beat-up appliances and a used microwave and coffee urn.

Lisbeth, who lived in an upscale condo in an exclusive part of town, deemed the space 'adequate' but even she was impressed with the bathrooms. Unlike Michiel's last campaign office where the toilets flooded on a regular basis, these bathrooms boasted state-of-the-art sinks and toilets, well-stocked soap and paper towel dispensers, and indirect lighting that flowed over the edge of the drop ceiling and bathed the room in a luminous glow.

Lisbeth was already at her desk when I arrived. She was dressed for the heat, wearing beige linen slacks, a white cotton T-shirt, and J'adior slingback shoes. I was wearing an old pink shirt too big for me, tight jeans, and flip-flops. I was beginning to feel underdressed. Her personal and campaign cell phones were neatly arrayed in front of her. She was about to pick one up when she saw me. "Good. You're here."

"What are you working on?" I asked.

"Volunteer orientation sessions. Three this week. The first one is tonight. Judging by the on-line registration we can expect seventy, eighty people. Can you sort out the food?"

Can I sort out the food? I love food. Especially junk food, which is why I run every day. "No problem."

She nodded, her jet-black hair hiding her face as she leaned forward and picked up her phone. She'd already moved on to the next item on her to-do list.

By mid morning the office was buzzing. Bernie the sign guy was fighting with a computer program, trying to plot the most direct route between households requesting lawn signs. Jamal, the get-out-the-vote guy, was entering voter data into the GOTV computer program. He wanted the door knockers to plug the data into their iPads right on the voter's doorstep, but the older volunteers couldn't get the hang of it and jotted the information down on scraps of paper that they'd bring back and drop in his lap. It drove him mad.

A worker dropped something on the concrete floor above

us. Metallic ringing reverberated across the empty space, no one flinched.

I was sorting the *#VoteMichiel* T-shirts into small, medium, and large piles for the volunteers who'd signed up for tonight's orientation session when my phone buzzed and flashed: *Keith Lawson*.

"Evie, can you come by the office?" He sounded breathless. Very un-Keith like.

"Is something wrong?"

"Nope, all good," he said. "Can you come this morning?"

"Of course. I'll be right there." My plan was to spend mornings at the campaign office and afternoons and evenings as needed at the law firm. I'd also promised to be available whenever the firm needed me. This would be more of a challenge in September after we shifted into 24/7 campaign mode so I'd better pile up my brownie points now while I have the chance.

~

"Morning, I didn't expect you till one." Bridget, our admin on the front desk, greeted me with a cheery smile. She's a twenty-something blonde who has a knack for making everyone, be they clients or couriers, feel welcome when they set foot in the Lawson Valentine reception area.

"These are nice," I said as I buried my nose in the bouquet of pink, white and blue sweet peas sitting on the corner of her desk. The fragrance was summery, brimming with promise. "Is Keith in his office?"

"Conference room."

Our office is relatively small but the reception area and conference room are, in my humble opinion, stunning. They have a fresh contemporary feel with just enough mahogany to project an air of gravitas without becoming stodgy or oppressive. The conference room is at the back of the building. Its large windows overlook the river which shifts from a placid ice-covered ribbon in the winter to a roiling torrent in the spring, and a gentle stream in the fall; it really comes alive in the summer when it's packed with raucous teenagers bobbing along on air mattresses and inner tubes. Luxury townhouses run along the riverbank across from us and if you use binoculars you can see right into their living rooms. Not that anyone would ever do that.

Keith was hunched over a stack of papers at one end of the conference table, surrounded by piles of binders, file folders and maps. As long as I've known him, he's worked in a state of controlled chaos.

He looked up, eyes sparkling, as I slid into the chair beside him. "I just finished meeting with Sam Calhoon."

"What? *The* Sam Calhoon of Calhoon Developments Corporation?"

"That's the one. He wants us to represent him."

"On which project?" Calhoon made a fortune building commercial office towers and had recently branched out into residential developments.

"That's the best part. *All* residential projects."

"Really? What happened to Gates, Case and White?"

Keith shrugged. "Damned if I know. All Calhoon said was he wants to spread his work around. The commercial stuff will stay with Gates, the residential stuff is coming to us."

"And he came directly to you? No beauty contest, nothing?" This was highly unusual. Big corporate clients never hand out lucrative work without first asking for proposals from four or five firms setting out the calibre of their lawyers, their billing rates, and why they're the best law firm for the job. Managing partners and their marketing directors turn themselves inside out dreaming up new ways to say: *We're the best, we understand your business, we'll provide quality service at reasonable prices; did we mention we love you*? While at the same time building enough wiggle room into the bid price to give the client a ten percent discount if the client asks for it. And they always ask for it.

"No beauty contest," Keith said.

"Why not?"

"Because we've got an excellent reputation, that's why not."

"Keith, we have an excellent reputation in regulatory law for green energy. Real estate and municipal law aren't a huge part of our practice."

He looked out the window, staring at the luxury homes nestled among the poplar trees on the opposite bank. "You could count the lawyers who do municipal law in this town on one hand," he said, then he listed four lawyers who specialized in the area, including the one who had recently had a stroke and wouldn't be back to work for months.

"That's true, but the best muni lawyer in town is Archie Williams, did he get a chance to bid on it?"

"I don't know, Evie." Keith sighed, settling back in his chair which creaked. It was a nice-looking Eames highback chair. I'd picked it out myself. "Why are you fussed about this? Calhoon's work will give us a nice buffer, top up our billings as the regulatory files ebb and flow." He shifted and the leather chair creaked again. "Oh, and he wants you to be the lead lawyer on this file."

Before I could point out that of the two of us, Keith had considerably more municipal law experience than I did, a voice, the memory of my mom, whispered in my ear. *Don't look at the horse's mouth.* As a Hungarian who emigrated to Canada in her twenties, she had a knack for garbling clichés. Once she toasted my sister with the heartfelt desire to throw mud in her face. But Mom was right. It was time to move on.

"Does Calhoon have a big application coming up or something?"

"As a matter of fact, he does." Keith picked up a yellow legal pad covered with his flowing handwriting. Some words were fiercely underlined.

"You know the Glen Park lawn bowling pavilion?"

I did. My dad, an Englishman, loved that place. He bowled there for 40 years. The pavilion was a bit rickety, having been built in 1912. He and his bowling buddies fixed it up every decade or so, trying to restore the structure to something approximating its original splendor. But Dad was an accountant, not a carpenter. He soon discovered his time was better spent leading the charge to designate the pavilion a heritage building than hammering a nail in sideways and having to yank it out again. Dad was elated when the city finally bought the property and turned it into a park. He remained active with the league, shouting helpful hints at the younger players when he became too arthritic to hold a bowling ball.

"Does Calhoon know I'm dividing my time between the firm and Michiel's campaign?"

Keith grinned. "He does. He said having a personal connection to the mayor was an added bonus."

"So what's he like? I hear he's Godzilla if he doesn't get

his way." Like many men of great wealth, Calhoon had a reputation for bending others to his will. Those who refused to bend snapped into little tiny pieces.

Keith considered this for a moment before replying. "He's very businesslike, he got right to the point, but seems pleasant enough. He's got to be in his mid-sixties; looks fit for his age, though."

"Well, that's a bonus, we can't have our newest client kicking off before we send him the bill."

"Oh yes, about that—"

"What's the discount?" I cut in before Keith could finish. It's a bad habit. I've got to stop doing that.

"We didn't actually discuss a discount, so let's assume we're charging him the usual rate."

I stared at Keith in disbelief. "Hold on, the biggest developer in town drops a huge file in our laps and he *doesn't* ask for a discount?"

Keith shrugged and I decided to stop complaining about our good fortune. We'd just landed a big client who was prepared to pay full fees. *Don't look at the horse's mouth.*

4

Lisbeth had been the mayor's government relations manager for the last four years, she knew Michiel's habits and predilections better than anybody. She swore, hand to heart, that not only would Michiel show up on time for tonight's volunteer orientation session, he'd charm and bewitch the crowd. 'Michiel knows when to sparkle,' she said with an indulgent laugh. I replied that only Shirley Temple sparkled, the rest of us did something else, perhaps smiled winningly.

I did, however, agree with Lisbeth's premise that Michiel treated his volunteers with respect in order to gain their unbridled loyalty. Political volunteers are unlike other volunteers. They're sent into strange neighbourhoods and expected to connect with perfect strangers who often have no idea an election is on or even worse, can't stand their candidate. Assuming the volunteers aren't run off the property or verbally assaulted, they have to convince voters to disclose their personal information and load it into their iPads before the finicky GOTV app shuts down.

In recognition of the trials and tribulations of door

knocking I'd put a Brownie Points chart in the coffee room: 20 points for convincing the guy who hates Michiel to vote for him anyway, 15 for the weird guy from *Deliverance* or the zombie woman from *World War Z*, 10 for a naked man (many men lounging at home consider clothing optional) and one point for every cat or dog that squeezes out the door and tries to get flattened in traffic.

I reviewed the checklist for tonight's orientation session: fifteen large pizzas, coffee, tea, pop, junk food, (check, check, check), crudités and dips for Lisbeth and other healthy eaters (shudder, check), and fifty chairs neatly arranged in front of the low dais where Michiel would be speaking, with plenty of room in front for The Brat Pack to tweet, Facebook and Instagram to their hearts' content (check).

It was well past two by the time I sorted out the details. I was ready for a break and asked Lisbeth if she wanted anything from the deli down the street.

"No, just a coffee." She rubbed her temples with her delicate fingers, her voice as tight as a bowstring. I studied her more carefully. In high school she would have been one of the mean girls with glossy hair and expensive clothes, but today she just looked small and anxious.

I make it a point not to pry into the affairs of people I barely know, especially when they're referred to as the Ice Princess behind their backs. But we were going to be cooped up in this concrete box of a campaign office for the next two months; it was worth a try.

"Why don't you come with me?" I asked. "Janet can cover your desk for a few minutes." I glanced at the middle-aged volunteer rummaging in a cardboard box on the swag shelves. "A change of scene will do you good, come on."

Lisbeth's silver and black sapphire bracelets jangled against the metal arm of her chair. She looked from Janet to me and said, "Sure, why not."

Soon we were outside on the pavement, suffocating in the hot still air and exhaust fumes. Luckily Delano's was only a half a block away. They didn't serve the best coffee in the city, or even on this block, but we both liked the proprietor and his wife, an old couple who insisted on being paid in cash. We took our coffees back outside and sat on a bench under the canopy of a heavily graffitied bus shelter.

"So, what's wrong?" I asked, tentatively.

With a heavy sigh she said, "I'm worried about Nicholas."

"Nicholas? Whatever for?"

She fiddled with her bracelets, twisting an elaborate silver hoop around and around her delicate wrist. "I think there's something going on between him and Michiel."

"Like what?" I hadn't noticed anything, but unlike Lisbeth I hadn't spent the last four years working shoulder to shoulder with the two of them.

"They argue all the time now. Always sniping at each other, here and at City Hall. Nicholas is Michiel's campaign manager, for God's sake, he's supposed to support Michiel, not harangue him. It isn't good for Michiel, and it's not good for the campaign."

I took another sip of coffee (it truly was awful) and considered what to say; this was not the time to share my reservations about Nicholas.

I'd met Nicholas back in law school when he still went by Nick. We were in the same graduating class and took many of the same courses over the three-year program. He was extremely clever, and unlike the other students who believed their success hinged on another student's failure,

Nick was willing to help those who didn't catch on to the nuances of trusts or constitutional law as quickly as he did. Grateful classmates would cluster around his cubicle in the library, their heads almost touching, as he explained the rationale of a case in his slow, patient way. No one was surprised when he graduated in the top ten percent of the class and landed articles at Gates, Case and White. I ended up there as well and witnessed Nick's meteoric rise to the top. He made partner in record time: five years instead of the usual eight. There wasn't a CEO in the city who didn't have Nick's number on speed dial.

But something happened to Nick after law school. He used to say he worked hard and played hard, but soon he became too busy to 'play' with his old friends. *City Magazine* named Nick, hereinafter known as Nicholas, one of its "Top 40 Under 40." The article fawned over his achievements, running a photo of a scrawny kid raised by hardworking Brazilian immigrants (his dad was a geologist, his mom a homemaker) next to a photo of an elegantly dressed urbane sophisticate—business trips to New York City were never complete without a stop at his favourite tailor for a bespoke suit. The world was coming to Nicholas now; anyone who thought otherwise was sadly mistaken.

Lisbeth reached into her mini clutch bag for a Kleenex and delicately dabbed the corner of one eye. I pretended not to notice. Had she twigged onto something real or was she simply overwhelmed by the responsibility of keeping 250 volunteers focused on Nicholas' campaign strategy? Come to think of it, what *was* Nicholas' campaign strategy?

She pursed her lips. The topic was closed. By the time we returned to Campaign HQ she was calm, her distress as short-lived as a summer squall.

My phone rang when I sat down at my desk. It was Madeline: AJ and I were booked into a meeting with Calhoon on Thursday at 3 p.m. and Calhoon had already signed and returned the retainer letter. Apparently Keith was right, Calhoon was happy to pay full price for our legal services.

When I thanked her she replied, "Nothing but the best for you, Evie."

I met Madeline on my first day of articles at Gates. She was an intimidating corporate paralegal and I was the latest in a string of articling students (commonly referred to as 'junior chipmunks') trying to hide my terror under the usual camouflage, a tailored navy suit and crisp white shirt. Gates prided itself on its collegial work environment, but the camaraderie described on Gates' website was a far cry from the cauldron of unbridled competition that was everyday life for articling students and lawyers clawing their way up the partnership ladder. Madeline decided she liked me and stepped in from time to time to save me from being eviscerated like a goldfish in a shark tank. I was grateful and asked her to come with us when Keith and I created our own firm. Our compensation package was no match for the one she enjoyed at Gates, but she accepted anyway. "It's not about the money, darling."

~

That evening, Campaign HQ buzzed like a concert hall waiting for a rock legend to grace the stage. Political junkies traded gossip; volunteers who hadn't seen each other since Michiel's last campaign became reacquainted. I greeted them as they streamed off the elevators, curious about why they were volunteering for Michiel instead of one of the other candidates. The consensus was they trusted Michiel, he was not just another sleazy politician.

My phone rang: it was the pizza guy. He was standing outside a half-finished building that had our address scrawled in white paint on a piece of wood tacked over the front door, was he in the right place? I assured him he was exactly where he was supposed to be. When Lisbeth and I got to the lobby we found a sweaty middle-aged man bent double under the weight of fifteen large pizzas boxes hanging from a strap contraption around his neck. We loaded the boxes onto a trolly and trundled back into the elevator.

"I love the smell of pepperoni and cardboard, don't you?" I said on the ride up.

"The elevator will reek of pizza for days, it'll drive the workmen nuts." She laughed.

Soon it was 6:50 and still no sign of Michiel. I was peering out the large windows anxiously scouring the streets when a white BMW eased up to the far curb. Michiel hopped out of the passenger side and bolted across the street into the building. Nicholas opened the driver side door, hesitated for a moment, then plunged into traffic after Michiel.

The elevator door slid open and Michiel bounded out, his thick brown hair dishevelled by the slight breeze. "Evie! How's the best office manager in the city?"

"Michiel, I love living in your world, everyone you know is the best at something or other."

He gripped both of my hands and looked me square in the eye. "I mean every word," he said. He sounded so sincere I almost believed him.

He cocked his head, listening to the excited chatter that flowed like a rising river all around us. "How's the crowd look?"

"Good. There are about sixty-five people, standing room only, they've eaten something and they're ready for you. It's the usual drill, Lisbeth will welcome everyone and introduce Nicholas, Nicholas will say a few words and introduce you, then you'll work your magic."

"Sounds good," he smiled, and a dimple appeared in his left cheek.

Lisbeth came around the elevators and gave Michiel a big hug before stepping back to tell him to stay out of sight until Nicholas finished his introduction.

"Whatever you say, ma'am," he replied. Was there anyone else on the planet who could call Lisbeth *ma'am* and get away with it? She smiled indulgently and returned to the main room.

"People, people." She stepped up on to the dais and clapped her hands together to silence the boisterous crowd. "We're about to start the evening."

Lisbeth stood tall and surveyed the audience. The teary-eyed woman I had comforted this afternoon was gone, replaced by a self-assured businesswoman on a mission. She started by introducing herself and explaining that her role as volunteer coordinator was to pamper her precious volunteers, the door knockers, the phone bank callers, the lit drop people, the sign guys, anyone who was able to donate even an hour of their time to getting Michiel re-elected.

She introduced The Brat Pack, who she described in magical terms, they were meme wizards and pop-up event entertainers: Wendy, the campaign's social media strategist, was their fairy queen, although with her spikey blue hair she looked more like a pixie to me. Lisbeth introduced me, the trusty office manager; Jamal, the get-out-the-vote guy; Angie, who took care of fundraising; Bernie, the sign guy; and Clint, an older guy with years of experience in mainstream media. The volunteers chuckled when she said Clint's job would be considerably easier this time around, now that the media had finally learned how to spell Michiel's name.

Her face glowed when she turned to Nicholas who was sitting by himself in the front row. "Now, I'd like you to meet Michiel's campaign manager, Nicholas Silva. Most of you know Nicholas as Michiel's chief of staff, but you may not be aware that he's the man who propelled Michiel into the mayor's office the last time around." This was true. The pundits widely credited Nicholas as the political strategist who had transformed Michiel from who-is-that-guy to a serious contender. Nicholas was engulfed in a round of applause as he stepped up onto the dais.

He flashed a gentle smile, reminding me of the Nick I'd known in law school, and waited for the applause to die down.

He sketched the history of his friendship with Michiel, who was somewhat of an enigma in law school. Unlike the other students, Michiel had absolutely no interest in landing articles at one of the Big Five law firms. He refused to waste what he called the best years of his life 'on a soulless quest for a fat paycheque.'

"Make no mistake," Nicholas said, "Michiel had the brains to be a damn fine lawyer but he believed public service was far more important than cranking out mega-deals and exploiting technical loopholes to help criminals get away with murder—" this drew a pitter patter of applause "—so I wasn't the least bit surprised when Michiel quit law after finishing his articles to join a non-profit group working on poverty reduction."

Just then a murmur rose from the crowd. Michiel strolled around the corner of the elevators, moving with the feline grace of a model on a Parisian runway.

"You're interrupting my flow, man." Nicholas smiled, waiting for the hubbub to subside.

Michiel raised his hands in surrender. "Carry on, my friend, carry on."

"Too late now, you've ruined the mood."

The volunteers chuckled as Nicholas motioned for Michiel to join him. Michiel hopped on to the dais, threw his arms around Nicholas, clapped him on the back, and whispered something in his ear. Nicholas smiled and the crowd cheered as if they were at a Tragically Hip concert.

"Thanks everyone, thanks," Michiel nodded, gesturing for the crowd to settle down. "And thank you Nicholas, for everything you've done and everything you're going to do!" He cocked a finger at Nicholas who nodded with mock gravity.

Michiel turned his attention to the crowd, his charismatic personality on full throttle. Lisbeth was wrong: Michiel didn't sparkle, he blasted energy like a supernova.

"As Nicholas said, I started with The Shoebox, a poverty reduction coalition, but soon realized the only way to make lasting change in this city was to get inside the bureaucracy where the real power lay. At first I thought I'd start small, maybe run for the school board or city council, but Lisbeth quickly disabused me of that idea." He turned to look at Lisbeth. "It was that come-to-Jesus meeting around your kitchen table, remember? You said go big or go home."

She flashed a wide smile.

Michiel continued. "So, against my better judgment I

threw my hat in the ring and for a while there it looked like the city was going to toss it right back at me." The audience giggled, what a ridiculous idea. "Then we started the '*Every Kid Deserves a Summer*' campaign, we took off like a rocket…and here we are today.

"These two," he spread his arms wide to encompass Nicholas and Lisbeth, "are the reason I got into politics, and you people," he extended his arms to include the crowd, "are the reason I'm staying."

The room exploded with wild applause.

He talked about continuing the good work he had started in his first term and tackling the new challenges created by the precipitous drop in oil prices. He promised to do everything in his power to make the city the best place in the world to work and play.

Then he dropped his voice and put a finger to his lips. "Can I tell you a secret? If you promise not to repeat this, I'll tell you my most important campaign promise."

The room became so quiet I could hear the coffee urn burbling.

I glanced at Lisbeth. She was staring at Nicholas, her lips slightly parted. For a moment Nicholas looked perplexed, then his face settled, tight and impassive.

The audience leaned forward in their chairs. *Yes, tell us a secret.*

Michiel waited a beat before continuing. "The only way to fund the things we need, affordable housing, transit, the arts, is to raise taxes, right?" The audience groaned. No one gets elected by promising to raise taxes. "Wrong," Michiel said. "We don't need to raise taxes; we just need to make sure everyone pays their fair share."

The audience squirmed in their seats. What was he

talking about? They all paid their fair share of taxes—as far as they were concerned they paid *more* than their fair share.

Michiel's face was grave. "We don't collect enough taxes to pay for essential services. Why? Because after the oil companies left town, there were fewer businesses in the downtown core, this means lower revenue from business property taxes and not enough money to pay for existing and new services."

I wondered where Michiel was going with this, it was his 'most important campaign promise' after all.

Michiel smiled sympathetically. "I know, I know, many of you are afraid that if we can't attract more businesses to the downtown core, we'll have to cut services or raise your taxes."

Yes, that's exactly what they're worried about.

"Well, that's not going to happen. Because here's what I'm going to do. I will encourage developers, incent them, to build more residential housing in the downtown core. That way we'll get the housing we need *and* generate extra tax dollars from the additional people and the businesses in the downtown core. And that, folks, is how we're going to keep your taxes low."

I frowned. It made no sense. Inner city land is expensive. Was Michiel going to turn the city into Paris or Milan where the rich can afford to live downtown and everyone else is jammed into ticky-tacky developments in the suburbs, chewing up two hours a day commuting to and from work?

People started clapping. Apparently, it didn't matter what I thought. Michiel said it would work and they trusted him.

Michiel looked at a woman in the front row and winked. She blushed and whispered shyly to the woman sitting beside her. "Now remember what I said, this is a secret. I'm announcing it to the media tomorrow at ten o'clock. Can I trust you guys to keep it quiet until then?"

Absolutely! The audience whooped. They were thrilled to be a part of the inner circle.

Michiel glanced over at Lisbeth who realized with a start that he was finished speaking and it was time for her wrap up. Nicholas sat as still as a statue, his face expressionless.

Lisbeth stepped back up on the dais and gave Michiel a quick side hug before turning back to the crowd. She thanked everyone for coming and reminded them to leave their contact information on the sign-in sheets on the table by the elevators.

Michiel waved and shouted, "Have a good evening everybody, and welcome to the campaign!"

The crowd broke up into small groups, chattering with excitement. Several volunteers clustered around Michiel, shaking his hand and telling him how much they admired him. Others milled about with their friends, speculating whether Duffy O'Halloran, Michiel's only real competition, stood a snowball's chance in hell at beating their guy.

O'Halloran was a middle-aged businessman who'd made a fortune in investment banking before becoming an entrepreneur and a vociferous critic of Michiel's administration. O'Halloran believed government should be run like a business. The lower the taxes, the better; what could be privatized should be privatized. The business community loved him.

An hour later the volunteers were gone. The blood red rays of the setting sun fell across the table where Michiel, Nicholas, Lisbeth and I sat drinking tepid coffee and room temperature fizzy drinks. Nicholas was quiet, content to listen as Michiel and Lisbeth gossiped about people I didn't know. After a few minutes he hustled Michiel downstairs and into his car.

Lisbeth and I barrelled around the room, picking up sign-in sheets and sorting the trash into recycling and garbage. Soon I was heading into the elevator, dragging two gigantic trash bags behind me. I rode down to the main lobby and went out the back way to toss the bags into the industrial trash bins scattered about in the alley. When I returned to the back door I discovered the wind had slammed it shut. It was locked and I would have to go all the way around the building to re-enter through the front door.

It was after ten o'clock and just light enough for me to pick my way down the alley which was littered with bits of rebar and clumps of dirt kicked up by the construction vehicles. The "Re-elect Michiel" sandwich board was still propped open by the main doors which meant Lisbeth had not locked up yet. I dragged the sign inside and crossed the lobby to the stairs leading down into the underground parkade. One of the elevators whirred. It was heading up; Lisbeth was ready to go home.

As I walked through the parkade to my car, I forced myself not to replay that movie scene where some poor schmuck is mowed down by a bad guy in a black SUV. *Give your head a shake; the garage is clean and well lit, there's no reason to be nervous*. My Mini Cooper was parked at the far end of the garage next to a floor-to-ceiling enclosure we called 'the cage.' It's a chicken wire pen where we store campaign signs, heavy wooden stakes, and thin metal set-stakes designed to hold the small signs we plant on people's lawns. The signs were neatly sorted and stacked by size. The metal set-stakes leaned in tidy piles against the back wall. The cage was securely locked. Everything looked fine.

I hopped into my car and headed home, hoping I'd have enough energy left to review the Calhoon documents before falling into bed.

5

It was dark by the time I pulled up in front of my house. I glared at the thing that passes for a porch light over the front door, fumbling to get my key in the lock.

Quincy appeared out of nowhere, crashing into my knees when I opened the door. “Bloody dog!” I muttered. He stood at my feet, tail whipping back and forth, refusing to budge until I patted his rock-hard head. This is how Quincy greets us after any absence longer than ten minutes. I rubbed his ear and he skittered across the hall tiles to Louisa, who was standing in the kitchen in a T-shirt and flannel pyjama bottoms. People say we look alike, but other than our colouring—dark hair, fair complexion—I don’t see the resemblance.

“Aren’t you hot?” I asked.

“No,” she replied. Of course not. We shared a bedroom when we were kids and battled constantly over whether the window should be open or closed. One night I flew into a rage when I didn’t get my way, kicking the walls and hurling dolls and stuffed toys all over the place. Mom sat me down on the edge of the bed and explained that anger could be a dangerous thing. It had to be controlled. 'Think of it as your superpower, Evie. Use it for good, not evil.' That sounds corny now, but to an eight-year-old who loved the X-Men it made perfect sense.

"How did it go?" Louisa asked. "Did Michiel have them eating out of his hand?" Louisa met Michiel a couple of years ago at a fundraiser. She thought he was charming and sexy in a Cary Grant kind of way.

"Yes, he did," I said. "Although it got a bit strange at the end."

"Strange, how?"

"Yeah, well, Michiel told us, a 'secret'…all sixty-five of us."

She wiggled the kettle at me. I nodded, yes, I would have some tea.

"That's weird," Louisa said, "sixty-five people can't keep a secret."

"No kidding. I'm an official member of the campaign team and I'm blabbing it to you."

She rubbed her hands together. "So what is it?" Her eyes sparkled with mischief and I was reminded of the little girl who was constantly getting me into trouble. As the older sister it was my job to keep her in line, as if anything could stop Louisa once she got an idea into her head.

I shrugged. "Something about making the city great and funding everything we need by building more residential units in the downtown core."

"What if I don't want to live in the city?" she asked.

"You *do* live in the city, well, the inner city."

"Yes, I *know* that." She plopped two tea bags into two mugs and poured boiling water over them. "I don't mean me, personally. Lots of people with young families want to live in the burbs, they like the big backyard, the slower pace." She wrinkled her nose. "Although how they put up with the daily commute is beyond me."

"Me too," I stroked Quincy's head, "we'd never have time for a W-A-L-K, would we Quincy." He cocked an ear at the sound of his name.

Louisa pulled a packet of honey grahams out of the cupboard and broke one in half. She raised an eyebrow at me, I shook my head. Too much junk food already today. "What I don't get is why Michiel told you guys 'the secret' in the first place. Isn't it a cardinal rule in politics that no one leaks anything because they'll screw up the message?"

I had second thoughts about the honey grahams and pulled one out of the packet. "Yes, you're right. The only good leak is the one leaked by the politician to a reporter they trust. They don't just blurt things out willy-nilly to a room full of strangers."

I shook my head and went into the study. "I need to check my email, I'm expecting stuff from the office."

Louisa was horrified. "Oh Evie, it's almost eleven. Can't it wait until tomorrow?"

"Just a quick peek, don't want to get caught with my pants down."

She looked down at Quincy who was eyeing her graham cracker. "Come on bud, let's go to bed." Quincy leapt to his feet and trotted after her.

My study is a peaceful room: small, with just enough space for my desk, a Stickley table actually, that sits in front of the French windows overlooking the river, and two well worn leather chairs on either side of the fireplace on the opposite wall. Beside one chair is a small marble-topped table with a brass reading lamp. The other chair is tucked in the corner next to a tall mahogany bookcase. A Persian carpet covers the hardwood floor. Dad gave it to me after Mom died. Louisa got the other one which is in our TV room. Quincy, bless his little doggy heart, decided neither was edible.

I opened my laptop and scrolled through my email. There were two notes from the office, one from Madeline attaching the Calhoon file and the other from AJ updating me on his progress. He had downloaded the city's rezoning regulations and all the applications he could find where the city pulled parkland out of reserve and sold it to private developers. There weren't many examples.

I sent two notes back, one thanking Madeline and the other asking AJ whether he'd be available tomorrow to go over the file. I was surprised when he responded to my email almost immediately with a text saying he was open all afternoon.

Why are you still working? Don't you have a personal life? I texted.

My life is the law! He replied.

I sent him a shocked face emoji and went to bed.

6

Lisbeth was livid when I arrived at Campaign HQ the next morning. She had just learned that Duffy O'Halloran, Michiel's only real competition, had told a reporter the televised candidates' debate was on the same night as the Heritage Awards Gala, an event Michiel had hosted every year for the last four years. Lisbeth had spent weeks negotiating with the TV station and the candidates' teams to ensure the two events would not conflict and O'Halloran upended all her hard work with a careless comment to a reporter.

She grabbed her phone and punched in the number for O'Halloran's campaign manager, whispering to me that she wouldn't be joining our morning conference call, and then snapped to attention when O'Halloran's staffer came on the line.

I went into the 'war room' which is the only room in the campaign office with a real door. In theory Nicholas and Michiel would use the room to dream up campaign strategy; in practice no one used it for anything other than Nicholas' morning conference calls with the team. I was dialing the call-in number when Wendy, our social media strategist, strolled in. Her blue pixie cut wasn't quite as spikey as usual and her dark eyes were bloodshot. She looked like she'd fallen into a caragana hedge.

I raised an eyebrow. "Late night?"

She took a sip of her latte. "You know how it is, The Brat Pack never sleeps."

Clint, the mainstream media guy, was already on the line, talking to someone about last night's volunteer orientation meeting.

"…caught me by surprise…"

I cut in to let them know Wendy and I were here.

"Hey Evie, great event last night." That was Angie, our head of fundraising.

"Yes, everyone was pretty pumped."

We heard some muffled noises and Bernie, the sign guy, and Jamal, the data input guy, came online.

"Anyone know where Nicholas is?" I asked.

"I'm here," he said. "Let's get started." *How long had he been lurking on the line*?

Clint cleared his throat. "Nicholas, about Michiel's secret announcement last night…?" He paused to give Nicholas an opportunity to speak. Nothing. After an awkward silence Clint continued. "I'd like to talk with you and Michiel about how we're going to manage the media."

"Me too." That was Wendy. "Michiel's message—and I'm still not sure what it is—won't be easy to squash into 280 characters on Twitter."

Silence on the line.

"Nicholas…?"

"Yeah, I'm here." His voice was edged with irritation. "I'll set something up."

"About the presser this morning…?" Clint continued. "I don't have anything on it, no media packages, nothing." Once again he waited for Nicholas to respond. Again, silence. Clint continued, his voice firm. "If there's a media release coming from this campaign, I'm the guy who should be drafting it. Media is my responsibility."

"Clint, this is the twenty-first century for God's sake, you have to move fast." Nicholas spoke very quickly. "If Michiel says the press will be here at ten, they'll be here at ten. He gave them notice."

Even I knew this was highly unusual. It was Clint's job, not Michiel's, to liaise with the press.

Nicholas continued. "Wendy is doing her thing building buzz on social media, Evie will tune up HQ, call in a squad of volunteers to man the phones and stuff envelopes, whatever it takes to make the place look alive."

Wendy and I looked at each other. This was news to us.

There was an uncomfortable pause before Clint came back on the line. "I want to meet with you and Michiel at your earliest convenience." His voice was low, frustrated. I understood exactly how he felt.

"Fine, after the presser."

"Fine."

"Well, if there's nothing else, we've got a lot of work to do between now and ten o'clock." Nicholas hung up.

A lot of work indeed. Wait until Lisbeth finds out we have less than an hour to round up twenty volunteers for a photo-op.

"No rest for the wicked," I said to Wendy.

"Right-o," she said. "Time to dream up a snappy Twitter thread about God knows what Michiel is going to say at ten. Hey, maybe that's the hashtag: *#Godknowswhat*, or

#MichielFullOfSurprises." She laughed and wandered out.

Lisbeth was getting off the phone when I reached her desk. Her blue eyes glinted with satisfaction. "There! I told O'Halloran's assistant if he tries to fuck with me he'd better think twice; they said it was all a big misunderstanding and it won't happen again." *Note to self: don't mess with Lisbeth.*

"When's the debate?" I asked.

"September twenty-second, the same date it's always been," she said with a smug smile.

"Perfect." I sat down at my desk, stalling a little to give her more time to simmer down. "So, Lisbeth, you know that presser Michiel mentioned last night...?"

"Hmmm…"

"Nicholas wants the office humming when the reporters arrive. We have to get a bunch of volunteers in here, working the phones, stuffing envelopes, whatever, by ten o'clock…"

"This morning?" She blinked a couple of times; before she could say anything I handed her a volunteer contact sheet and started dialing.

By the time the reporters and camera crews clattered off the elevator, we had cajoled thirteen volunteers into coming in. Some were babbling into their cell phones while others were sorting campaign postcards into packets of 50 and securing them with rubber bands. Everyone smiled sweetly when Michiel and Nicholas rolled in with Clint trailing behind them.

Michiel greeted the reporters warmly and shook their hands before stepping up to the front of the room. He painted a glowing Norman Rockwell picture of the future of the city, which would include a vibrant downtown core with accessible transit, busy shops, crowded restaurants, museums and art galleries, all supported by additional taxes flowing from inner city residential housing units, a veritable fountainhead of new revenue. It was a mesmerizing image and not one esteemed member of the press asked whether any developers were onside with his plan.

Wendy videoed the whole thing. She would use snippets in a *#WheresMichiel* social media campaign in which Michiel would unveil his campaign promises from various locations around the city. She structured it like a contest, asking his followers to guess where Michiel was when he made the announcement. There was no prize other than the glory of outsmarting the rest of Michiel's 350,000 followers. She dreamed the whole thing up in 30 minutes. That's why she's the fairy queen of social media.

I was chatting with Wendy when my phone buzzed with a text from AJ.

When will you be in today?

1 hour, what's up?

Not sure, talk when I see you.

I promised to buy him lunch and turned my attention to proofreading Lisbeth's memo to the volunteers about their roles. It started with the statement: *Volunteering for Michiel is ALL about protecting Michiel's brand—authentic, trustworthy, intelligent, and engaging. A true leader.* I wondered whether Lisbeth had a memo describing what we were supposed to do if our intelligent and engaging leader went off the rails and started dreaming up campaign promises without vetting them first with his campaign manager. Given her mood I decided not to ask.

~

An hour later I hauled open the heavy glass doors of Lawson Valentine. I've done this almost every day for the last four years and still my heart sings at the sight of Keith's last name and mine etched on the glass next to our logo, a Möbius strip. I can't remember why we thought a curly one-sided band was the best representation of our law practice but it's been on our letterhead from day one and it's staying there.

Madeline was manning Bridget's desk.

"What's up?" I asked.

She brushed her thick auburn hair away from her face. Madeline is in her mid forties, unmarried, and men still fall all over themselves begging for her phone number. A vixen in the old Hollywood sense of the word.

"I don't know," she said. "AJ asked me to print off a stack of documents this morning. He's in the conference room."

I found AJ at the conference table placing cups on the corners of a large architectural rendering to keep the corners from curling up. He greeted me with a broad grin. With his sandy blonde hair, square jaw and lean body he looks more like a soccer player than a lawyer. "Bridget's getting us something from Bun Boyz."

I returned his smile. The food truck is perennially parked outside our building; we've been customers for so long that we know the names of the proprietor's kids, their ages and where they go to school.

"What have you got?" I asked.

"I'm not sure." He thumped a law book down on the last corner of the drawing. "I was reviewing the documents Calhoon left with Keith, but couldn't make out some details so I called Calhoon's office and asked for a larger version.

Bev, his executive assistant, sweet lady, couriered over a USB stick. Madeline took it to Staples to print it off." He ran a hand across the drawing to smooth it down. "Here, take a look."

He pointed at a beautifully drawn rendering labeled Pavilion Plan A. The pavilion glowed white against a pale blue sky. Hip-looking people wandered in and out of cafés and book shops. On the other half of the site happy families played on manicured lawns outside pristine white townhouses accented with gleaming black doors and boxwood shrubbery along the foundations.

"This is the same as the drawing Calhoon left with Keith. Calhoon says he wants to buy the parkland from the City and divide it in half. He'll keep the pavilion half intact, restoring the lawn bowling hall for commercial use, shops, maybe a restaurant or something, and build nine three-storey townhouses here, on the other half, nestled among the trees."

"It's lovely," I said. "Those trees are more than a hundred years old." It takes a lifetime to grow trees in this climate; new subdivisions are bleak tracts dotted with sad little saplings, nothing more than buggy whips, desperately trying to take root before they're destroyed by hail or vandals.

"So, what do you make of this?" He pulled out a second drawing and lay it on top of the first. It was labeled Pavilion Plan B. It too was beautifully drawn, but the pavilion and the townhouses had vanished, replaced by a ten-storey glass and concrete tower with commercial space on the first floor and residential units above. It sat in a sea of asphalt that obliterated the ancient woods, leaving nothing but a two-metre-wide strip of grass dotted with concrete planter boxes pressed up against the sidewalk.

"Where did you get this?" I asked.

"The USB stick. It has two versions of the development. Plan A, *with* the Pavilion, is the drawing Calhoon left with Keith. Plan B, *without* the Pavilion, showed up on the USB stick. Madeline printed out two copies, one for me, one for you." He nodded toward a red cardboard tube lying on the credenza behind me.

"Plan A, Plan B? I don't get it," I said.

"Neither do I."

"Maybe this will help." Bridget appeared in the doorway, holding up a large bag of banh mi sandwiches and drinks. We sorted out who was eating what while we pored over the drawings.

What was Calhoon planning to do? If he went with Plan A, the pavilion and the ancient elms and ornamental apple trees would be saved. If he went with Plan B, the pavilion and pretty much everything else in the park would fall under the wrecking ball.

Demolishing old buildings is tricky in this town. Even buildings riddled with asbestos have their champions. The public has no patience for politicians who let developers bulldoze their history to clear the way for glittering office towers and pricey condominiums, *pied-à-terre* for jet-setting oil executives who would rather live in Houston. Michiel responded to the public's concern by becoming an advocate for heritage preservation. He seems to know what the public wants before they do. He created the Heritage Awards Gala to honour developers who preserved historic buildings or incorporated historic elements into their projects.

Plan A was exactly the kind of development worthy of a Heritage Award—assuming Calhoon built it. If not, this project was going to get very ugly, very fast.

"Leave it with me," I said as I gathered up the drawings.

AJ put his hand on top of mine. "Nope, this one's mine. Yours is on the credenza."

I scooped up my poster tube and said, "I'll talk to Keith and check whether Calhoon said anything about Plan B to him."

"You can't, he's gone until Monday." That was after our meeting with Calhoon.

"Not a problem, I've got his cell."

AJ shook his head and mumbled through a mouthful of salad roll. "Can't call. He's houseboating on Shuswap Lake; reception's crappy."

I had forgotten this was Houseboat Week. Keith and his brother, an accountant, always get together in mid-August for a mini family vacation. Despite his complaints about clogged toilets and party boats with drunken half-naked revellers hanging off the side, houseboating had turned into an annual event.

I left Keith a message anyway but wasn't optimistic he'd return my call before AJ and I met with Calhoon.

After a couple of hours of burrowing through zoning regulations, I'd lost the ability to concentrate and wandered over to Madeline's office to see if she had any sweets in the antique glass candy dish that sits on the corner of her desk.

"Werther's? All you've got is Werther's?" I sniffed. "That's old people's candy."

"Stop complaining and try one. You're no spring chicken, you know."

"No one says that anymore, Madeline, and for the record you're older than I am."

She raised her eyebrows at me. I chuckled, popped a

candy in my mouth and wandered back to my office to call Lisbeth. She picked up right away. "How are things going?" I asked.

"Good."

"Do you need me down there?" For once I hoped the photocopier was out of toner and I could ditch the Calhoon file for a couple of hours.

"No, we're good here."

"Damn."

She laughed and said she would see me in the morning. AJ and I were meeting Calhoon in the afternoon so I had time to drop by Campaign HQ for our morning conference call with Nicholas.

I was staring blankly into space when Madeline popped her head in the door. "You're not getting much done, are you?" she asked.

"This is my 'what-if-it-all-goes-pear-shaped' face."

"Ah," she said. "I know what you need. Food. And I need a drink."

Bridget called out from her desk, I swear she has the hearing of a bat, "Yeah, you do, Evie. Eat something, you'll feel better."

A moment later Madeline and I were melting into the stream of humanity heading home for the day. Humanity looked the way I felt: hot, tired, and cranky.

Instead of opting for a table on a patio at one of the many bars and restaurants that dot Seventeenth, we headed to Monro's, a small bar on the main floor of the Alt hotel. It was upscale without being too pricey; better yet, it's cool, dark, and within walking distance of the office.

Soon we were perched at a two-top waiting for the server to take our order. A nice-looking young man wearing a black shirt, black pants, and a black tie approached us with menus and the bar list. I waited for Madeline to do her thing. I don't know what it is about that woman but when she focuses her green eyes on a man, they're gob-smacked.

"I'll have a Pimm's Royal please," she purred. The server stared at her, then got a grip on himself and said "Absolutely!" He had no idea what a Pimm's was, but he would crawl over broken glass to find one.

He looked at me. I ordered a grilled cheese sandwich and a club soda. I didn't purr, purring is not my style.

The nice thing about Madeline is when we're out of the office we never talk shop, we talk about Madeline's amazing social life. Madeline inherited a tidy sum from her mother before she moved here from Montreal. She immediately connected with up and coming businessmen who showered her with jewelry and exotic holidays, but it was their investment advice she wanted. Over the years Madeline's contacts had made her rich.

"What are you wearing to the Heritage Awards Gala?" she asked.

The Gala is a huge event on the city's social calendar. Everyone who is anyone would be there, especially with the municipal election just a few weeks away. The theme may be heritage preservation, but the function is an excuse for developers, investment bankers, and lawyers to schmooze with the mayor and the city councillors who will ultimately decide whether a project gets the green light or dies a miserable death on the drawing board.

It would take a crowbar to force Keith to attend, so I was Lawson Valentine's designated representative and I had asked AJ to be my plus-one.

The server returned with our order. When Madeline

took a grateful sip of her drink, I thought he would melt right before her eyes. She shooed him away with a wicked smile; he returned to the bar and pretended to polish the wine glasses.

"I'll probably wear the white sequined thing I wore last year." I bit into my grilled cheese sandwich which lived up to Monro's high standards and far exceeded my own.

"You absolutely will not!"

"Why not? I've only worn it once."

"You're Sam Calhoon's lawyer, he'll want to show you off."

I put the sandwich back down on my plate. "Madeline, I am not a prize heifer to be trotted around the barnyard before it's auctioned off." Good Lord, we live in the third millennium and women were still considered arm candy in this town.

"I didn't mean anything like that." She clinked her glass to mine. "You just need to look confident, to take charge of Lawson Valentine's newest client, that's all."

I nodded, mollified. "Maybe I can borrow something."

She brightened. "That's a wonderful idea. I have some gowns that would fit you." They might fit me, I thought, but I've seen Madeline's closet. It's stuffed with bustiers and boas, I wouldn't be surprised to find a whip stashed in the corner.

"Um, thanks, I didn't mean borrow from you…thanks though—" She cut me off with a laugh.

"We'll figure it out," she said and took a large swig of her Pimm's.

After twenty minutes of small talk I glanced at my watch and realized it was time to get back to the office. I caught the server's eye and waved my hand in the universal gesture for 'cheque please.' He raced over to our table and did not take his eyes off Madeline until we paid and were safely back out on the sidewalk.

It was almost nine by the time AJ and I finished 'war-gaming' our strategy for the Calhoon meeting. I've always thought the phrase 'war games' was silly—a way for lawyers who are chained to a desk to feel like they're doing something more meaningful than arguing over the placement of a comma—but after years of working with these guys I'd adopted their lingo. I just hoped I didn't sound as pretentious as they did.

~

Louisa and Quincy sprang to their feet when I finally came through the door that evening, struggling to keep my grip on my briefcase, purse, and the poster tube.

"Need a hand?" asked Louisa, while Quincy huffed and puffed.

"I've got it," I said through gritted teeth as I juggled my way into the study and dumped everything in an untidy heap on my desk. When I returned to the TV room Louisa was curled up in her comfy chair with Quincy slumped at her feet. He raised his head and glared at me before dropping his head back down on his paws.

"I think I scared him," I said.

"Well, that was quite an entrance," Louisa said. "Did you eat?"

"Yes…but…" I eyed her Girl Guide cookies and she tossed me one. I caught it before Quincy realized there was food flying around the room.

I dropped onto the sofa, drumming my fingers on its

leather arm.

"You're fidgety tonight," she said.

"Trying to figure out what to wear to my meeting with Calhoon tomorrow."

She shot me a quizzical look. "I've never seen you fuss about what to wear to a client meeting before." Louisa is not one to be impressed by designer labels, or any labels for that matter. "What's up?" she asked.

What's up, indeed? I've had my fair share of regulatory applications go sideways when someone finally admits they were overly optimistic about the level of community support or the size of the market, but I'd never started a case not knowing which of two scenarios, one a slam dunk and the other a gong show, I'd be advocating for. This had to be resolved tomorrow. I don't like uncertainty.

I leaned over and scratched Quincy's head. He wagged his skinny tail; I was forgiven for scaring him half to death. "I don't know, Louisa, there's something about this file…"

"You'll sort it out. Mom always said you were like a dog with a bone, you wouldn't let things rest until you were satisfied. It drove her crazy."

"*Cat*. Mom always said I was like a *cat* with a bone. She never could get her clichés right." Mom died a year and a half ago; Dad passed away a few months later. Louisa and I thought he died of a broken heart. It was months before we could talk about our parents, but whoever said time eases the pain of loss was right.

What they don't tell you is every death creates its own unique trauma.

7

The pigeons were having a party on my windowsill. They'd built a nest under the eaves last year and managed to save their chicks from marauding crows and magpies and appeared to be settling in for the long haul, much to Louisa's chagrin. She says they're messy, depositing sticky pigeon fluff everywhere, but I find their murmurs and the flutter of their powdery wings soothing.

And today I was in need of soothing. I stood in front of my closet, flicking through the hangers. My wardrobe does not rival Meghan Markle's or even Lisbeth's, but what I have is of good quality. After discarding various outfits as being too formal or too casual, I settled on a pair of light grey slacks, a white short-waisted jacket with matching silk top and black patent heels. I was good to go, and still had time to pop in at Campaign HQ before picking up AJ and heading over to Calhoon's office.

Lisbeth was already at her desk when I reached the fourth floor. With her hair pulled back in a chignon and her slim body wrapped in a flowing summer dress, she was better dressed for a day of volunteering than I was to meet Lawson Valentine's most lucrative client. She spotted me the instant I came around the elevator bank. "Please tell me you brought coffee." Only the volunteers drink the campaign coffee, the rest of us bring in something decent from outside.

"Don't you ever sleep?" I handed her my Verona Blend.

Her eyes lit up as she raised the cup to her lips. "You're just in time for the morning call. Nicholas is poking around in the swag area looking for a T-shirt in his size and Wendy is on her way up with muffins."

I was trying to picture Nicholas wearing a *#VoteMichiel* T-shirt under his Armani jacket (he could probably carry it off) when Wendy swanned in. We squabbled over the chocolate chip muffin on our way to the war room. The others were already on the line. Everyone sounded tired, which was a bit unsettling given that there were still many weeks to go.

Nicholas spent a good deal of time lauding Wendy's *#WheresMichiel* social media campaign. It was trending on Twitter which in turn generated some good mainstream media coverage. Wendy ducked her blue pixie head and said The Brat Pack deserved all the credit.

I slipped out of the room when the meeting shifted to gossip about what the other candidates were doing, always a pointless exercise in my mind, and ran into Bernie who was making a racket by the elevators.

A heap of lawn signs and set-stakes lay in a tangled mess on the floor. He was struggling to free a set-stake which was jammed between the rubber bumpers of the closed elevator doors. He yanked it free with a tremendous grunt. "Great," he said, "now it's bent." A set-stake is a wire frame, the top half holds a small lawn sign, the bottom half is nothing more than two pointy metal legs which are jabbed into the ground. The legs on this set-stake were bent at corkscrew angles. They weren't going to poke into anything anymore, not that that stopped Bernie from trying to twist them back into shape.

When I returned to Lawson Valentine I found AJ and Madeline huddled over Bridget's desk. Bridget was showing them photos of her new puppy, she had just dropped him off at puppy daycare. It was his first day but I was sure the puppy, a funny looking pudgy thing, would do just fine.

"He's adorable," I crooned. Bridget beamed like a new mom.

I tipped my head at AJ who followed me into my office and dropped into my visitor's chair. "Are we ready?" I asked. "No new developments since last night?"

He shook his head, his sandy hair falling into his eyes. "Nope, we're good to go." We spent the next hour reviewing the City's rezoning regulations before heading back out into the rising heat of the parking lot.

I waited patiently while AJ, half in and half out of my Mini, fiddled with the lever under the passenger seat, trying to push the seat as far back as it would go. Finally he folded himself into the seat, his knees up around his chin, and announced he was ready to roll.

"You're sure," I asked, "got your seat belt on, feeling comfy?"

He stopped, glancing at me comfortably positioned behind the steering wheel. "You think this is funny, don't you?" he asked with mock indignation. I suppressed a smile, pushed in the clutch, and glided smoothly into first and then second gear.

"It's a standard," he said with a hint of surprise.

"Yes, a real one with a gearbox and everything, not one of those shiftable automatics. Can you drive stick?"

He snorted. "Of course I can drive stick. I'm a farm boy, remember. I learned to drive my Granddad's tractor when I was twelve. Tractors, balers, Minis, they're all the same to me."

AJ wasn't exactly a hayseed farm boy. His grandfather owned an agricultural conglomerate headquartered in Saskatchewan and was constantly pestering AJ to join the family business, but AJ refused, wanting to make his own way in the world.

"We're a dying breed," he said.

We *are* a dying breed, I thought, and not just because we drive stick. AJ, like Keith and me, wanted to practice law the right way, not padding our billables or taking shortcuts to boost our profit margins. What brought that on? I wondered, my eyes flicking across the rear-view mirror.

We found a parking space a half a block from Calhoon's building. AJ grabbed his briefcase and the poster tube while I reached into the back seat to haul out my briefcase and purse, which was packed with my wallet, emergency makeup, dog treats, Kleenex, a small notepad, three pens (likely dead), loose change and Lord knows what else. Why do women let fashion designers talk them into buying handbags bigger than suitcases?

Calhoon Tower occupies an entire city block. It's a glittering monument floating in a sea of hard and soft landscaping that looks stunning all year round. The grounds are studded with urban art including a gigantic silver sculpture of a bird which is actually a million tiny birds that shimmer and chime with the slightest breeze. This is a windy city, it's a wonder the sculpture is still intact.

We entered the lobby and approached a long reception desk staffed by two attractive young women wearing matching pale blue outfits. They didn't sport company name tags, just the company's logo, CDC, which appeared as a discrete embroidered flourish over their left breast pockets. They could have been models for Vera Wang. One woman looked up at us expectantly. When I said we had an appointment with Mr. Calhoon she checked her computer and asked for identification. We handed her our drivers' licenses and she created two temporary passes complete with our names and photographs. I glanced at AJ. "I guess we're in the Calhoon database now."

The elevator to the thirty-sixth floor floated up the centre of the building and opened onto a plush lobby decorated in soothing earth tones, punctuated here and there with a shot of red or yellow. We were greeted by another young woman, this one not wearing a pale blue CDC outfit. She waved a graceful arm in the direction of three long sofas arranged around a heavy marble coffee table and said she would inform Mr. Calhoon's executive assistant we had arrived.

AJ sank into a beige leather sofa, but I remained on my feet. I'm not very tall, about five foot five, and discovered early in my career that extricating myself from squishy low sofas did not create a brilliant first impression. Far better for me to stand around pretending to admire the artwork which in this case looked like Soviet Art Deco; brightly coloured, but not to my taste.

Calhoon's EA glided down the hall, her hand extended. "It's so nice to meet you, Ms. Valentine, I'm Bev." She was a well maintained fifty-something woman; Madeline would describe her as an 'Office Wife,' a loyal secretary who is ready day or night to pick up Calhoon's dry cleaning or drive his kids to the airport.

I shook her hand. "I'm Evie."

She smiled and trained an inquisitive eye on AJ. "And you must be Mr. Braxton." He grinned and asked her to call him AJ.

We followed Bev past a row of large offices with floor-to-ceiling glass walls. The office furniture was sleek and modern; ergonomic leather chairs with shiny metallic arms were positioned behind glass-topped tables which, depending on the occupant's tolerance for clutter, were either buried in mounds of paper or completely bare. Each desk had a keyboard and wafer-thin dual screen monitors. Based on the steel name plates affixed to their doors, all but the vice president of human resources were men.

Bev stopped at Sam Calhoon's door. He had his back to us and was staring out a large plate glass window. The view from his corner office swept over the western half of downtown and wheeled north across the river. Bev cleared her throat and he turned slowly to face us.

Calhoon's silver-grey hair was swept back off his forehead, his face was tanned. An easy smile played across his lips as he rose to shake our hands. "Thanks for taking the trouble to come downtown," he said. His voice was surprisingly soft for a man his size.

"It's no bother," I said. "I've wanted to see the view from up here for a long time."

He chuckled. "It's not the tallest building in town, but it's got a sightline right down Third between the Richards Parkade and the Wilson Building, clear out to the Ridge and the airport."

"It's spectacular," I said.

He turned back to face the window. "You can see the

planes coming and going all day long. It's like watching fish in an aquarium. Peaceful." I followed his gaze. He was right, all those planes dropping out of the clouds were mesmerizing.

We accepted Bev's offer of coffee and watched her bustle down the hall. Calhoon directed us to two long sofas facing each other across a large glass coffee table at the far end of his office. The room was the size of a tennis court. We were settling ourselves on the sofa (another low squishy one) when Bev returned carrying a tray bearing porcelain mugs, coffee, cream, sugar, and a plate of palmier cookies. The coffee was delicious. No doubt freshly ground, there would be no Nespresso capsules cluttering up Calhoon's break room.

I told Sam how pleased we were to be working with Calhoon Developments Corporation on their residential applications and asked him to describe his vision for the pavilion project. There isn't an executive on the planet who doesn't relish an opportunity to expound on their schemes and dreams.

Calhoon was no exception. His grey eyes lit up as he explained that he'd named the development 'The Pavilion' in honour of its long history as a lawn bowling facility. The townhouses would be traditional in design, none of this modern concrete slab stuff that would clash with the Pavilion's fine architecture. He was looking forward to restoring the historic building and while he recognized there would be some architectural challenges, there always were with these wonderful old buildings, he was confident they could be overcome.

Calhoon stood and walked over to an antique walnut cabinet that looked like it belonged in a British map shop.

He pulled a drawing out of one of the flat oversized drawers and lay it gently on the coffee table. It was the same as the drawing he had left with Keith: Plan A.

"Sam..." I looked at him carefully. "I wonder if you could clear something up for me."

He smiled in that indulgent way older men do when young women ask them questions. "Fire away." For a second I thought he was going to add 'little lady.'

"This drawing is the same as the one you left with Keith last Monday. It depicts a three-storey, nine-unit townhouse development and a restored pavilion. Plan A, right?" I paused, reminding myself to soften my tone, I wasn't cross-examining the guy.

He looked guarded. "Yes."

I picked up AJ's poster tube and tapped it gently. Plan B slid out and landed with a soft plop on top of Plan A.

"But this one for the same site is different. The Pavilion and the townhouse development are gone, replaced by a ten-storey tower four times the footprint of Plan A."

Calhoon became very still. His eyes narrowed. "Where did you get this?"

AJ explained he needed a more legible drawing and Bev sent him a USB stick. Now we had two very different renderings for the same site.

Calhoon crossed his arms. An emotion I couldn't read flickered across his face.

I continued. "Sam, just to be clear, this isn't a problem. We need to confirm which proposal is going forward to City Council. Plan A is relatively straightforward, but if you intend to build Plan B, we'll need to build in some extra time for public consultation. This will delay the process by a month or more depending on the level of opposition."

Calhoon looked steadily at me. "There will be no delay to the process. Plan A is the correct rendering. The Pavilion will be preserved. That is how the application will be presented to the City." He sounded like a drill sergeant, the words rattled out of his mouth like marbles.

"Glad to hear it," I smiled, attempting to lighten the mood. "Public hearings are contentious at the best of times, public hearings concerning the demolition of historic buildings even more so. Remember the ruckus over the Wilson Building, the developers promised to save the Art Deco exterior; by the time they were done with it all that was left was the marquee. The Heritage Preservation Society went ballistic."

AJ opened his mouth, took one look at Calhoon's face and wisely said nothing.

"Right, then," I continued brightly, "the application should move through the bureaucracy quickly and, as an added bonus, Calhoon Developments will be showered with praise for going the extra mile to restore the Pavilion and preserve the existing landscape—"

"—Good." Calhoon cut me off in mid sentence.

There was an uncomfortable pause. The electric hum of the HVAC system filled the silence. I set my coffee cup down on the table, the porcelain clunked when it touched the glass surface. "Sam, who should we deal with from the company? There's no need for us to bother you with trivial questions."

He hesitated, as if he'd temporarily forgotten the name of his right-hand man. "Garry Johnston, VP for Business Development, Bev can introduce you." He paused again. "No, wait, Garry's out of town until next week. Bev will give you his contact information."

I gave AJ my 'we're done here' look, he nodded and started rolling up the drawings to stuff them back into the poster tube.

Calhoon placed his hand flat on the edge of the Plan B drawing. "Leave it." He sounded like Louisa telling Quincy not to touch something vile on the sidewalk.

"Certainly." AJ slipped Plan A out from under Plan B, rolled it up tightly and slid it into his poster tube.

Calhoon thanked us again for making the trip downtown, we told him it was our pleasure and the three of us went out to Bev's desk where he instructed her to give us Johnston's business card. She stepped over to her credenza and rifled through a lacquered red box. She probably had the details of every single member of the management team including their anniversaries and children's birthdays in that box. She gave each of us one of Johnston's cards and Calhoon said she would show us out. Bev went ahead to call the elevator while we shook hands with our client. Sometimes it takes longer to say goodbye after a meeting than it takes to have the meeting itself. This was not one of those times.

We returned our temporary passes to the women in matching outfits at the main reception desk and stepped out into the late afternoon sunlight.

AJ turned to me. "Is it just me or did something weird just happen?"

"It's not you, something weird just happened."

Sam Calhoon built a multi-billion-dollar real estate empire in a city where fortunes rose and fell on the price of oil. Only those with the sharpest instincts and steadiest nerves survived. I had expected him to laugh off the mix-up with the drawings, instead it stopped him cold. Was he just another thin-skinned executive embarrassed by a subordinate's sloppy mistake? I told AJ to forget about it, we had our marching orders.

Madeline was sitting at Bridget's desk when we returned to Lawson Valentine.

"Where's Bridget?" I asked.

"That puppy daycare place. She's worried sick about the dog. God knows why; if the Facebook photos are anything to go by, he's having a fantastic time."

"They post pictures of the dogs on Facebook?"

"Indeed, all dolled up with sunglasses and tiny hats, they look better than I do on the French Riviera."

I had a fleeting impression of Madeline and the pudgy puppy wearing matching caftans and sun hats.

"Speaking of being dolled up, have you figured out what you're wearing to the Gala?" Madeline asked. "It's next Wednesday, you know."

AJ glanced from Madeline to me, "If you two are going to talk clothes and dogs in funny hats, I'm outta here," and ambled down the hall to his office.

"Madeline, why are you so curious?"

She smiled coyly. "I'm going with Duffy O'Halloran."

"You've got to be kidding! O'Halloran is running against Michiel, you know that right? And since when do you know O'Halloran?"

"I know everyone, darling."

Madeline *did* know everyone. She knew them when they were nobodies, years before they became somebodies. If she ever wanted to blackmail this crowd she'd be set for life, well, more set than she already is.

"Won't this be fun," I grumbled. "Michiel and O'Halloran circling each other like a cobra and a mongoose, the press hoping one or the other goes ballistic, and you and me trying to smooth things over with small talk."

"Not me, darling," she said, a dreamy smile on her lips, "I'll be sipping champagne and dancing to the music. There are better ways to spend an evening than watching two men in tuxedos go at it *mano a mano*."

I laughed and went to find AJ who was working on his computer. He had pulled up the City Planning website and was downloading additional information. The application should be relatively straightforward from here on in.

8

The heat shimmered across the alley as I pulled into the underground parkade at the campaign office. I ran up the basement stairs and picked my way through the spools of thick wire and batts of insulation that littered the main lobby.

Lisbeth was in the coffee room chatting with some volunteers about an upcoming pamphlet drop. She smiled and tipped her head in the direction of the war room. "Nicholas is waiting for you."

Nicholas was sitting at the conference table, his arms crossed behind his head, his chestnut loafers up on a chair, watching a video on his laptop. Even sprawled across the furniture he looked elegant.

"Good, you're here," he said, swinging his feet to the floor. "Michiel wants to push a message about preserving the city's natural amenities. Which of these clips do you like better?" He turned his laptop to face me.

"Hey Nicholas," I said dryly. "Nice to see you too."

A puzzled look crossed his face, then he grinned and said slowly, "Well hello, Evie, how nice to see you. Doing well

I trust?" I replied I was just dandy and sat down beside him while he opened links to videos of Michiel extolling the virtues of nature in the city. The first clip showed Michiel on a leafy riverbank, against a backdrop of silvery wolf willows and rustling cottonwood trees. The second placed him in front of a large pale brick house that had once been the home of Maclean Jones, a respected politician, now long dead.

"Well, it's pretty obvious, Nick…em, Nicholas. If Michiel is going to talk about nature on our doorstep, he should be out in the wilds, not preaching from the heart of the concrete jungle."

Nicholas snapped the laptop shut. "That's what I told him, but he wants to do it in front of the Mac Jones House."

"Why? Is he trying to create a subliminal connection with one of the greatest politicians we've ever had?"

He chuckled. "I hadn't thought of that."

"I was being sarcastic."

Nicholas sat up in his chair. His smile faded as he moved his empty coffee cup round and round in tiny circles on the worn tabletop. "I don't know what's up with him lately."

"Michiel?"

"Yeah, he's distracted, irritable…" Nicholas stopped, his eyes flicked to the window and back.

"Well, he *is* campaigning to be re-elected as mayor, that would be a major stressor for anyone, even Michiel who's one of the most optimistic and laid-back people I know."

"Yeah, well, he wasn't this erratic the last time around, and back then we thought he'd lose." The coffee cup stopped moving. "He's ridiculously confident one minute and convinced he's going down in flames the next."

This didn't tally with the Michiel I'd seen over the last

few days. "Give me an example."

"Debate prep." Nicholas shot an uneasy glance out the door at Lisbeth. She was at her desk, head bent over her laptop, long fingers motionless over the keyboard. Nicholas lowered his voice. "I want to schedule a half day mock debate so he'll be rock solid on live TV, but he refuses to put in the time." His eyes flicked back to Lisbeth, then to me. "I get it, Evie, he's smart, articulate, charming…but that's not enough against O'Halloran."

"O'Halloran? Surely O'Halloran's not a serious threat. He has all the money in the world, but the polls I've seen say people don't trust him. He's just another rich, bored businessman who's doing this for a lark. God, Nicholas, if we've learned anything over the last few years, it's that rich men dabbling in politics are a menace to the public."

Nicholas put his elbows on the table and started massaging his forehead. I recognized the signal from our law school days. It meant Nicholas was either very frustrated or very disappointed, likely both.

"Nicholas," I touched his sleeve. He looked up and I noticed it for the first time—he was exhausted. "Is there something happening at work that's bothering him? A project off the rails or over budget? Union strike? Sex scandal?"

He snorted. "You just described my typical day, and no, there's nothing out of the ordinary. I just don't get it. His approval ratings are strong, way better than O'Halloran's and significantly better than Sarah Hamilton's; yet one day he's too cocky for debate prep, the next day he's wringing his hands, convinced the campaign is going to hell in a handbasket…"

Sarah Hamilton. I had almost forgotten about Sarah

Hamilton, the city councillor and single mom who'd entered the race at the last minute. Apparently the only thing Michiel and Nicholas agreed on was that Sarah was a non-starter.

"Can you have a 'come-to-Jesus' talk with him?" I probed gently.

"I've tried. He just changes the subject. When I push it, he shuts down."

"Do you want me or Lisbeth to talk to him?"

"Lisbeth *has* talked to him. She got nowhere. And no offence, Evie, but he doesn't know you well enough."

"None taken," I said. "Well, if he won't talk to anyone, all we can do is keep him focused on the campaign. You know what they say, a busy candidate doesn't have time to get underfoot and screw things up."

Nicholas' face relaxed and he laughed. "Spoken like a true political operative, Evie."

"Anytime, Nicholas."

I gave him a reassuring smile and returned to my desk to check how we were doing on office supplies. I thought I'd hate this part of the job, but the Staples website is a goldmine of esoterica. Who knew they carried pencil sharpeners shaped like pig snouts or bouncy castles?

9

LATE AUGUST 6 weeks to Election Day

"You look amazing!" Louisa said as she secured a diamante clip in my hair.

"You approve?" I twirled in front of the full-length mirror. Tonight AJ and I were attending the Heritage Awards Gala. My designer gown, midnight blue with tiny sparkles that glimmered like stars in a velvety sky, came to me direct from Dream Closet, a rent-the-runway store, and would go straight back there tomorrow because I'll be damned if I'm going to spend thousands of dollars on a dress I'll only wear once.

Louisa was in charge of my hair and makeup. My dark hair was swept up in soft waves, my eyes were smoky, my lips were ruby red. Usually I look like a no-nonsense lawyer, chin-length hair, minimal makeup, well-designed clothes, but tonight I looked like a movie star straight out of the 1950s. *I'm ready for my close-up, Mr. DeMille.*

I checked my watch. It was almost seven. "AJ will be here soon."

He may be my plus-one but this wasn't a date, it was a business function: we'd cover twice as much ground with two of us schmoozing the movers and shakers…still, I was going to a black-tie function with AJ. This was going to be fun.

My phone buzzed.

I'm here. AJ texted.

Coming down. I replied.

Louisa pointed at my phone. "Mom would kill you if she saw you doing that. She'd say it was as bad as some yahoo pulling up in front of the house and leaning on the horn."

"That's true," I replied. "But this is a work thing, it's not a date."

Louisa harrumphed. I slipped my phone into a tiny silver handbag (borrowed from Madeline) and tried not to wobble in my stilettos as I made my way down the front steps to AJ's car.

"You look fantastic!" AJ and I said it simultaneously. Any man looks better in a tuxedo, but with his sandy hair and strong features AJ looked like a secret agent on his way to save the world. "Thanks," I said, feeling a tad embarrassed. He grinned and off we went.

Rutherford Hall is a magnificent sandstone building that started life as a teachers' college before being converted into a banquet hall for swanky events. AJ pocketed the valet ticket and I slipped my arm through his as we crossed the street and passed through the massive brass doors. We went up a short flight of stairs and entered the main hall which was jammed with sparkling rainbow dresses and stiff dark suits. Peals of laughter punctuated the silky sounds of a string quartet. Waiters drifted through the crowd bearing trays of canapés and champagne flutes.

Madeline appeared out of nowhere and graced us with a smile. "You two look lovely." She was wearing an off the shoulder beaded red gown and a diamond necklace that sparkled so brightly I thought I'd go blind.

"Madeline, you're beautiful, as always," I said. "So, where's the inimitable Mr. O'Halloran?"

She waved vaguely toward the centre of the room. "Duffy's in there somewhere hobnobbing with the kingmakers and bagmen." She laughed and floated away as gently as a soap bubble.

I looked at AJ. "Shall we mingle?"

"Sure, meet you back at our table when dinner starts."

We'd checked the seating plan when we arrived. We were seated at Table 15, which was nicely placed in the middle of the dining hall. Our dinner companions, the City Solicitor and his wife, also a lawyer, an investment banker and his girlfriend, and a social media entrepreneur and his husband, promised an evening of lively conversation.

The roar of the crowd increased as I pressed into the centre of the room. I heard a distinctive laugh and spotted Michiel in a perfectly tailored tuxedo and highly polished shoes, chatting with a small group of people. Louisa was wrong, with his dark hair and deep brown eyes Michiel looked more like a young George Clooney than Cary Grant.

"There she is," he said when he spotted me, "the best office manager and regulatory lawyer in the city." Would he ever tire of that line? Would I?

"Hello Michiel," I laughed, and air kissed his cheek.

He took my arm and drew me closer. I strained to hear

what he was saying over the excited chatter. “Nicholas says someone broke into the campaign office last week.” Michiel was referring to Lisbeth’s suspicion that someone had rifled through her desk after she’d gone home for the day. She always arranged her stapler, pens, and papers just so. ‘A place for everything and everything in its place,’ she said in a tone that defied anyone to disagree. One morning she found her coffee cup on the wrong side of her desk. She was convinced we’d had a break-in. I checked the coffee room, the bathrooms, even the cage in the parkade; everything was as it should be. Nevertheless, the coincidence was unsettling. A few days earlier Keith had arrived at the law firm, fresh off his houseboating adventure, and found the coffee room window wide open and the shelves in the supply room in disarray. Nothing was missing and we put the incident out of our minds.

“Lisbeth is just a little stressed, Michiel,” I whisper-yelled in his ear. “She thought it might be someone from the O’Halloran campaign doing oppo research.” I shook my head. Opposition research? Had she lost her mind? This was a couple of guys running for mayor, not for president of the United States.

A shadow of concern crossed Michiel’s face. He’d known Lisbeth since elementary school, they’d always been close. I told him not to worry, I’d talk to her.

“Where is she?” I asked, scanning the crowd.

“In there somewhere,” he said, glancing over my head. “She invited the head of the university’s business school to be her guest. She’s probably talking his ear off about setting up an internship program with the City.”

A booming voice cut off the rest of our conversation. “Hey you two. Is this a private conversation or can anyone join in?" Duffy O'Halloran was bearing down on us with a couple of minions in tow. No sign of Madeline, no doubt she was sipping champagne and dancing to the music.

Michiel whispered, "Here goes." He grinned and extended his hand. O'Halloran is a good four inches taller than Michiel and was trying to look even taller. He too was wearing a custom-made tuxedo, nothing off the rack for these two. With his curly black hair and green eyes he looked very Irish. Attractive in an overconfident, 'I'm rich' kind of way.

Michiel and O'Halloran engaged in small talk while people from the media edged closer to catch what they were saying.

"Can we get a photo, fellas?" A scruffy-looking photographer from *The Journal* held up a tiny camera. The fellas obliged him with three or four shots before shooing him away.

"Good turnout," said O'Halloran.

"It gets bigger every year," Michiel replied. "Like the Academy Awards for developers who care about heritage buildings. Instead of getting an Oscar, they get a bronze lion."

O'Halloran tried to interject, but Michiel kept on talking. "As you know, the lion is a copy of the ones outside City Hall. And those are copies of the ones at the base of the Nelson monument in Trafalgar Square. A nice historical touch, don't you agree?"

O'Halloran brushed aside this bit of trivia and changed the topic to the upcoming candidates' debate. Michiel flicked his eyes in Nicholas' direction. Nicholas caught the signal and materialized by Michiel's side to hustle him away.

O'Halloran turned to me—*great, now I'm stuck with this*

guy—but just then I spotted Sam Calhoon and an attractive middle-aged woman engaged in an intense conversation by the bar. She was staring down into her cocktail; he was talking to the top of her head. I smiled sweetly at O'Halloran and said I'd catch up with him later and struck off in Calhoon's direction.

Calhoon greeted me with a broad smile as he introduced his wife, Marianne. She offered her hand and allowed me to shake her fingertips.

"Where's Keith?" Calhoon asked.

"He's recovering from sunburn and houseboating, long story." This was a little white lie. Keith did have a touch of sunburn but given the choice between the Gala and a root canal, Keith would choose the root canal.

Calhoon erupted with a loud laugh. Marianne managed a tight smile. When Calhoon told her Keith and I were representing the company on the Pavilion file she took a big swig of her martini and tuned out completely. Apparently, the only thing Marianne found more boring than her husband was her husband's business.

In stark contrast to the unsettling mood that marked our last meeting, tonight Calhoon was voluble. He bounced from topic to topic: How long had I been with Lawson Valentine, why did I leave Gates, Case and White, where did I go to law school? These were the kinds of questions a client asks a lawyer before they decide to place their business with the firm, not afterwards.

It was a relief when a bell chimed three times indicating it was time for dinner. The crowd quickly got its bearings and flowed like an amoeba into the dining hall, a large airy room with tall windows that splashed red-gold light across the glittering tableware. I made my way to AJ who was standing next to Table 15, placed my tiny purse beside my plate and sat down. Unlike most convention halls that jam guests in so tightly you can't lift a fork to your lips without elbowing your neighbour, here we could breathe. As we waited for our table to fill up, AJ leaned close to say he had connected with Garry Johnston, our contact on the Pavilion file.

"Oh, what's he like?" I asked.

"What you'd expect: smooth, slick, but always probing beneath the small talk. Seems to know his stuff though, from the few minutes I talked to him."

Our dinner companions settled in their chairs while we waited for Michiel to step up to the podium. The microphone squealed, he laughed and said now that he had everyone's attention he was delighted to welcome us to this glorious event. He invited us to enjoy the music, the delicious food, and the fine wine, and promised to return during dessert to present the awards.

The conversation at our table quickly moved to the upcoming municipal election; by the time we finished our quinoa salad we'd reached a consensus: O'Halloran would be lucky to garner thirty percent of the vote. We started our grilled chicken and fingerling potatoes with an animated debate about American politics and were well into our coffee and hazelnut chocolate tart when Michiel returned to the stage to kick off the formal part of the evening.

His presentation started well with a reminder of the importance of the city's heritage buildings—they tell us who we were and where we'd come from—but went sideways when he presented the Best Heritage Developer award to the company that had been universally vilified in the media for reneging on its promise to preserve the iconic Wilson

Building. Then it got even worse. Michiel gave the Best Heritage Champion award to the woman, a well-respected university professor, who'd organized a city-wide protest to pressure City Council to save the Wilson Building, only to see it fall under the wrecking ball. The room gave her a standing ovation when her name was announced, making it clear to the developer—and to Michiel—whose side they were on.

Our table tried to understand Michiel's bizarre decision. Why honour the developer who'd obliterated a historic landmark as well as the woman who'd fought him tooth and nail, refusing to give up until the building was pulverized?

I leaned closer to AJ, whispering in his ear. "When the Wilson Building was slated for demolition, it fell to Nicholas to deflect the blame from Michiel. He spent months in the public eye, fending off angry citizens and antagonistic reporters who refused to believe the building was too far gone for restoration. The controversy finally died down… until tonight." Voices barely under control rolled across the room while Michiel smiled calmly, thanked everyone for attending and wished them a good evening. *What on earth was he thinking*?

An hour later AJ and I were pressing our way through the crowd in search of the valet station. AJ handed in his ticket and we waited in silence for the car. He tipped the valet and opened my door before I could beat him to it.

"Well that was strange," I said.

"No kidding. You could have cut the tension in that room with a knife." AJ pulled out into traffic. The air was soft. I could barely make out the shapes moving in the dusky shadows on the sidewalk.

I said, "For a moment I thought that poor woman was

going to refuse the award."

AJ nodded. "That would have been hugely embarrassing for Michiel."

"Maybe that's what he was banking on, that she wouldn't make a scene in front of all those people." *Why do politicians use our inherent decency against us*?

AJ glanced at me. "You've got sparkles in your hair." I could not see his face clearly, but he sounded like he was smiling.

I laughed. "My dress is shedding." It was a lovely evening, but I was tired and looking forward to getting home. "I'll see you in the office tomorrow. We can put the finishing touches on the Pavilion application."

"I'm meeting with a client in the morning but…" he pretended to look at his watch, "…I can squeeze you in, say, late afternoon?"

I chuckled. "Sounds good. Around four o'clock, then?"

"Sure." He pulled up in front of my house and I stepped out of the car.

"Thanks for being my date tonight, AJ."

"My pleasure, ma'am."

I knew Louisa would be in bed by now, she was on days tomorrow, but that did not stop Quincy from thundering down the stairs and bodychecking me into the closet.

I rubbed his ears and told him he was a good dog. He had sparkles on his snout. "Good grief, Quincy, you're ruining my dress, go back to bed." He trotted back upstairs to Louisa's room and I kicked off my shoes and hiked up my dress to avoid leaving a trail of sparkles from the front door all the way up to my bedroom.

Tomorrow was media day. I was assigned to drive Michiel to interviews all over the city. It would be grueling.

None of us expected a warm reception from the media, the esteemed members of the Fourth Estate.

10

"Well, this looks ominous." Lisbeth and I were standing next to the floor-to-ceiling windows at Campaign HQ, peering into the grey morning light. Heavy raindrops splashed against the glass and the spindly ash trees planted in holes carved into the sidewalk whipped from side to side.

"I hope whoever designed this building knew what they were doing or we'll be sliced to ribbons," I said as the windowpane shuddered in its frame.

"Did you bring a raincoat?" Lisbeth asked. I was tempted to say no so I could borrow hers, a sleek black Alto Cappotto coat that would be more at home in the back seat of a limousine than scrunched up behind the wheel of my Mini.

"It's downstairs in the car. I'm ready for anything, rain, snow, hurricanes, King Kong, you name it."

"That's Sim City," she laughed. "Come on, let's figure out where you're supposed to be today."

Lisbeth opened her laptop and checked the emails from media outlets requesting interviews. Michiel was going to blitz the newspaper editorial boards today, the interviews would go online tonight and into the print editions tomorrow. He wanted the stories to settle over the weekend before following up with the TV and radio talk shows next week. That would put him squarely in the public eye in the first week in September, boosting momentum in the final sprint to election day.

I looked at the media lineup. Were any of these interviewers hard-hitting crusaders for justice or simply hacks, purveyors of click-bait and thirty second sound bites? Not that it mattered much. Michiel's approach to the media was simple: dazzle them with charm and refrain from being drawn into a slagging match over anything, period. He believed the public had grown weary of non-stop negativity, so he defaulted to cheery optimism every chance he got.

I printed off our schedule: *The Journal* at 11:00, *The Sun* at 12:30 and *The Star* at 2:00. Lisbeth wished me luck as I grabbed my purse and went downstairs to the parkade to fetch the car.

The Mini shuddered in the wind when I slowed down in front of City Hall. Michiel was standing outside in the rain, staring at the pavement. His raincoat flapped around his knees and his dark hair stood straight up. I pulled up at the curb and rolled down the passenger side window. "Where's Nicholas?" I yelled over the wind.

Michiel struggled to pull the passenger door open. "God, this is a small car."

"Get in. Where's Nicholas?"

"Getting lunch."

Just then Nicholas appeared clutching a soggy paper bag. He handed it to Michiel and looked at me, incredulous. "This is your car?"

"Get in the back, Nicholas." I hopped out, pushing my seat forward so he could squash his damp body into the back seat. "Try not to get too crumpled back there." I managed to keep a straight face while he fussed with his seat belt.

Michiel settled in the front seat and opened the paper bag. *Bam*! The car smelled like a Happy Meal.

"Jeez Michiel…" I wrinkled my nose in disgust.

"No time to stop for lunch," he mumbled through his first bite of a McChicken burger. This was true. *The Journal*'s office is in the northeast quadrant of the city, *The Sun* and *The Star* are in the northwest. The last thing we wanted to do was parade a hungry, crabby Michiel before the press.

Nicholas pulled a page of talking points out of his briefcase and passed it to Michiel.

"Good," Michiel said, "you added a bullet point about increasing the number of residential units in the downtown core."

Nicholas nodded. "You may get some questions about the Heritage Awards, given the controversy over the Wilson Building."

"What controversy?" Michiel asked mildly. Was he kidding? Did Michiel truly not understand the hypocrisy of giving the heritage preservation award to the developer who'd demolished the finest Art Deco building in town?

I glanced at Nicholas in the rear-view mirror. He rolled his eyes.

Fat raindrops splatted on the windshield and the windows steamed up as we zipped between semis rocketing down the highway. Siri had a minor meltdown when I detoured around some road construction but otherwise did a fine job of getting us to *The Journal*'s office on time.

The rain eased off a bit by the time I pulled into the

parking lot. We piled out of the car, glad to be out in the fresh air. Our reflections rippled across the reflective glass walls of the building as we approached the main entrance. Michiel, Nicholas and me, our dark raincoats billowing in the wind, the sky a luminous pearl grey behind us; we looked like something out of *The Matrix*.

Nicholas hauled open a heavy glass door and we filed past him. I told the young woman sitting behind the front counter we were here for a meeting with the editorial board.

"Wait there, they're almost ready for you." She pointed to a row of chairs pressed against the wall in the reception area where a very wet young man was scrolling through his Twitter feed. None of us sat down.

A door banged open in the back of the building and we heard O'Halloran's voice booming down the corridor. Soon he appeared, flanked by his campaign manager and two young guys in lumberjack shirts, too sloppily dressed to be part of O'Halloran's team.

O'Halloran spotted us and strode purposefully toward Michiel. He clapped Michiel on the shoulder with more force than was necessary in any setting other than an arrest and said, "How are you doing, buddy?"

Michiel gave O'Halloran that two-handed handshake politicians favour nowadays: one hand gripping O'Halloran's upper arm, the other vigorously pumping his hand.

"You're doing the circuit, I see," Michiel tipped his head in the direction of the checked-shirt guys, who stared wide-eyed as if they were suspended in amber. What did they expect, that Michiel and O'Halloran would knock each other down like rams in mating season?

"How's it going?" O'Halloran asked.

"We're getting a good response at the doors, how about

you?"

"Lots of feedback. Michiel, my man, you're in trouble." O'Halloran's eyes glinted.

Michiel laughed. "Duffy, all that matters is the feedback on election day."

O'Halloran glanced over his shoulder at one of the checked-shirt guys. "Rupert, you take good care of my friend here." His campaign manager told the wet young man in the reception area to bring the car around. O'Halloran guffawed, saying a little rain never hurt anyone and barged out the door. The other two sprinted to keep up.

We turned to Rupert who indicated we should follow him. He snapped his fingers at the young woman behind the counter and shouted "Coffee." At us? At her? It was hard to tell. We declined and followed him through to the conference room. Rupert introduced us to a paunchy middle-aged man hunkered down like a cane toad at the far end of the table. This was Bob, the managing editor, Rupert was the deputy editor and the other lumberjack-shirt guy was Malcolm, the city editor.

Bob did not bother standing up, he barely extended his hand, clearly expecting Michiel to come around to his side of the table; a show of deference, I suppose. Instead Michiel quickly shook Bob's hand, then sat down at the other end of the table with his back to the windows. Now Bob would have to squint against the glare to gauge Michiel's reaction every time he asked a question. I glanced at Nicholas who cracked an insincere smile and we took our places next to Michiel. We were off to a great start.

Bob said, "Now that you've met the editorial board of this great paper, let's get started." *Great paper*? A hedge fund had taken over the paper years ago, they fired half the staff and pulled most of their content from head office in Toronto. Bob turned *The Journal*, which had once been a decent paper into a slightly more refined version of *The Sun*, a junky tabloid complete with scantily clad Sunshine Girls on page three.

Bob peppered Michiel with pointed questions: Why was City spending out of control? Why were the unions running roughshod over City administration? Isn't it true that Council was so hopelessly divided that nothing gets done? It's the mayor's job to deliver the programs but people say Michiel couldn't deliver a pizza if his life depended on it.

None of it fazed Michiel. He's from a large Dutch family where everyone talks at once, yelling to get their points across. Law school had sharpened his mind and he easily avoided being dragged down a rabbit hole. He deflected every insulting question by turning it into the question he wanted to answer, not the one he had been asked, working in his talking points so all Bob had on tape was Michiel at his charming best.

It was a virtuoso performance but it troubled me. Despite Bob's hostile attitude, he raised an important point when he asked who called the shots at City Hall, the developers or the public, because development after development had been approved notwithstanding the public's objections.

Forty-five minutes later we were back in the car.

"Fucking idiots," Nicholas fumed. As chief of staff he could shield his boss from the hostile media, but as campaign manager he couldn't run interference without making Michiel appear weak and incompetent.

Michiel pulled his phone out of his pocket and clicked onto his Twitter account. His fingers flew across the tiny keyboard.

"What are you doing?" Nicholas asked warily.

"How's this sound?" Michiel replied. "Great meeting with #*Journal* editorial board. Thanks guys. Enjoyed it. #*VoteMichiel* #*MuniElex*."

Unlike other politicians who think tweeting in full caps bristling with exclamation points is a sign of intelligence, Michiel was an accomplished member of the Twitterati. Nicholas retweeted Michiel's message. The Brat Pack was on it before we left the parking lot.

The interviews with *The Sun* and *The Star* ran more smoothly, but then again *The Journal* had not set the bar very high.

~

I dropped Michiel and Nicholas off at City Hall before returning to Lawson Valentine. The sun danced around the edge of a cloudbank, raindrops glittered like diamonds on the poplar trees in the woods behind our parking lot.

AJ was hanging up the phone when I entered his office. "How did it go?" He asked.

"Don't get me started on the quality of journalism in this town."

"That bad, huh?"

I slumped down in one of his visitor's chairs.

He smiled. "Well, this should perk you up. I talked to my friend at the City law department. The easiest way to proceed is for Calhoon to meet with the Mayor to see if he'll support the project. If the Mayor likes it, he'll hand it off to his Chief of Staff." AJ nodded at me. "That would be Nicholas, who'll quarterback the project through Corporate Properties, Planning and Legal. Assuming those departments are happy, Calhoon and the City staff will sign a nonbinding Memorandum of Understanding which will be put before City Council a week or two later."

"Doesn't the release of parkland require public notice?"

"That comes later. City staff will present the MOU to City Council behind closed doors—to protect commercially sensitive information and all that—and if Council approves it, then the City will transfer the property to Calhoon. Then Calhoon has to file a rezoning application to split the park in two and build townhouses on one half. That's where the public hearing comes in."

I was dubious. "Sounds like a lot of 'ifs' to me."

"My friend in the City law department says it shouldn't be a problem because Calhoon is restoring the Pavilion, not tearing it down."

"We need to set up a meeting with Michiel and Calhoon as soon as possible—" Suddenly I had an awful thought. "God, I hope Calhoon hasn't donated a bundle to Michiel's campaign. The optics would not be good."

AJ shook his head. "No worries, I've already checked." He turned to his computer and pulled up Michiel's campaign website—Michiel and O'Halloran agreed to disclose their donor lists prior to election day, candidates are all about transparency these days—and scrolled down until he found Calhoon's name. Calhoon, like all the major developers in town, was one of the big spenders, both in his personal capacity and through his company. His donations were large, but not as large as the top donor.

"Not only that," AJ said, "Calhoon contributed the same amount to O'Halloran's campaign."

Smart businessmen always hedge their bets. O'Halloran may have zero chance of winning, but it never hurts to slip a few dollars to the powerbrokers in this town.

"Right. AJ, you set up the meeting: you, me, Calhoon, and Garry Johnston, at any time that suits Michiel. The sooner the better, his schedule is tight and it's going to get a lot tighter in September."

AJ nodded, then stretched and crossed his arms behind his head. "That was a fun event last night, wasn't it?"

Suddenly I felt awkward. *It wasn't a date*. "Yes," I said, "as corporate wingdings go, this one was right up there."

He laughed. "You mean shindigs."

"What?"

"Shindigs. Wingdings are a Microsoft font, like hieroglyphics; shindigs on the other hand are gatherings, like parties."

I rolled my eyes at him and left to check in with Keith.

Keith was absentmindedly winding his mantle clock when I arrived at his door. He smacked it with the palm of his hand, put it to his ear and, hearing nothing, smacked it again. The clock was an antique, crotchety and temperamental like many old things. When it stopped it wouldn't start again without this elaborate ritual.

"Does it need CPR?" I asked.

"Hmmm?" He listened to the clock again, it was ticking.

"You were a million miles away when I came in."

"Was I?" He waved me in. "Have a seat." He placed the clock on his credenza, carefully positioning it dead centre under a large painting, a bright blue and white representation of the mountains.

"Is something bothering you?" I've seen Keith like this before, he floats around in a fog until he gets whatever it is off his chest.

"Bothering me? Nothing really." He settled comfortably

behind his desk. "I was talking to Curtis Chan over at Gates..." Curtis was a member of the regulatory bar. He and Keith wrangled on the opposite sides of countless files over the last four years.

"And...?"

"And we started talking about this Julianna thing."

Julianna? It took me a moment to place the name. Julianna was the young lawyer who had fallen to her death from the forty-fifth floor of Gates, Case and White.

"Oh, has something happened? The last I heard the police were still investigating."

Keith nodded slowly. "Nothing new so far, but Curtis says Gates is seething with rumours. Some people say she committed suicide because her marriage was in trouble, others are convinced she screwed up royally on a big file and killed herself out of shame, a few say she was murdered, why else would the police still be investigating."

"Well, the suicide scenario makes no sense to me," I said. "Wouldn't she kill herself at home if she were having marital problems? Kind of a *see-what-you-made-me-do* message to her husband? And if she botched a major file Gates would cut her loose. By all accounts she was smart and ambitious. She'd demand a big severance package and land a new job at one of the Big Five before word of the screw-up got out on the street. But the murder scenario? Why would anyone murder one of Gates' lawyers?"

Keith turned his chair slightly to look out the rain-specked window. The sunlight glistened on the wet cotoneaster bushes on the other side of the glass.

"It's pretty out there, isn't it," he said quietly before turning back to face me.

"I don't get it, Keith. Why are people at Gates still

buzzing about Julianna? Don't they have better things to do?"

He snorted. "It wouldn't surprise me if Dennison is fueling the rumours, the suicide ones, at any rate. To him, the firm's reputation is everything."

"What are you saying? That Dennison *wants* people to think his standards are so high that if his lawyers make mistakes their only option is suicide? The Dennison version of seppuku? God, that's mercenary."

We locked eyes and he said, "Things were bad when we were there. Can you imagine the stress the lawyers are under now?"

I remembered the newspaper photo of Julianna and her husband laughing for the camera. "I wonder how her husband is holding up."

"According to Curtis they had the funeral a couple of weeks ago. Curtis didn't really know Julianna, he's more a friend of her husband, they play in the same hockey league or something. Anyway, Curtis said the husband is really torn up. He doesn't believe Julianna killed herself."

"Well, I certainly don't understand it, but who knows what lurks in the hearts of man."

Keith gave me a look that implied we were getting much too philosophical for his liking and shifted the topic to the Gala. He hated the idea of getting gussied up in a penguin suit, but he loved hearing all about it afterward.

After a few minutes he asked how things were going on Michiel's campaign. For some reason I was hesitant to discuss it. Maybe it was the escalating tension between Nicholas and Michiel or maybe it was Lisbeth's suspicion that there had been a break-in at Campaign HQ; something was making me uneasy.

11

EARLY SEPTEMBER 4 weeks to Election Day

Lisbeth had said there's nothing to it. Like a fool I believed her. However, the strain of volunteering for Michiel while carrying on my law practice, even at two-thirds time, was beginning to wear on me and I was relieved to be heading home, to push these responsibilities aside if only for a couple of hours. My townhouse is in the inner city, nestled among the birch and weeping willows that grow along the riverbank; we have all the amenities of urban living plus the freedom of the countryside. Last week Quincy and I spotted three coyotes trotting down the street, one had a magpie in its mouth.

I parked the car in front of the house, gathered up my purse and briefcase and went up the front steps to the door. The key clicked in the lock when I heard a sound behind me. As I turned my head, my cheekbone cracked into the oak door and the door banged open. I tripped over the threshold and fell face down into the foyer. Someone slammed down heavily on top of me, crushing the air out of my lungs. Pinpoints of light swirled around me. Then I heard a deep growl, the weight shifted and something—a switchblade—skittered across the floor.

A man with greasy black hair was splayed on the floor beside me. Quincy was standing on his chest. The dog's head was down, his powerful jaws clamped on the man's throat. Quincy made a strange guttural sound. His teeth sank deeper into the man's neck. God, the dog was going to tear his throat out. Shred every cord, every muscle, every tendon until the man suffocated in his own blood. I was suspended, frozen, in a pulsing silence.

"Quincy! No!" Louisa screamed as she flew down the hall.

Quincy growled. The man's eyes rolled up at Louisa as the dog tightened his grip.

"Quincy! Stay!" She yelled, tearing at my arms, trying to haul me off the floor. Quincy followed her with his eyes but did not release his grip.

Louisa spoke slowly. "Quincy. Stop. Don't hurt him. Please don't hurt him." The dog looked at Louisa. *He's not going to let go.* I staggered to my knees. Louisa crouched next to me.

"Are you hurt?"

"What?"

"Are you hurt!"

I could hardly hear her. Blood pounded in my ears. "Get the knife!" I pointed to the switchblade which was now wedged between the baseboard and the back leg of the foyer table.

"Jesus." She whipped around to face the guy spread-eagled on the floor like a frozen starfish. "If you move a muscle this dog will tear you to pieces," she hissed.

"Louisa! Get the knife!" The buzzing in my ears got worse. My heart pounded so hard it hurt. She picked up the knife.

Then my thoughts slowed, became clear. We had to get Quincy to release this guy before the dog filleted him. "Louisa, we have to tie him up, immobilize him."

"The basement." Louisa gave me the knife—*Jesus*—and raced down the narrow stairs to the basement. The knife was heavier than I'd expected. Shiny pointed blade, well balanced, nice heft. I looked back at the man. His breath came in harsh puffs, but he'd stopped squirming.

Then Quincy growled. "It's okay, she's coming back." But it was not okay. A stranger attacked me, the dog had him by the throat, and I had a switchblade in my hand…I stared at him, memorizing his features. The idiot looked like Moe from The Three Stooges, same stupid hair cut, same piggy eyes. Louisa came pounding up the stairs. She had something in her hands.

"Bolt cutters? I said tie him up, not castrate him." The man blinked rapidly.

"Wire cutters," she said as she snipped a metre of wire off a small roll and wrapped it around the man's ankles. He moaned when the wire bit into his flesh. Quincy snorted, drool ran out of his mouth, down the man's neck, forming a puddle on the floor.

Louisa moved up to the man's hands which were pressed into the floor, palms down. "Good boy, Quincy, good boy." The dog made a guttural sound.

The man's eyelids fluttered. Beads of sweat appeared

on his forehead. *Yes, be afraid. Be fucking afraid.* Quincy rumbled louder.

"Put your hands up, over your head. Slowly!" Louisa hissed. "Press your palms together, slowly or I swear he'll kill you." She cut another length of wire and looped it around the man's wrists. She sat back on her heels when she was finished. I found my purse under the hall table and pulled out my phone. Quincy was absolutely rigid, lethal as a loaded bear trap. He was making sharp snorting noises. *It wouldn't take much to trigger him.*

I dialed 9-1-1. I told the operator there was an intruder in the house, my sister and I had immobilized him. We needed the police. The operator asked for my address and said the police were on their way. She continued to talk to me until a police car arrived ten minutes later. It felt like an eternity.

The gravel crunched as the squad car rolled up to the curb. The car door popped open. How were we going to get Quincy to release Moe? Would Quincy attack the cops? He doesn't like strangers, especially men.

I stepped onto the stoop. A lanky policeman stood next to the cruiser, his partner was opening the driver side door.

"Stop! Don't come any closer, please," I called out. "I have to come to you." The cop stopped at the bottom of the steps. Stay there, he motioned to his partner.

"I will bring you in. If the dog sees you with me he'll know you're a friend." Would he?

I forced myself to relax and met the cop halfway up the front steps. We entered the foyer together.

"Hello, um, Sergeant?" I said politely as if he were coming to tea. "Quincy, look who's here, it's a nice policeman." Quincy swivelled an eyeball in the cop's direction. Moe thrashed, Quincy snarled, and Moe became still. Maybe he's not as stupid as he looks.

"It's okay, Quincy." Louisa stroked Quincy's ear. "Everything is okay now. The nice policeman is here. He'll take this bastard away."

"Jesus," the cop said under his breath, his eyes darting around the foyer before coming to rest on Moe.

We stood quietly in the doorway while Louisa, crouching next to Quincy, patted his back and crooned in his ear. "Leave it, Quincy, leave it, please." Gradually the dog relaxed his grip on Moe's throat. Then he turned to Louisa and dropped his head into her lap.

"Good boy!" she whispered. "Good, good boy!" Blinking back tears she slipped her hand under Quincy's collar and hauled him off into the powder room, shutting the door.

Moe, wriggling on the floor like a jellyfish, unleashed a stream of obscenities and demanded that the fucking dog be shot. He shut up mid rant when Quincy hurled himself against the powder room door which shuddered on its hinges. The cop, a lean, middle-aged man, looked down at him and said, "Buddy, if you know what's good for you, you won't say another word." He cuffed Moe before reaching for the wire cutters to free Moe's hands and feet.

"They trussed you up like a turkey," he shook his head in wonder.

"Fuck off," Moe said as the cop led him out to the squad car where his partner eased him into the back seat.

The cop, who introduced himself as Sergeant Pritchard, returned to take our statements. Quincy barked and thumped against the powder room door and I told Pritchard Louisa would have to let Quincy out or he'd break down the door. Pritchard had the good sense to sit quietly at the kitchen island while Quincy sniffed his shoes. Satisfied that

Pritchard wasn't a threat, Quincy yawned to show Pritchard his teeth and lay down at Louisa's feet.

Pritchard pulled a notepad out of his pocket and I described what had happened, starting with unlocking the front door and ending with Quincy slamming into Moe so hard he lost the knife.

"What knife?" Pritchard asked.

I looked down at my hand. Where was the knife? I glanced around the room and spotted the knife resting on the table in the foyer. I didn't remember putting it there.

"I'll get it." Louisa stood up.

"No, I'll get it on the way out."

Louisa said, "Quincy grabbed him by the throat and would not let go."

"Yeah, I noticed that," Pritchard said dryly.

I touched Louisa's hand. "I've never heard him make that sound before."

"Neither have I." She shuddered and I put my arm around her.

Pritchard stopped writing for a moment, then said, "Any idea who he is?"

"Not a clue."

"You called him Moe just now."

"Oh, that." Now I was embarrassed. "His hair. He looks like Moe from The Three Stooges."

Pritchard nodded and looked at Louisa. "You know him?"

She shook her head.

He glanced at his notes. "Anything going on in your lives that might account for this?"

"Nope," I said. "Nothing out of the ordinary, I mean other than the campaign." He waited for me to elaborate. "I'm volunteering on Michiel Van Dijk's re-election campaign."

Pritchard scribbled something in his notepad and flipped it shut. "This will do for now," he said. "Here's my card. You two will need to come down to the station to file a formal complaint. Feel free to call me if you think of anything else, okay?"

"What about Quincy?" Louisa's voice quivered. "Will he be put down for attacking Moe?"

"Not a chance," Pritchard said. "The dog was defending its owners against an armed intruder." The interview complete, he crossed over to the table in the foyer and nudged the knife into a baggie.

It took me two tries to lock the front door after Pritchard left, my fingers kept slipping off the lock. I turned to Louisa and hugged her very hard.

"Louisa…"

"I know."

I shuddered. "For a moment…I wanted Quincy to kill him."

"I know."

"It was like…"

"Shhh. Don't." She stroked my hair.

I scooped up the spool of wire and the wire cutters and set them on the kitchen island. "Where did you get this stuff?"

She smiled. "If you paid any attention to your surroundings you'd have noticed I'm building a clematis frame next to the garage."

"Well, good for you and your green thumb." I hugged her again. Her body, like mine, was trembling. Quincy shoved his head between our knees. "Oh, Quincy." His ears popped forward at the sound of his name. "Do you want a treat? You deserve one." He snuffled in the pantry cupboard while I rummaged in the treat bag.

"How about you Louisa, want a drink? We certainly deserve one."

Louisa isn't a big drinker. Neither am I, not anymore, but we filled two crystal glasses to the brim with wine and downed them faster than freshmen playing a drinking game. I stalled as long as I could before going to bed, afraid I'd have nightmares. But other than a strange dream about a three-headed hound that wouldn't let me pass, I was fine.

12

Is that a black eye?" Keith peered at my face.

"My, aren't you observant."

Keith and I were catching up over a cup of coffee in his office. The early morning sunlight bounced off the river, nicely illuminating my bruises. Pain shot up from my cheekbone into my temple when I bit into my chocolate donut.

"You should see the other guy," I said.

"That's what they all say," he replied.

"No, I'm serious, Quincy almost killed him."

"What…?"

I'd just gotten to the part where Louisa appeared with the wire cutters when the others piled into Keith's office and I had to start all over again from the beginning.

"Jeez Evie, are you sure you're all right?" Bridget peered closely at my face. She'd swaddle me in cotton balls given the chance.

"Yes, we're fine."

"Do the cops know who he is?" Madeline asked.

"They think he's a petty criminal."

AJ frowned. "A home invasion in broad daylight, with a switchblade? Doesn't sound too 'petty' to me. Why'd he target your place and not someone else's?"

I had managed to convince myself this was just some random attack, all Louisa and I had to do was take the usual precautions, keep our doors and windows locked, stay alert for strangers in the street, but nevertheless AJ's comment worried me.

"I don't like it," he said.

I tried to make light of it. "Are your spidey senses tingling, AJ?"

"Ha ha."

We went back to his office so he could update me on the Calhoon file.

"We've got an appointment with your good friend the Mayor on Friday," AJ said. "I confirmed with Calhoon's office—oh, did you know Bev retired? Her replacement is a woman named Brock."

"Brock?"

He shrugged. "It will be Calhoon and the business development guy, Garry Johnston, you, me, Michiel, pardon me, the Mayor, and Nicholas, in his role as chief of staff, not campaign manager—these guys wearing two hats is getting confusing. We're meeting at eleven."

"Sounds good." I entered the date and time in my cell.

AJ continued. "I'm meeting with Johnston later today to make sure we've got our ducks in a row. He'll brief Calhoon and we should be all set. Have you got time first thing Friday morning to touch base?"

"Absolutely. I always have time for you, AJ." I smiled. "I'll get Madeline started on the corporate searches, I want to ensure the park property is transferred to the right Calhoon company."

AJ looked puzzled. "I assumed it would be Calhoon Developments Corporation."

"Not likely, developers create separate standalone companies for each project they build. If the building is defective, say leaky windows or a sinkhole swallows the parking lot, the developer is only on the hook for whatever that subsidiary has in the bank, which isn't much, just enough to pay the trades, hookups to City utilities, builder's liens, that kind of thing."

"Ah yes," AJ said, "the corporate veil."

"Indeed. Madeline can confirm with this Brock person which sub should be named in the MOU and do some searches. For all their smarts, these big companies have a habit of forgetting to file their annual returns at the Corporate Registry, especially if they have a lot of subs like Calhoon does."

I found Madeline arranging a stack of papers into a tidy pile on her desk. Her eyes lit up when I told her I needed a detailed corporate search on CDC. Madeline is one of the few people I know who'd jump at the chance to run something through CORES, the corporate registry system.

~

Lisbeth's teal blue skater dress flared gently around her legs as she hustled back and forth between the filing cabinets and a small group of volunteers sipping coffee in the coffee area. One of the volunteers spotted my black eye and I had to repeat the intruder-with-a-knife story all over again.

Lisbeth set down the pamphlets she was carrying and

dragged me over to the window so she could better examine my bruises. "It's a good thing you didn't fracture your cheekbone," she said. "You have lovely high cheekbones, it would be a shame to ruin the symmetry."

"The symmetry? I'm just grateful we all survived."

She grinned and said, "You didn't miss much on the morning conference call. Nicholas said Michiel wowed the editorial boards—" this was an overstatement but I let it go "—and Clint and Wendy were pleased with the print and online versions of the story. But Evie, did you see the comments?"

"I never read the comments. They're usually written by idiots."

"Apparently some people don't like Michiel's appearance."

"Why? What's wrong with his appearance?"

"They say he's a hipster, as in avocado toast eater, or too Euro-sophisticate, whatever that means."

"That's strange," I said, "his appearance didn't seem to bother them the last time around." *What did they want, a cowboy covered in dung*?

Lisbeth and I were working at our desks when the elevator pinged. A slick looking man in a flashy suit strolled around the corner, propelling a frail old man in a yellow cardigan ahead of him. Lisbeth was on the phone and it fell to me to be the welcome committee.

"Hello," the flashy man's voice filled the corners of the room. He thrust out his hand. "I'm Salvatore Cancio. Where's Michiel? I want a sign." He grinned, baring teeth that were very white. "Three signs. Huge ones." He spread his arms wide. "To put on my restaurants." This was unusual. Commercial establishments generally avoid displaying political paraphernalia lest they offend their customers.

He continued to grip my hand in a crushing manly-man handshake while I explained Michiel was not here. He peered around the office; did he think I had stashed Michiel in a cupboard somewhere? I promised I would tell Michiel he stopped by and assured him Michiel would be very pleased to have his support. This placated him somewhat and he turned to the thin old man standing quietly by his side.

"This," Salvatore said, shoving the old man toward me, "is my father-in-law, Al Alfonsi. Al and Sal, Sal and Al." He laughed heartily. Clearly, he had made this joke many times before and still found it amusing. I laughed politely and shook Al's birdlike hand. The old man looked at me, bewildered, and then back at Sal who was still chuckling at his display of wit.

"Salvatore…" I said.

"No, no, call me Sal." Again with the loud voice. Was poor Al deaf? Is that why Sal yelled all the time?

"Okay, Sal. We'd be happy to deliver the signs, I just need your contact information." I picked up a clipboard and a pen.

"No." Sal shook his head. "My car is here, I will take the signs now." I told him we stored the giant signs offsite, but we had some good-sized ones in the cage downstairs that would fit into his trunk. He said that was acceptable but since they were small he would take six, not three.

I parked Sal and his father-in-law in the coffee room and signalled to Lisbeth that I was going downstairs to the cage. By the time I reached the elevator she was off the phone and was offering them coffee. Sal declined, he was too busy ogling her legs, while Al peered up at her from the depths of the saggy old couch; he had lost the thread ages ago.

I ran into Bernie in the downstairs lobby. “Thank God, you’re here,” I said. “I need six biggish signs.”

“How biggish?”

“Biggish, but not so biggish they won’t fit into the trunk of a car.”

We clattered down the cement stairs to the parking garage, Bernie unlocked the cage and dragged out six signs. We lugged them up to the main lobby and propped them against the wall by the front door.

Lisbeth was back at her desk by the time Bernie and I returned to the fourth floor. She smiled as we rounded the elevator bank, carefully avoiding looking at Sal. I introduced Bernie to Sal who puffed up like a Brahma rooster when Bernie said Michiel would be very pleased to have his support.

Sal said, “They’re going on the restaurant wall, outside, two restaurants and on the overpass beside my biggest restaurant, Adriano’s, everyone will see them.” Bernie told him he couldn’t put any signs on the overpass, it was city property, but it was okay to put them on the restaurants’ walls if he owned the property. Sal nodded vigorously, yes, yes, that was what he said. No, that wasn’t what he said, but I wasn’t about to argue with a guy taking six signs.

“You make sure you tell Michiel that Salvatore Cancio took six signs, six big signs. He knows me. Tell him to come back for dinner, and bring his friends, that pretty lady—” he nodded in Lisbeth’s direction “—it’s on the house.” He looked meaningfully at Bernie, then at me; he wasn’t sure who was ‘the boss,’ me or the man schlepping the signs.

He repeated his name carefully, enunciating every syllable, and marched toward the elevators. Bernie snatched the clipboard off my desk and raced after him, desperately trying to scribble down Sal's contact information.

Just as Sal stepped into the elevator I noticed Al, the old man, still wedged in the corner of the sofa in the coffee room, staring blankly at nothing at all.

"Sal," I yelled. "You forgot Al."

"Al is fine," he said, dismissively. "He can stay for an hour." The elevator doors snapped shut and he disappeared. Bernie shot me a glance and busied himself with the clipboard. I looked at Lisbeth who rolled her eyes. We have a strict rule against babysitting volunteers' kids, but neither of us thought we'd need a rule against babysitting someone's dotty old father-in-law.

Lisbeth led Al to a worktable buried under boxes of campaign literature and sat him down in front of a stack of brochures. She showed him how to fold the brochures so the words were on one side and Michiel's smiling face was on the other. Her tone was surprisingly gentle. Al sucked in his lips and with a trembling hand reached out and touched the brochure on the top of the stack.

When she returned to her desk she said, "I'll check on him in a few minutes to make sure he hasn't gotten it backwards. The last thing we need is a crease across Michiel's 'Euro-Sophisticate' face."

"Michiel would not be pleased," I said.

"No, he wouldn't. Creased clothes are bad; a wrinkled face? Unforgiveable!"

I laughed. It's not every day the Ice Princess cracks a joke.

~

That afternoon I was back at Lawson Valentine scrolling through my emails when Madeline swept into my office and parked herself squarely in front of me.

I raised an eyebrow. "I've seen that look before. What's up?"

"This CDC search." She had an oversized sheet of paper in her hand. "I just got off the phone with Brock—" she grimaced "—what kind of name is *Brock*?"

"Go on," I said patiently.

"Brock says the property is going to Calhoon Developments Corporation. But that can't be right. There's no way Calhoon would put the Pavilion in the parent company, they'd want to use a sub to shield the parent company from liability."

Madeline placed the sheet of paper on my desk. "And, surprise, surprise, that's exactly what they've been doing, it's standard business practice, no matter what this silly Brock person says. I ran a corporate search on Calhoon Developments Corporation. There are more than a hundred Calhoon subs, a whole bunch of them called Calhoon Developments Ltd. with a year added to their names, probably the year they were incorporated for a specific project."

"Wow," I whistled under my breath. "Calhoon's built himself quite a spiderweb of companies." She was going to like what I said next. "So, Madeline, given that we'll be representing Calhoon on all his residential developments in the future, it wouldn't hurt for us to understand how all these companies fit together. Could you do a deep dive on Calhoon's corporate structure and prepare a simple, and I do mean *simple*, corporate structure chart for me?"

Madeline's eyes gleamed. "Darling, I thought you'd

never ask." With a dramatic swish of her retro skirt she returned to her office.

I poured myself a fresh cup of coffee and went down the hall to see what Keith and AJ were up to. Keith had left for the day, but AJ was still in his office. I knocked on his open door and asked how it was going.

"Good," he said. "Your eye's looking better." AJ was right, the bruising had settled down and with a liberal application of makeup it was barely noticeable.

"I met with Garry Johnston this morning," he said.

"Oh yes, and…?"

"Very knowledgeable, knows the history of the property like the back of his hand. Told me all sorts of stories about 'the good old days' when the crème de la crème of society held lawn bowling tournaments. Picture this, Evie: they'd get all decked out in their whites for back-to-back matches, pressing on regardless of the weather. At the end of the day they'd change for dinner." He flashed a wicked grin. "After a sumptuous meal the men would send the ladies into another room so they could enjoy their port and cigars in peace. It was all very genteel, you'd have loved it."

"Indeed I would," I snorted, and then looked at him carefully. "Do I sense a 'but' in there somewhere?"

He sighed. "Clearly Johnston is very good at his job, Calhoon wouldn't make him VP of business development if he wasn't, but there's something odd about this guy. I get the feeling if you scratched the surface you'd find a used car salesman ready to sell you a beater that falls apart the minute you drive it off the lot."

My eyes widened. "Whoa, that's quite a statement coming from you, AJ."

He shrugged. "Just a feeling."

I said, “It will be interesting to see how Calhoon and Johnston play off each other at the meeting tomorrow.” Executives who have been together a while develop a rhythm in negotiation meetings, like a good cop bad cop routine but less aggressive. Friday’s meeting wasn’t a hardcore negotiation—based on what AJ’s contact at the City said we were reasonably certain the City would sell us the parkland, but nothing is a sure thing.

AJ tapped his pen on the desk. It sounded like the woodpecker who spent last weekend trying to drill a hole through my eavestrough. “I suspect Calhoon will open the negotiations and let Johnston handle the details,” he said.

“I suspect you’re right.” I glanced at my watch. “I’ve got some work to do before I head back to campaign headquarters tonight.”

“Have fun,” he said.

I spent the rest of the afternoon immersed in an application to build a small solar farm next to a country residential estate. The residents were concerned, well, frantic actually, that it would scorch the countryside and fry the wildlife. My client and I would have to mount an intense community engagement program to allay their fears.

13

Long feathery clouds stretched across the sky and the air was still. I wanted to enjoy the last of summer so I left the Mini in the law firm parking lot and walked over to Campaign HQ. Unlike AJ who can't wait for the onslaught of winter—skiing, snowboarding, snowshoeing!—I detest the cold and would gladly spend the dark months of winter dozing in front of a fire with a good book propped open in my lap.

I stopped at Little Spice to pick up a samosa, its fragrance filled the elevator as I rode up to the fourth floor. Lisbeth was packing up when I arrived.

"How did it go with Al?" I asked. "Did Sal pick him up or is he still doing origami in the coffee room?"

She hesitated for a second, then remembered Al, the befuddled old man who'd spent the morning folding brochures. "Oh, yes, Sal retrieved him after two and a half hours. Sweet old guy."

"Well, you certainly don't look any worse for wear." Given that she'd spent the day fielding phone calls, organizing volunteers, accepting donations, giving out

T-shirts, and babysitting seniors, she looked remarkable, blue eyes bright, lipstick perfect.

She tucked a strand of hair behind her ear and smiled. "There was a lot going on today. I was on the phone half the morning confirming Michiel's TV interviews for Monday." She made a face. "He forgot to mention he has to be at ACE-TV at six-thirty in the morning for *The Breakfast Show*. He needs a driver. I can't do it. Luckily, Wendy's available."

"What about CTV and CBC? They're at ten and noon if I remember correctly."

"Wendy will do those too."

"So, all's good until Tuesday when he does the radio shows?"

"Yes," she said absently. "All's good." She tossed her phones and her laptop into her Fendi tote bag and rummaged around for her car keys. I wished her good night, but she didn't reply.

I studied the volunteers' Brownie Points sheet while I ate my samosa. Looks like we have a new category: people who throw a tantrum and spit, literally, at the mention of Michiel's name. Decorum is dead.

Three groups of door knockers trickled in over the evening. They reported good vibes on the doors and just one family pet, a belligerent Siamese, that clamped on to a volunteer's ankle and came *this close* to being booted into traffic. I thanked the volunteer for her selfless sacrifice to the cause.

The sun was sliding behind the buildings across the street, dusk settled over the city. It was time to lock up. Nicholas did not like having volunteers working alone late at night. He said you just never knew what kind of crackpot might wander in. The fact that the office was on the fourth floor of a building still under construction didn't help, there wasn't a soul in the place after the construction guys left for the day.

I had just finished putting the poll kits away when the elevator pinged. Had Lisbeth forgotten something? I was about to call out her name when I heard someone say, "Stay here, watch the elevators."

I froze.

It was the voice that told Sergeant Pritchard to fuck off. The intruder with the switchblade. Moe was here. I was caught in the middle of the room, halfway between my desk where I'd left my phone and the elevator bank. Trapped like a rabbit on the highway.

Heart pounding, I crept across the floor, keeping the elevator bank between me and Moe. Maybe I could reach the door to the stairwell, it was next to the elevators in the lobby, and make it down the stairs. I stuck my head around the corner of the elevator bank.

A scrawny man with curly hair squashed under a blue baseball cap was on the far side of the lobby with his back to me. Curly was staring at a large poster of Michiel, who was grinning from ear to ear. Could I slip into the stairwell without Curly seeing me? He turned slowly. I ducked back. The cupboard doors in the coffee area slammed open and closed. Something metallic bounced lazily across the floor.

What is he looking for?

I pressed against the wall.

Moe's shoes squeaked as he crossed the concrete floor, heading toward our desks at the far end of the room. When he gets there he will find my phone and my purse and he'll know I'm still here.

The ladies' bathroom was to my left, built into the

concrete core that houses the elevator, the stairwell, and the utilities. If I hid in the bathroom and they found me, I'd be cornered with no way out. But standing here with Moe on one side and Curly on the other was no better.

I crept along the wall, eased open the bathroom door and slipped inside. There was a moment of inky darkness before the halogen lights clicked on, illuminating the sinks, large glass bowls positioned on an iridescent tiled shelf. *God damn modern design, nowhere to hide a roll of toilet paper let alone a human being.*

Five toilet stalls with floor-to-ceiling doors ran across the back wall. The doors were wide open, a sparkly decorative ledge ran across the back of each stall about waist height. Another useless element of modern design—

—I peered up at the ceiling. A false ceiling dropped down about a foot below the real ceiling. It stopped a foot short of the back wall and was edged with LED lights that reflected off the glass tiles, bathing each stall in a luminous glow.

Could I get up there and hide? Was the drop ceiling strong enough to bear my weight?

Moe yelled to Curly. He'd discovered my purse and phone.

Christ!

I rushed to the bathroom stalls, closing all the cubicle doors, except the one at the far end right next to the wall. If the drop ceiling was attached to the wall as well as the concrete slab above it, it would be better anchored here than in the middle of the room. I slipped into the cubicle and slid the metal latch shut. Gingerly I placed one foot on the toilet seat. Steadying myself against the cubicle walls I stepped up onto the ledge, testing my weight. It felt solid.

Thump. Moe banged open the bathroom door.

I put both feet on the ledge, held my breath, and scrambled up, mashing my body between the real ceiling and the drop ceiling suspended below it. The space was dirty and dark, littered with screws, bent nails, and oddly shaped hunks of wood. But it felt solid. I was safe…for now.

“Check the stalls,” Moe growled.

Curly started at the far end, flinging open each door until he reached my stall. “It’s locked.”

He rammed the door with his shoulder a couple of times. The hinges groaned but the metal latch held.

“Get out of the fucking way!” A scuffling noise.

The door was made of heavy wood with decorative slats running across the bottom half. I wondered what they were made of.

Moe threw his weight against the door, once, twice. It didn’t budge. He let out a string of obscenities and told Curly to stay put. The bathroom door banged open and slowly hissed shut. Curly didn’t move a muscle. Neither did I. We waited. The bathroom door opened and hissed shut again.

“Break it down,” Moe said. Metal things clattered across the tiled floor.

“What’s this?” asked Curly.

“Kitchen junk.”

Moe snarled. “It won’t be long now, sweetheart.” Fear and rage engulfed me.

Then a loud crack. A slat shattered.

“Well, don’t stop now shithead, rip ‘em out.” Slats cracking and splintering.

Then silence. Curly stopped. “There’s no one here.”

“What the fuck are you talking about?”

"See for yourself," Curly said. I imagined Moe peering through the broken slats. For one insane moment I wanted to be down there so I could stab a shard of wood into his eye.

"She's got to be here," Moe muttered. Slats splintered and bounced across the floor.

"Well, she's not," said Curly.

Moe didn't reply. Someone kicked the door again and again. It boomed, the noise reverberating off the sparkling glass mirrors and the thousand tiny tiles embedded in the walls.

I held my breath.

Moe erupted into a lurid description of what he'd do to me when he found me. *Not if I can help it, jackass*!

The stream of obscenities faded as he dragged Curly out of the room. The pneumatic door hissed shut for the last time. I didn't move. Thirty seconds later the halogen lights clicked off. I was wrapped in darkness, comforting and still.

Eventually, the elevator pinged.

I waited. Were they really gone? I would stay up here in my pitch-black hidey hole all night if I had to. Twenty minutes later the elevator pinged again. My heart began to race.

"Evie?" Someone called my name. It barely registered up here in the dead space between the drop ceiling and the concrete floor above.

Then louder. "Evie, are you here?" It was AJ. I had to get out of the ceiling. I was stiff with fear and anger. I flexed my hands. Start moving, just start moving.

I inched to the edge of the drop ceiling and swung my legs down, flailing around in the dark, searching for the tiled ledge. My belt caught on a clip that anchored the LED lights, it snapped off and I half slid, half fell onto the ledge and bounced to the floor, landing winded between the toilet and the cubicle wall. A shard of wood nicked my ankle. I reached out blindly until my hand touched the door. The metal latch was loose but intact. I jimmied with the lock and threw my body against the door. It popped open and I fell out on to the floor. On my hands and knees I picked my way through the broken slats and kitchen utensils littering the floor, crawling forward until I reached the opposite wall. Feeling my way I found the door, yanked it open and stumbled out into the light.

"AJ?" I coughed.

"Jesus, Evie!" He rushed over and steadied me as I swayed uncertainly on my feet. *Just what I need, another face plant*. Suddenly my legs turned to jelly and I sat down. AJ sat down with me.

"Evie, you're a mess. What happened?" I was caked with plaster dust and metal shavings. My eyes stung and I couldn't stop shaking. "What happened to you?"

"Moe and Curly," I pointed at the bathroom. "Trapped. Ceiling."

"Trapped?"

"Bathroom ceiling." I shook my head to give myself time to calm down.

"I need a drink," I said, firmly.

"You need a doctor," he replied.

"A drink…my place."

"Okay," he said, "but I'm driving."

"Good, my car's…" I couldn't remember where my car was.

"First we call the cops."

"No need," I gulped. "I know who…explain in the car."

He shook his head. I stared him down with bloodshot eyes and he relented. We gathered up my phone and purse. My wallet, credit cards and cash were untouched. What did they want?

"Why are you here?" I was breathing more steadily now. "Not that I'm complaining."

"We'll talk when we get you home."

We took the elevator to the lobby and drove in silence to my place. I felt jittery, my stomach heaved. He told me to take deep breaths. I tried to speak, to assure him I was all right, but the words wouldn't come.

~

Except for the kitchen light, the house was dark. Louisa and Quincy were already in bed. Quincy grumbled when we came in; I called to him to reassure him it was only me. I told AJ to pour himself a beer while I had a fast shower. I felt prickly, like I'd rolled in pink insulation. AJ was sitting at the kitchen island looking at his cell phone when I returned with a bottle of wine. He listened carefully when I described the attack, interrupting only when I referred to my assailants.

"Moe and Curly?"

Embarrassed, I explained. "I remember people by associating them with film stars. When our parents took us on vacation, Louisa and I would amuse ourselves at airports playing the Movie Star Game. You know, who looks like a famous movie star but is actually a schlub. I set the all-time record with the most Tom Cruise sightings at Heathrow."

AJ smiled and gestured for me to continue.

It took me fifteen minutes to get the entire story out. "If I were a teenager with a cell phone glued to my hand, I could have called for help, but I left my phone on my desk."

"I know," he said. "I've been calling you for hours. I left you four messages."

"Really?" It was a relief to focus on something other than myself. "Why?"

"Madeline found something odd in her CORES search. When I couldn't reach you, I tried Louisa, she said you were at the campaign office. And that's where I found you." He smiled at me.

"Pried me out of the ceiling is more like it."

"Things are never straightforward with you, Evie."

"So, Madeline? CORES search…?"

AJ pulled up a photo on his cell. "Right. Madeline says CDC was incorporated in 1983 when Calhoon took over the business from his dad. Calhoon Sr. started the business in 1964, building houses. He shifted to commercial buildings a couple of years before Calhoon Jr. came on board. They built a good chunk of Fairfield, you know."

"No, I didn't know," I said.

"Yeah, a real up and comer, our Sammie is."

I stifled a yawn. "AJ, you're talking Yoda-speak." I made a motion indicating he should speed it up. "Tired I am…"

"Right, the CORES search shows CDC has been incorporating and dissolving subsidiary CDC companies since 1983."

"Yes," I said, "it's prudent business practice. If something goes horribly wrong—"

"—Yep, got it, but what we can't figure out is this." He swiped the screen. A second photo appeared. This one showed a simplified corporate structure chart. The parent company, CDC, appeared at the top of the chart, dozens and dozens of little boxes dangled below it. Each had a name, Avro Building, New Cube, and so on. Some of the boxes were white, most were black.

"What do the colours mean?" I asked.

"It's Madeline's colour code. A white box is a sub that is still active, the building is under construction. A black box is a sub that's been dissolved because the construction is complete and the limitation period to sue for deficiencies is long gone."

"What's this?" I pointed to a small red box sitting by itself at the edge of the diagram. AJ enlarged the photo with two fingers. It was a numbered company: 1817245 Ltd.

"That's just it. We have no idea. Madeline connected all the other boxes, white and black, to actual Calhoon properties. There are over eighty commercial and retail projects in the city, a half a dozen parking lots, and eleven residential high rises, some are rentals, some are condos. But she found nothing corresponding to the red box."

I poured myself another glass of wine. "Maybe it's the Pavilion box, red to signify the project is waiting for approval and they'll change its name to a CDC corporate name once they get the green light from the City."

"Nope." AJ pointed to a white box nestled under the parent company. "Here's the Pavilion box. That's why I called you. We're meeting Calhoon and the Mayor tomorrow. Is this important?"

"I haven't got a clue, but I doubt it's relevant to the application." I frowned. "We've got two choices here, we can ask Calhoon about it or we can let it go because we already know which company the Pavilion is going into." I looked steadily at AJ. "Maybe it's because I spent half the night in the ceiling but I'm inclined to let it go unless, or until, it becomes germane to the application."

AJ laughed. "You're sounding very lawyerly this evening, Ms. Valentine. Well, except for the ceiling part."

I smiled and shrugged.

"Fair enough," he took another sip of beer. "That's why they pay you the big bucks."

We were discussing the logistics of getting to the mayor's office—it's easier to lay down a line in *Tetris* than find a parking space near City Hall—when AJ said he'd better be on his way. After he left I realized why: I looked like I'd been hit by a truck, I was exhausted.

AJ texted me just as I slipped into bed: **Call the cops!**

I will. I replied, but I didn't. There would be plenty of time to call them tomorrow.

14

God, what a mess!" Lisbeth was standing in the ladies' room muttering to herself when I arrived at Campaign HQ the next morning.

"Tell me about it," I said.

She started involuntarily at the sound of my voice, then narrowed her eyes, appraisingly. "You know what happened, don't you?"

"As a matter of fact, I do, I—"

"—Wow! Looks like Jack Nicholson took an axe to the cubicle door." Wendy appeared in the doorway. The expression on her face looked as shocked as her hair which was standing straight up in short blue tufts.

Lisbeth leaned against the iridescent counter and crossed her arms, silver bracelets jangling in the tiled room. "So what happened? Take me through it from the beginning."

My throat tightened when I started describing how Moe and Curly trapped me in the bathroom. My voice faded to a husky whisper.

Lisbeth touched my shoulder with a gentle hand. "It's

okay, you don't need to go through all the details. What did the cops say?"

"I haven't called them yet."

"What?" Her eyes grew round. "Why not?"

"I don't know. Too tired and freaked out last night, I guess. And it just didn't seem that serious in the cold light of day."

She waved a hand at the shredded cubicle door, the splintered wood and twisted kitchen knives strewn all over the floor. "Are you kidding me? Have you looked at this place? Evie, you have to call them now."

She was right, of course, but it sounded like she was issuing an order and for some reason this annoyed me. I tamped down my irritation while I fumbled in my purse for Pritchard's card. Lisbeth and Wendy hunched over my shoulder as I dialed his number, Lisbeth pressed her glossy black head close to mine, straining to hear what Pritchard said. He'd send some officers around to assess the damage and collect evidence, assuming there was any. And, when I had a moment, could I stop by the station and give another statement? I suppressed a groan. I had better things to do than hare back and forth to the police station but agreed to stop in after work.

"There, are you happy now?" I snapped at Lisbeth as I hung up.

She compressed her lips and said yes, then huffed back to her desk to report the damage to the building manager. Wendy looked at me sadly, shaking her head.

"What?" I demanded. She said nothing and I left the mess in the ladies' room and sat down at my desk to wait.

Thirty minutes passed and still no sign of the police. I snatched up my purse and announced I was leaving. Lisbeth replied, “Suit yourself.”

My hands trembled on the steering wheel as I revved the engine and raced up the exit ramp into the alley. Why was I so angry? Why was it so hard to tell Lisbeth what had happened? I’d managed to relate the story to AJ (admittedly, he’d been there) and Louisa, who also insisted I call the police. I didn’t snark at them. In fact by the time I strolled into the campaign office this morning I was convinced everything was under control. I’d reshaped the memory, shifting it from sheer terror to something merely unpleasant, like the nasty pills we give Quincy wrapped in cheese slices. But when Lisbeth asked me about it, the memory resurfaced so sharp and jagged it took my breath away.

A horn blared behind me. The driver jabbed his finger in the air. Green light. All right, all right! The Mini shot forward. I couldn’t dwell on this any longer. In a couple of hours AJ and I were meeting with Calhoon and the Mayor. The firm’s representation of our newest client had to be flawless. I stowed the memory in what Louisa calls my Scarlett O’Hara box; I could think about it tomorrow.

~

City Hall is a majestic sandstone building, built around the turn of the last century. It sits next to the Municipal Building, a glass and steel monstrosity that looks like it’s trying to muscle the smaller building off the block.

“Did you know City Hall was designated a national historic site thirty years ago?” I asked AJ. The stone walls bounced the September heat into our faces as we walked up the steps to the front door.

“No, I didn’t know that.”

"Yes, it's one of the few, quote, monumental, unquote, civic halls left on the Prairies."

"And you know this why?" AJ held the door open and I stepped into the cool, dark lobby.

"Google. I'll be damned if I'm going to look like an unschooled rube when Michiel launches into his favourite topic, the preservation of historic buildings, not that you'd know given his performance at the Heritage Awards Gala."

AJ coughed quietly. "This may not be the appropriate time and place to get into all that."

"Yes, you're right. So, would you like me to tell you about the clock tower and the arched entry, or maybe the Romanesque Revival flourishes?"

"No, that's fine, thanks."

A security guard sat at a small desk in the corner of the room. He invited us to look around while we waited for the rest of our party to arrive, pointing vaguely at some old photographs arranged on the wall across from his desk.

"Look, AJ, they've got pictures of the local constabulary." AJ joined me in front of a photo of the first police chief, a man who 'plowed heather as a farmer' in Scotland before becoming a policeman in Canada. His inspector, also a Scotsman, was a strict disciplinarian with 'a genial disposition' which sounded like an oxymoron to me. We were speculating about what it would have been like for the lone woman who worked for twenty-three men in the Electric Light and Power Department when the heavy front doors creaked open and a shaft of sunlight played across the stone floor. Sam Calhoon and Garry Johnston had arrived.

The security guard asked everyone to sign the visitors' logbook, a cheap red binder containing lined pages covered in indecipherable scrawls. Its purpose was to create a record of all the lobbyists visiting City Hall, but it seemed to me that anyone with nefarious intent would simply set up a clandestine meeting with a bureaucrat in a deserted parking lot or more likely, a private room in the back of a high-end restaurant.

We clipped our visitor badges to our jackets and waited for the security guard to inform the Mayor's receptionist we'd arrived. Then we waited some more while the receptionist advised the Mayor's staffer we were here.

Eventually an enthusiastic young man named Todd swept into the reception area and ushered us into a nearby conference room. He offered us refreshments and said the Mayor was running a couple of minutes late. In my experience, all leaders are a few minutes late, it's their subtle way of reminding everyone who's at the top of the pyramid.

Ten minutes later, Michiel breezed into the room accompanied by Nicholas. Today Nicholas was the deferential chief of staff, not the animated campaign manager. He flashed me a quick smile while Michiel vigorously pumped everyone's hand.

We settled around a conference table littered with the detritus of earlier meetings, and I thanked the Mayor for seeing us on such short notice. I explained that Mr. Calhoon had an idea we thought might be of interest to the City. Michiel said he was intrigued, and I turned the meeting over to Calhoon and Johnston.

Calhoon's words were humble but his tone was that of a man accustomed to getting his way. "Mr. Mayor, I know you're an extremely busy man, so I'll get right to the point. City Council is grappling with a shortfall in tax revenue due to reduced business activity in the downtown core."

'Grappling' was putting it tactfully; the councillors almost came to blows at the last budget meeting.

Michiel acknowledged that yes, 'robust' discussions were par for the course these days. He pushed his dark hair off his brow and sighed. "Unfortunately, some councillors fail to grasp the big picture. We can't spend money we don't have." He shot a sideways glance at Nicholas. "We have to be creative, innovative, think outside the box."

"Exactly," Calhoon said. "Think outside the box. I'd like to propose a project that will increase tax revenues *and* preserve an important part of the City's heritage at the same time."

Michiel raised his eyebrows, his eyes alive with interest. Nicholas sat back in his chair, crossed his arms and waited, watching Calhoon carefully.

Calhoon turned to Garry Johnston. "Garry, why don't you take these fine folks through the details?"

"Sure thing," Johnston said. He focused on Michiel with such intensity that the rest of us melted into the woodwork. His spiel mirrored the speech Michiel had given to the volunteers on orientation night, the only difference being Johnston's specific references to the lawn bowling pavilion. Michiel nodded in appreciation. Nicholas brought his hand to his chin, one finger covering his mouth.

"Garry," Calhoon said, "they say a picture is worth a thousand words, why don't you show the Mayor the renderings."

Johnston pulled a large, heavy sheet of paper out of an oversized portfolio case and lay it in front of Michiel as if it were the Magna Carta.

A small box in the lower right-hand corner identified the drawing as "The Pavilion on the Green." The pavilion, a low white building with a steep slate roof, was nestled among mature trees stretching their limbs up into a crystal blue sky. It was no longer a lawn bowling pavilion but a series of trendy little shops and bistros opening out to a slate patio. Johnston directed our attention to the nine-unit townhouse development across from the Pavilion and the grassy berm and thick hedge that would muffle the sound of activity coming from the Pavilion. Happy families lolled on the berm eating ice cream and watching their dogs gambol in the sunlight. Plan A.

"Will there be any lawn bowling?" Nicholas asked. His voice was low and caught me by surprise, he hadn't said more than two words since the meeting began.

"No," said Calhoon, "there hasn't been any lawn bowling, or any kind of organized recreational activity, on the site for a good twenty years."

"That's a shame."

"People aren't interested in the games of yesteryear," Calhoon said dismissively.

I cocked an eyebrow at AJ. Women were no longer interested in being sent out of the room so the gentlemen could enjoy their port and cigars in peace.

Johnston locked eyes with Michiel, ready to close the pitch. "Mr. Mayor, we understand that some members of the public won't like the idea of taking parkland out of inventory and selling it to a private developer, especially when a proposal involves a quasi-heritage building," he paused for effect, "so we would be open to applying for a heritage designation for the Pavilion if that would allay the public's concerns."

Michiel gave Johnston a megawatt smile. "A heritage designation, great idea Garry." He turned to his chief of staff. "Nicholas, this is exactly the kind of creative solution I've been talking about. I want you to quarterback…what's it called," he glanced at the drawing, "the Pavilion, through the process. Call Jake Santos in Corporate Properties, tell him you want someone really senior on the file, preferably Santos himself. Make sure Jake understands this is a win-win all around."

Nicholas fixed his dark eyes on Calhoon. "Just so I'm clear, Sam. Not only do you want to preserve the pavilion, but you're prepared to apply for a heritage designation, if that's what it takes to get this project over the finish line."

Calhoon gave a curt nod. "That's what I just said." His tone was gruff and he smiled to soften its impact.

Nicholas promised to get right on it but Michiel wasn't finished yet. "Give the Law Department a heads up and tell them you'll be personally involved. I expect you to review the Memorandum of Understanding when it's ready. We don't want the lawyers sitting on this one too long." The Mayor grinned at Calhoon. "Having a lawyer as your chief of staff makes things so much simpler."

Calhoon chuckled and said, "Having our lawyer on your campaign team comes in handy as well." Everyone laughed but for the life of me I didn't see why the comment was funny.

"Nicholas," I said. He pulled his gaze away from Calhoon to focus on me. "I'll touch base with you later today to get the name of our contact in the City's Law Department."

"Sounds good," he said.

There was a quick rap on the door. Todd the staffer poked his head into the room. "Mr. Mayor, your eleven-thirty is here." The room filled with the sounds of briefcases snapping shut and chairs being pushed back as we rose to leave. Calhoon wished Michiel good luck in the campaign and said he had no doubt Michiel would sweep back into office with a resounding majority. Michiel told him not to jinx it and we all laughed.

Soon we were out on the sidewalk congratulating ourselves on how well the meeting had gone. I told Calhoon that AJ and I would connect with Garry that afternoon to finalize the key terms of the Memorandum of Understanding; we wanted to get it into the City's hands as soon as possible. Calhoon instructed Garry to do whatever was necessary to move the deal along.

Twenty minutes later, AJ and I strolled into Lawson Valentine, debating what to have for lunch. Bridget summarily informed us we were getting chicken pitas from the food truck outside. AJ and I looked at each other.

"Works for me," I said.

"Sounds great." AJ nodded.

"You guys back already?" Keith's voice rang down the hall. "How did it go?" We found him bent over his desk, trying not to get tzatziki sauce on his shirt.

"Let me guess, Bridget got you lunch. Is she on commission or something?"

He grinned. "And? How'd it go?"

"I thought it went really well. What did you think, AJ?"

"I agree, Calhoon and Johnston were smooth as silk, although I must admit I expected Nicholas to be more engaged in the discussion."

"Well," I said, "he might be a bit gun-shy after the Wilson Building fiasco."

Keith swallowed a bite of pita. "Yeah, it became really acrimonious. First the developer, some one-off company no one had ever heard of, promised to save the building, the next thing you know all that's left is the bas-relief plaque over the front entrance. Nicholas ran interference for Michiel and was crucified."

"Sacrificial lamb," AJ said slyly. "It's part of an underling's job description."

I raised a skeptical eyebrow. "As if you've ever been a sacrificial lamb."

Just then Bridget appeared, carrying two large paper bags bearing the food truck's logo. "Are you guys eating here or the conference room?"

"Conference room." I turned to Keith who asked how Michiel's campaign was going.

"Good," I said, raising my voice so Bridget could hear. "This being an office manager, it's a piece of cake."

"Yeah, right," she said, returning from the coffee room and handing us two plates. "For your pitas, they're leaking." I tipped my head in a deferential bow.

AJ and I spread our files across the conference table, hunching over our plates to avoid making a mess of our clothes. He pulled up a precedent MOU form on his laptop and we began. AJ and I both think out loud when we work, often interrupting each other in mid sentence as we bounce ideas back and forth. It's like a verbal tennis match, chaotic but surprisingly effective.

We were finished with twenty minutes to spare. I was back in my office cruising through my inbox when my phone buzzed. A text from Nicholas. The name of the City lawyer assigned to our file? No, this was personal.

How about drinks sometime? My place?

I had never been to Nicholas' home. Intrigued, I replied. **Sure, when and what time?**

Next Wed 7 PM?

Works for me. Address?

I was entering his address into my contacts when AJ appeared in my doorway; he had Johnston on the line.

Johnston had anticipated the issues we'd flagged as possibly contentious and instructed us not to take a hard line with the City. Feel free to posture all you want, he said, but know that CDC is fine with letting the City win on every point, even the dicey one: how much money CDC was prepared to spend to restore the Pavilion to meet its heritage designation. AJ looked up from his notepad and made a *who knew* face.

The only thing that was non-negotiable was the closing date. The MOU had to be signed, sealed, and delivered a week before the election. This left us a month to close the deal. A month is not a long time to close a commercial transaction of this complexity, even with Nicholas leaning on the City's bureaucrats, but we assured Johnston it was feasible.

~

It was almost 7 p.m. by the time I returned to Campaign HQ. As I stepped off the elevator I was immediately engulfed by a chatty group of volunteers who flowed past me like a school of fish. They waved their poll kits at me—door knocking!—before the elevator doors closed, carrying them away.

"Evie," Lisbeth looked relaxed in an oversized white shirt and dark blue leggings, "come look at the door knocking map." She tipped her glossy black head at a large map of the city.

"It's more green than white now," I said. Green

represented neighbourhoods the door knockers had finished canvassing, white represented virgin neighbourhoods they had not yet visited. This much green a month out from the election was reassuring.

She raised her arms and spread them wide, her silver bracelets jingling as they slipped up almost to her elbows. “Isn’t it beautiful? Michiel stopped by this afternoon; he’s very pleased.”

I was relieved to hear it. If I’d learned anything over the last few weeks, it’s that Michiel’s opinion means the world to Lisbeth. They’d met in the third grade and had a lot in common, two bright, inquisitive kids who grew up on the wrong side of the tracks. Their parents could not afford dance classes or piano lessons so they’d spend Saturdays at the local library learning about spiders and coding and the solar system. Their friendship endured through university and after Lisbeth obtained an advanced degree in political science, she joined Michiel in the non-profit sector and later followed him to City Hall.

Lisbeth handed me a sheet of paper. “Look! The results of the latest internal poll. Michiel is going to knock this one out of the park.”

“Fantastic. Is he going to match the support he got the first time around?”

Her face fell but she recovered quickly. “Well, no. No one expects Michiel to get the same turnout this time around, but the good news is he’s polling a solid twenty points ahead of Duffy O’Halloran.” She licked her lips. “Mr. Look-at-me, Mr. Self-Made Millionaire, who suddenly saw the light and decided to go into public service; he’s in for a horrible shock come election night.”

I smiled. “What’s the plan for this weekend?”

She pointed at the whiteboard calendar hanging outside the war room. Each date box from now until election day was jammed with events scrawled in coloured marker. This Saturday and Sunday would be devoted to 'press the flesh' events at seniors homes and community halls and Sunday evening was reserved for a social media taping with Nicholas and Wendy.

I examined the whiteboard carefully. "I don't see debate prep. Isn't the debate coming up fast?"

"The debate isn't for a couple of weeks. Michiel's a natural, he won't need much prep."

"True, but I thought Nicholas wanted Michiel to block off some time to prepare."

Her face closed. Her words clipped, she said, "I wish Nicholas would stop haranguing Michiel about that stupid debate. If Michiel says he's ready, he's ready, and Nicholas banging on about it isn't helpful."

A number of responses popped into my head, starting with Nicholas is Michiel's campaign manager and perhaps his advice should be taken seriously, but Nicholas and Michiel had had this conversation many times before; nothing would be gained from me arguing the point with Lisbeth.

15

MID SEPTEMBER 3 weeks to Election Day

Of the six candidates who had entered the race, only three had enough momentum to stay in it. Election day was approaching at warp speed and Michiel, Duffy O'Halloran and Sarah Hamilton were in 24/7 campaign mode.

I asked Nicholas if he'd like to postpone drinks at his place but he said no, a couple of hours away from the grind of the campaign would do us both a world of good.

So here I was, standing in front of Nicholas' building, wondering why it was called The New Cube when it wasn't a cube at all but a skinny glass silo, home to the city's wealthy trendsetters. I entered the foyer, a dizzying space of glass and metal, and pressed the buzzer. Nicholas told me to come right up, the door was open.

A tantalizing aroma wafted into the hall as I crossed his threshold. Nicholas was standing in the kitchen, arranging morsels of food on a cobalt blue platter. A long black apron protected his clothing and his lightly tanned face glowed from the heat of the oven.

"Nicholas, are you cooking? You said this was a drinks invitation." I handed him a bottle of wine and a small jar of rose petal and gewurztraminer jelly. I had no idea what gewurztraminer jelly was, but it sounded like something he would enjoy. He accepted it graciously and said it went well with cheese. "You read that on the label just now, didn't you?" I teased.

He smiled and set two wine glasses and a plate of hot appetizers on the kitchen island.

My mouth began to water. "Cox…cox…cox something and pastel something, right? Is this your mom's recipe?" The last time I had homemade Brazilian food was ten years ago when Nicholas took pity on our study group and started sharing the snacks his mom packed for him 'to keep his strength up.'

He laughed. "Coxinha and pastelzinho. Don't you remember anything I taught you in law school?"

"You didn't make this yourself, did you?"

He looked a little sheepish. "Well, truth be told I had a little help."

"Uh-huh."

"Okay, when I told my mom you were coming over she insisted I couldn't serve you reheated frozen appetizers."

"So she 'helped'…?"

"All right, she made the whole thing. But hey, I had to heat it up in the oven, set the dials and stuff."

"Hence the need for the apron, right?"

He held up a hand and laughed. "Enough. Take this to the living room."

I carried the wine glasses and food platter to a low marble coffee table and settled in one of the two grey sofas strewn with oversized tan pillows. Other than the vibrant artwork on the walls there was very little colour in the room: was this Nicholas or the light touch of an interior designer? Nicholas put another tray of appetizers into the wall oven and sank into the matching sofa across from me.

We talked about his mother's culinary skills; after Nicholas' father died, she took refuge in cooking and spent hours cruising the internet looking for new recipes from around the world. He asked how Louisa and Quincy were doing after Louisa's divorce. That surprised me, I had forgotten how well he knew my family. Soon we relaxed into being the Nick and Evie we'd been at law school.

"Ready for a second round of coxinha?" he asked.

"Absolutely," I said, "But first a trip to the powder room." The powder room was as sleek and shiny as the rest of the condo and I was wrestling with the faucet, a curvy goosenecked thing with no obvious way to turn it on, when I noticed a small white card lying on the floor. Nicholas' business card. I slipped it into my pocket. A splash of colour caught my eye as I stepped into the hall: a piece of art in his study. I went into the study to better examine it.

"Nick?" I called out. "Is this an authentic Andy Warhol?"

He joined me. "It is," he said proudly.

I had seen photos of Warhol's ubiquitous *Marilyn* but I'd never seen the real thing up close. The colours were crisp and vibrant. "It must have cost a fortune." The minute I blurted it out I regretted it. "Sorry, none of my business."

"No worries," he said. "It was on auction at Heffel's. They accepted bids for an entire month. I thought I'd lose my mind waiting to see if I got it."

My eyebrows shot up. I had seen the Heffel's auction notice in the paper, the expected sale price was between $125,000 to $175,000. Lord only knows what Nick actually paid for it.

"It's breathtaking, Nick."

He beamed, his eyes lingering on the painting, and said, "Let's go out onto the balcony. The view to the west is spectacular at this time of day."

I picked up my wine glass and followed him out through the patio doors. We settled into black metal chairs that were more comfortable than they looked.

"The sun gets huge when it dips below the horizon," he said softly. "And when the moon is full, Evie, if you look at it long enough it will swallow you whole."

"Nicholas, you missed your calling, you should have been a poet."

He laughed and said, "I like to come out here to think. Sometimes I think too much." He glanced at me out of the corner of his eye. "Evie, have you ever wondered what life would be like if Michiel had not won?"

"Not won the first election?"

"Yeah."

"Well, he almost didn't win, remember, your *Every Kid Deserves a Summer* campaign pushed him over the top."

Nicholas took a slow sip of wine. "Yeah, but what if he didn't win? What would the city be like? What would our lives be like...?"

He set his wine glass down on the table, picked up an appetizer and put it on the serviette in his lap without taking a bite.

"Well, we wouldn't have all those swimming pools for underprivileged kids, for a start."

He frowned. "Three of those pools will close permanently at the end of the year."

"After how hard Michiel fought to keep them open? Why?"

He shrugged. "No money."

"What a shame to have come this far only to lose them again."

He snorted. I glanced at him and he looked away, focusing on the gleaming horizon.

"Nicholas, what do *you* think life would be like if Michiel hadn't been elected?"

"Sometimes I wonder if it matters."

"If what matters?"

There was a long pause. The liquid voice of Holly Cole floated over the murmur of traffic below. Nicholas swirled what was left of the wine in his glass, tipped it back and finished it off.

"Any of it. If it matters who is elected mayor…"

I set my wine glass on the small table between us and pivoted in my chair to see him better. He stared into the twilight, a flurry of clouds ribbed orange and gold pressed against the darkening sky.

"I know Michiel can't impose his will on city council, not in our one-vote system, but Nicholas, you've got to admit he usually gets the votes he needs to push his agenda forward. Look at everything he's accomplished."

"What?" His tone was sharp. "What *exactly* has Michiel accomplished?"

"Good Lord, Nick, you know the answer to that better than anyone." I spread my fingers and started ticking off the highlights of Michiel's first term in office: improved transit, twenty more pocket parks, more supervised consumption sites. Nick's jaw was tight. He said nothing. "And let's not forget his promise to boost tax revenue by pushing inner city residential development."

His eyes flashed. "Do you seriously believe that's going to work?"

"I have no idea," I said with a surge of frustration. "You're the one working on the inside with city staff, city council, and the developers, not me. Whether it works or doesn't will depend on political will and the developers' pocketbooks."

"The developers' pocketbooks. It always comes down to the developers' pocketbooks." A look of disgust crossed his face. "The developers have millions of dollars on the line. They're pushing the administration and City Council really hard." He looked like he was going to say more but thought better of it.

He raised his wine glass to his lips before noticing that it was empty, then set it down again. Finally he said, "Evie, I don't know if I can do this anymore." He sounded very tired.

"Oh Nick, we're almost there. The election will be over soon."

"No, I—" he stopped, pressing his lips together.

The last ribbon of daylight was gone, I couldn't read his expression. "Everything will be back to normal soon. Just a couple of weeks, Nick, a couple of weeks."

He rose abruptly, snatching his empty wine glass and the serving dish off the table, "Yeah, you're right," and returned to the kitchen.

As I watched him bustling about, pulling a baking sheet out of the oven and skewering the cork in a fresh bottle of wine, I wondered why his question disturbed me so much.

Do you seriously believe that's going to work? When he set the food and wine on the table, I touched his hand. "Nick, what did you mean just now?"

He just smiled and said, "Here, try one of these so I can tell my mom you loved it." It was too late. The moment was gone.

We talked softly about everything and nothing—our vacations, our families, Louisa's work, the benefits and drawbacks of inner city living—and watched the sky fade to purple. It was all very pleasant, but I wasn't talking with Nick anymore. I was engaged in polite conversation with Nicholas, one of the "Top 40 Under 40" who could afford to live in The New Cube and buy Andy Warhol paintings on a civil servant's salary.

16

This made no sense. I stared out the window of the gloomy little interview room at the police station. It was very quiet in here. And cold.

The police brought me here to answer questions about Nicholas. I had to answer their questions carefully and to the best of my ability. I am a lawyer, I should be able to do this. I *had* to do this. Because Nicholas was dead.

I recoiled from the thought. How could Nicholas be dead?

I shook my head. At times I could hardly understand my interrogator, Sergeant Pritchard, the cop who answered the call when Moe attacked me in my house. Pritchard sounded like he was talking under water, muffled and far away. He introduced his partner, Officer Martinez. She was younger and looked more sophisticated than Pritchard, who reminded me of a cowboy.

"I'm sorry, what?" I forced myself to listen carefully to Pritchard's question.

"Miss Valentine, Evie, can you take us through it again."

Pritchard glanced at Martinez who turned a page in her notebook.

Take them through it again. Is this really necessary? Yes, of course it's necessary, because, Christ, Nick is dead.

I told Pritchard I'd arrived at the campaign office at 7:30 this morning and was surprised to find Nick's car parked next to the cage. Nick never shows up before 8:30.

When the elevator whispered open on the fourth floor the place was gloomy. On sunny days the office is so bright you practically need sunglasses, but today the sky was grey and dense with rain, and the exposed concrete sucked up what little light penetrated the windows. My first thought was Lisbeth isn't here yet, that's why the lights are off and the coffee isn't burbling in the dented urn in the coffee room.

I called out Nick's name. No answer.

I walked the perimeter of the cavernous space, searching for the lighting panel. It shouldn't be too hard to find, given the place was nothing more than a concrete box with windows. I looked everywhere. The coffee room, the war room, behind the metal shelving in the swag area. Nothing. Maybe the stairwell? It would be a stupid place to put a lighting panel, but where else could it be.

I pushed down on the metal bar that pops open the fire door. It opened a couple of inches then jammed.

I wedged my shoulder into the narrow space, forcing my way out on to the landing.

Nicholas was in the stairwell, on his back, the lower half of his body crumpled on the landing, his knees bent, legs blocking the fire door. His shoulders flopped across two steps leading down. His head tilted backwards as if he were staring down the empty stairwell. Blood everywhere. Smeared on the concrete wall. Pooling under his soft brown hair. Dark sticky blood.

I crouched down and whispered his name. One eye was open and blank. The other eye was a pulpy mess. His hand was ice.

The fire door clicked open behind me. A sharp gasp. I looked up into Lisbeth's pale face. She made a sound, like a whimper. Call 9-1-1, I said. She nodded and slipped back through the door. It closed with a loud click. A minute later the elevator chimed. She was heading downstairs to the lobby.

Pritchard and Martinez arrived. Moving briskly, they herded Lisbeth and me into the war room, then entered the stairwell. We could not hear what they were saying on the other side of the fire door. A few minutes later more official-looking people piled out of the elevator and crowded into the stairwell.

Someone drove us to the police station and left us in separate rooms. How long have I been sitting here in this sad little room, answering endless questions? I was tired. I wanted to go home.

Martinez's pen scratched across her notebook. Pritchard was the only one asking questions.

"Any idea why Nicholas went to the campaign office?"

I shook my head. "Not specifically, he comes in most days."

"Was he working on something important?"

"He's Michiel's chief of staff and his campaign manager, he's always working on something important."

"When did you last see him?"

"Yesterday, last night. Nick, Nicholas invited me over for drinks." *The sun gets huge when it dips below the horizon.*

"What time?"

"Around seven."

"Was he alone?"

"Yes, it was just the two of us. He answered the buzzer quickly as if he was waiting for me to press it. We had wine and Brazilian food. He's not much of a cook, his mother made the appetizers." I was having trouble swallowing. "His mother…someone needs to tell his mom."

"His mother has been informed." *Informed? This will destroy her.*

"I need to go to her."

"Soon. What was his mood?"

"His mood?" I shook my head. "What?"

"His mood last night."

I said Nick was relaxed, happy to see me. We gossiped about our families and our friends. It was like being back in law school. He showed me his new Warhol painting.

Pritchard stopped me there. "Warhol? As in Andy Warhol?"

"Yes, he'd made the winning bid, it was an art auction. He was thrilled." Martinez scribbled in her notebook.

"Then something happened, the conversation lurched off in a different direction. We both became irritable. It was like we were talking at cross purposes."

"Cross purposes? About what?" Pritchard asked.

I described Nick's criticism of Michiel's campaign promises and his desultory comment that it didn't matter who was elected mayor.

"That's an odd thing for a campaign manager to say, isn't it?" Pritchard's question hung in the air.

Then I was struck by a memory, as crisp and perfect as a snapshot, of the two of them in law school. Nick, casually elegant in a black turtleneck and chinos, and Michiel peering up at him through a stray lock of hair, tucked into a quiet corner at Starbucks, debating the merits of a submission to the *Law Review*. "They're an amazing team. Michiel has the charisma and street smarts, Nick is the big picture guy strategizing five years into the future." I stopped. I'd said it wrong, but I couldn't refer to Nick in the past tense. Not yet.

"And that was it?" Pritchard asked the question a second time.

I nodded.

"What time did you leave?"

"A little after nine."

"You were there for what, two hours?"

"That's about right."

"Did he say he was going anywhere, meeting anyone, after you left?"

"No."

"Did you see or talk to him after that?"

"No."

I shivered. It was cold in this dreary little room. "Sergeant Pritchard, how did he die?"

"All I can tell you is he was killed last night. We'll know more after the autopsy." He glanced at Martinez and they both stood up. The interview was over.

"Evie," he said, "the campaign office and the parkade are crime scenes, off limits until we're done."

The campaign? Who cares about the campaign?

"Has anyone told Michiel?" My voice cracked.

"We've contacted everyone who needs to know."

Pritchard said Martinez would drop me off wherever I wanted to go. She gave me a reassuring smile when I said I wanted to go home.

As the three of us walked down a narrow corridor toward

the front door Pritchard added, “Evie, I want you to be very careful.”

“Me? Whatever for?”

“You’ve been attacked twice.”

I frowned. Attacked twice? Once by Moe at my house, but twice? Oh, yes, when Moe and Curly trapped me in the ceiling at campaign headquarters and smashed the stall to bits trying to get me out. I had chosen to characterize that as a nasty scare, not an attack, because Moe hadn’t touched me. It was a coping mechanism.

I promised to be careful. I crawled into the front seat of Martinez’s car and texted Bridget to say I would be out for the day. She replied immediately: They’d heard about Nick. Did I need anything? It was barely noon. Four and a half hours since I’d found Nick’s body. How did the media get wind of this story so fast?

Of course.

Police vehicles blocking traffic outside the campaign office. Construction workers milling about on the pavement, grousing about being locked out of the building. Photos would be all over social media from the moment the cop cars screamed up to the curb until a stretcher rolled out of the lobby and deposited a lumpy black bag into the back of the coroner’s van.

~

It was drizzling by the time Martinez pulled up in front of my house. Louisa called as I unlocked the front door to say she’d be home in thirty minutes. I said she didn’t need to leave work early but was grateful when she said she’d already arranged to have someone cover her shift.

After ten minutes of talking nonsense to Quincy in a pathetic attempt to blank out everything that had happened, I needed something else to distract me and began to tidy up.

I was putting the silk top I had worn to Nicholas' place into the dry-cleaning bag when I felt something in one of the slim pockets. Nick's business card.

I sat down on my bed, gently holding the card between my fingertips. The city's coat of arms figured prominently, a yellow sun setting between a horse and a cow or was it a bull. They were standing on their hind legs. Muscular beasts, the horse was white and looked like a unicorn. The city motto 'No Limits' unfurled under their hooves. Nicholas' name and title were picked out in wavy gold font. He'd included his professional designation, LL.B, even though a law degree wasn't necessary for his chief of staff position. I smiled. *Once a lawyer, always a lawyer.*

Something was scrawled across the back of the card in black ink, a hashtag with seven random numbers, too cryptic for a Twitter hashtag, and no area code, so not a phone number. The number *8* was loopy, the number *1* had a little tail coming off the top. Not Nick's handwriting. I placed the card on top of my dresser.

I was scouring the kitchen sink when Quincy scrambled off the sofa to greet Louisa at the front door. She rushed past him and threw her arms around me. "Oh, you poor thing. Sit down and I'll make us a nice cup of tea." That was it. Everything poured out in a jumble of tears and anger.

Later I received a text from Lisbeth telling me to check my email. After her interview with the police she'd met with Michiel and the team to hammer out a communication plan. *Hammer out a communication plan*? I couldn't even think straight.

Attached to her email were two press releases: one for Michiel, the other for Nicholas' mother. Michiel expressed shock and sorrow at the death of a good and loyal friend, Nicholas' mother described the loss of a loving and supportive son. They both asked that people respect their privacy in the difficult days ahead. Naturally the media would ignore that last bit. Michiel would suspend his campaign for a couple of days—Lisbeth said he wasn't worried the hiatus would give his competitors an edge because they would follow suit; to do anything less would appear callous. Michiel would personally convey his condolences to Nicholas' mother at her home. This visit would be photographed and shared on social media which would ensure the photos would be picked up by the mainstream press.

Lisbeth said the purpose of the communication plan was to help Michiel stay ahead of the rumour mongers, but the whole thing sounded mercenary to me.

17

It was still raining the next day, but I decided to walk to work anyway. I thought the journey, block by slippery block, street light by shiny street light, would return me to the surface of normal life. Horror and disbelief would yield to a growing sense of equilibrium.

I was wrong.

Every red, blue and green newspaper box on my route was jammed with papers screaming variations of 'Mayor's Chief of Staff Murdered!' These headlines were slightly less lurid than yesterday's social media posts which roiled the curious and the mindless with ridiculous conspiracy theories and disgusting speculation about Nick's 'secret' love life. My nerves were a jangled mess by the time I reached the office.

Bridget hurried out from behind her desk when I opened the glass doors and enveloped me in a gentle hug. I could hear Madeline's stilettos clicking down the hall.

"Come," Madeline slipped an arm around my waist. Keith was right behind her and pressed a cup of hot tea into my hand.

"I'm so sorry, Evie," he said quietly.

Bridget asked, "Do they know what happened?" Madeline glared at her. Bridget pursed her lips and said nothing further.

"Evie, do you need anything?" Madeline asked. Yes, I did need something, something from Madeline, but I couldn't remember what it was. She saw the confusion on my face and squeezed my shoulder, silently assuring me everything would be all right.

Keith searched my face. "Should you be working? You've had a terrible shock. Take some personal time." I shook my head. One day at home was more than enough. The distraction of phones ringing, people talking, emails demanding answers, would keep me from sinking further into despair.

As it turned out I wasn't terribly productive, brief bursts of work were interspersed with long periods of staring out the window. Everything looked different now, even the river. Today it was a silvery snake sliding across the rocky riverbed. I was standing by the window lost in the mesmerizing movement of the water when AJ burst into my office, soaked with rain. He flung his briefcase down on my desk and scooped me up in a wet hug.

"Damn," he said when I stepped back, my white shirt blotched with damp folds.

"It's okay, it will dry."

"What about you, are you okay?"

"No, not really." My voice refused to stay in register and my legs felt unsteady. I sat down in one of my visitor's chairs. "I don't think I've really processed it yet."

He sat down next to me. "You two have a long history."

"AJ," I whispered, "it was me, I found him."

"Christ!"

"It was horrible."

He nodded. His hair was curly from the humidity.

"There was so much blood, AJ. I've never seen so much blood." The image was like a broken kaleidoscope; no matter how many times I rolled it over in my mind, the glass shards refused to settle into a coherent pattern.

~

The next day I remembered what I needed from Madeline. I found her in her office glaring at her computer screen, tapping one long red nail on the arm of her chair. Her face softened when I asked if she could look into something for me.

I placed Nicholas' business card on her desk. "Look at the back. What do you make of that?"

She examined the hashtag number. "If you ignore the hashtag this could be a numbered company identifier. They're seven digits long now." Her eyes narrowed. "I've seen this number before."

"Really? Where?"

"Give me a moment and I'll get back to you."

Just then AJ appeared at Madeline's door, asking if I had a minute.

He looked apprehensive and uncomfortable. "Calhoon's office just called. They want to know if Nicholas' death is going to slow down the approval process."

"God, they're not wasting any time grieving for the poor man, are they?"

"To quote Garry Johnston, business is business."

"I'll ask Michiel, I need to touch base with him anyway."

Michiel returned my call a couple of hours later. Our conversation was scattered and desultory. We discussed the media coverage of Nick's death, which was short on facts and long on wild speculation, and we agreed there wasn't much anyone could do about it. Michiel said Nick's mother wasn't holding up very well and I promised to look in on her after work. We both referred to Nicholas as Nick now, reverting to the name we knew him by when we'd met him in law school. For some reason that comforted me.

"Michiel, I don't mean to sound insensitive—"

"Yes?"

"—Calhoon wants to know how we should proceed now that Nick is…um…gone." Okay, that *did* sound insensitive. Nick was lying on a slab in the mortuary and we were already fussing about his replacement. Michiel said he had appointed an interim chief of staff, a guy called Mark Patterson.

"Can Patterson pull this off on such short notice?" I asked. "The closing date is just over a week away."

"Yeah, Nick did all the heavy lifting. Corporate Properties and Planning are on board. The Law Department is fine-tuning the legal documents. We'll meet Calhoon's deadline with a couple of days to spare."

Relief washed over me, then guilt. Was Nick really this expendable?

I was on my way down the hall to update AJ when Madeline called me into her office. She flashed a triumphant smile even before I sat down.

"Okay, what have you got?" I asked.

"It's the red box."

I had no idea what Madeline was talking about.

She spread a large sheet of paper across her desk. "Remember the CORES search I did on Calhoon Developments Corporation?" She flattened the sheet so I could see the big CDC box, the parent company, with little boxes dangling down like coloured bits off a baby mobile.

"Calhoon built over a hundred projects across the city. Every single project is represented here by a white or black box, except this one." She tapped the page with a crimson fingernail. "There's no project linked to the red box. It's an anomaly."

She lay Nick's business card down on the page. The handwritten number with the loopy *8* and the *1*s with the tails matched the number in the red box. 1817245 Ltd.

"Why would Nick have a CDC company, an outlier, scrawled across the back of his business card?" I squinted at the card. "Who wrote this?"

Madeline shrugged. "I have no idea, but I know how to find out."

"How?"

"I'm going to ask Calhoon's secretary, Bev."

I shook my head. "Why would she know, she's—" I caught myself before I said she was *just* a secretary "—retired."

Madeline reproached me with her eyes, then shifted her attention back to her chart. "Bev was Calhoon's office wife. She knows everything."

"Be that as it may, she's gone. Left the province."

"I know that. I just called her replacement, that Brock woman, and asked her what happened to Bev. Turns out she moved back to Quebec City to be closer to her grandchildren." She rolled her eyes. Madeline thinks grandchildren are as interesting as rocks.

"What's your plan then? You can't show up on her doorstep and pepper her with questions."

"Of course not, darling. I'm going to go back to the province of my birth for a well-earned vacation. Then I'll invite Bev to tea at the Château Frontenac—Brock gave me her contact information, that's a breach of privacy you know, that woman is an idiot—and *then* I'll pepper Bev with questions. Subtly, of course." Madeline arched her brow. "Well?"

"You know, that just might work. There's something in the Law Society's rules of conduct…Wait, I'll be right back." I scooped up Nick's business card and Madeline's chart and returned to my office to fetch my laptop.

I found Keith at his desk flipping through *Black's Law Dictionary*. He looked up when I knocked on his open door, a cryptic smile played across his lips.

"Guess what *conventio vincit legem* means." Keith wanders down these obscure little cul-de-sacs sometimes. It's best to go with him, resistance is futile.

"It's Latin for 'not today Satan,'" I replied.

He burst out laughing. "No, I mean, yes, it's Latin, but no, it's not 'not today Satan.' I like that by the way, is it yours?"

"Bianca Del Rio, the drag queen, she won Ru Paul's Drag Race in season six or seven."

"Evie," he said with a hint of admiration, "your interests are wide and varied." He dropped the dictionary on the corner of his desk. It landed with a satisfying thump. "*Conventio vincit legem* means the express agreement of the parties overrides the law."

"I see. Are you counselling a client to make an agreement that overrides the law?"

"No, but it's an interesting concept, that you can legally agree to override the law, like a Möbius strip that loops back on itself."

"Okay, now you've totally lost me."

He motioned toward a visitor's chair. "What's up?" he asked.

Good, he's back in the land of the here and now. "There's been a strange development on the Pavilion file. I don't know what it means, but I need to check it out…and checking it out invokes one of the Law Society rules." We always talk to each other before one of us does something that might trigger our professional code of conduct.

"Okay, walk me through it."

"This Plan A, Plan B stuff has me spooked."

He interrupted. "I thought Calhoon already confirmed CDC was going with Plan A."

"He did, but in my gut I don't trust him. Frankly, I'm worried Calhoon is doing a bait-and-switch. He's tricking the City into selling him Glen Park for peanuts, then he'll bulldoze the pavilion and destroy the park to make room for an ugly ten-storey building and make a killing in the process. I don't think Lawson Valentine should be a party to his shady business deal."

Keith looked thoughtful. "I sympathize with your gut—all kidding aside, there is something weird about this file—but before we toss our newest client into the street, don't we need more evidence?"

"We do. First, we have this." I put Nick's business card and Madeline's corporate chart on his desk and walked him through the bizarre coincidence of Calhoon's red box company number appearing on the back of Nick's business card.

Keith started to say something, I raised a hand to stop him. "This is a red flag. My gut and the Law Society say we should investigate."

"The Law Society? How? We're lawyers, not private detectives."

I placed my laptop on his desk, turning the screen so he could see it, and pointed to a paragraph that stated a lawyer who suspects an unscrupulous client is using them to 'do something dishonest, fraudulent, criminal or illegal' must make reasonable inquiries of the client and about whatever it is the client wants them to do. "Keith, we've already pressed Calhoon on this, I'm not satisfied with his response; now we have a duty to *make reasonable inquiries* about the project."

"Hmmmph," Keith said. "I've been practising for ten years, I didn't know we had a duty to investigate."

"Neither did I until recently, but like I said this file spooks me."

"Your gut," he said.

"My gut." I explained Madeline's plan to go to Quebec City and pump Bev for information.

Keith said, "You think Bev might know whether this red box company is connected to the Pavilion?"

"Bev knows everything. She's been with Calhoon since the beginning. Then immediately after Calhoon heard she'd given AJ the Plan B documents, she 'retired.' I think he was trying to get Bev out of the way. All of this is suspicious and—" I cocked my head at him "—we have a duty to investigate."

"When you put it that way, I would agree."

I returned to Madeline's office and told her to start packing.

~

A soft breeze kissed my cheek and the magpies squawked and dive bombed a crow struggling to fly off with a half-eaten donut, a fitting vignette for the excesses of consumerism or something. I was standing at a crosswalk, on my way home when my phone buzzed. It was Sergeant Pritchard calling to say Michiel was free to reopen the campaign office and asking me to stop in at the police station to sign my statement.

I found Pritchard chatting with a civilian working behind the counter in the reception area when I arrived. The lobby glowed in the late day sunlight, looking less bleak than the last time I was here.

Pritchard took me to a meeting room and slid a sheet of paper across the table to me. My heart flip-flopped in my chest as I reviewed my account of finding Nick's body. My pen wobbled as I signed the page.

I slid the page back across the table and said, "So, it's pretty obvious Nick didn't shove himself backwards through the fire door, crack his head on the cement wall and gouge out his eye, right?" That sounded more callous than I intended.

"Correct," Pritchard said.

"So, he was trying to get away from someone, right?"

Pritchard didn't say anything. I waited, drumming my fingers on the table. The room was full of tiny dust motes that sparkled in a long shaft of light.

"Do you have any leads? Are you making any progress?"

"I can assure you, Evie, this case is our highest priority."

"I certainly hope so. Can you at least tell me it was quick? He didn't suffer?"

Pritchard's eyes met mine. I hadn't noticed it before, but

one eye was blue and the other was brown. “We’ll get his killer, Evie. We need time to do our jobs properly. Do you understand me?”

“Yes, I understand.”

At the time I thought I knew what Pritchard was talking about. It turned out I didn’t understand a thing.

18

Here, you need this more than I do." Bridget placed a Danish and a steaming cup of dark coffee on the edge of my desk. Her cheeks were flushed and her blonde hair floated in wisps around her face.

"You ran down the street to Steff's?"

She nodded. "Nick's funeral is today, right?"

"Yes, AJ and I are leaving in an hour. I thought I'd get some work done before we head out."

"And how's that going?"

"Poorly."

"I'm not surprised." She sat down across from me. "Madeline called last night; I think she was at a bar."

"Madeline is always at a bar." I said it without rancour. Madeline in a bar is like a falcon in its nest, resting after a day on the prowl.

"True. Anyway, she said to tell you she was successful, she's flying back tomorrow and will bring you up to speed on Monday."

A glimmer of hope on a miserable day. Outside, the rain

continued to pelt down and the wind, which had turned my umbrella inside out in the parking lot this morning, was whistling into my office through a tiny crack where the seal had lifted from the window frame.

I thanked Bridget for the update and returned to a dispirited review of regulations governing the construction of wind farms.

An hour later AJ and I were hustling through the downpour to my car. AJ did not know Nick well, but agreed to step in for Keith who was not able to attend. I suspected the real reason AJ was hunched next to me in my clammy car was to offer moral support. As we eased into traffic I asked AJ if he cried at funerals, he said no, he tried not to think of the person who'd died. Wasn't that the whole point of funerals? I asked. Sure, he said, it's fine to remember the dead, but they weren't here anymore and a room full of wailing mourners could be overwhelming. To keep himself from slipping into despair he cleared his mind by counting backwards from one hundred; if that didn't work, he ran multiplication tables in his head.

I said, "Maybe that's why you're so good at figuring out the tip at lunch." It was an inane thing to say.

The chapel was a delicate, well-cared-for building, trimmed with ornate woodwork. The air was damp and heavily scented with lilies and grey and white roses. I didn't think the grey ones were real until I touched a soft petal. Grey, the colour of sombre sophistication. Nick would have liked them.

We were slipping into a pew at the back when Mrs. Silva, Nick's mother, spotted us and waved for us to come forward to sit with her. As we walked up the aisle we passed pews jammed with city officials, volunteers from Michiel's campaign, old law school friends, and partners representing all the major law firms. Even Phil Dennison, the managing partner at our old firm, Gates, Case and White, was here. Everyone was subdued and sodden with rain. Nick didn't have a large family, just he and his mother, and the family pew was empty except for Mrs. Silva, Michiel, and Lisbeth. Michiel was restrained. Lisbeth, her face pale and her eyes rimmed red, did not look up when Mrs. Silva gripped my hand and pulled me along the pew to sit next to her.

Everyone said the minister's words were uplifting when the service was over. Maybe so, but I couldn't remember a single thing he said. I was too busy running multiplication tables in my head.

The congregation followed Nick's mother downstairs to the tea room, a quaint space where the chapel ladies had laid out refreshments. I was pleased to see a large selection of Brazilian food, including coxinha, rolled guava cakes and little chocolate balls. "Mrs. Silva," I asked, "did you make all this?"

She smiled. "Yes, Nick was proud of his Brazilian heritage."

The image of Nick arranging appetizers on the cobalt blue serving platter the night he died floated into my mind. Then the tears came and I knew I had to get out of there. I apologized to Mrs. Silva for leaving early and went back upstairs.

As I threaded my way to the door, I felt rather than saw someone bearing down on me. Phil Dennison was plowing through the crowd toward me. He was a short square man, like a brick with a buzz cut. He hadn't played football in decades but still considered himself a jock. I had wasted far too much time pushing back on his sexist comments. 'Don't get all PC on me,' he'd say, 'it's just a joke.' His cavalier attitude set the tone at the firm and one night everything blew up. At the time I thought I could deal with it. I couldn't. So I quit and took Keith and Madeline with me. Dennison and I hadn't spoken more than two words to each other since.

"Hey, I want to talk to you," he said in a voice much too loud for a social gathering let alone a funeral. A few of the mourners glanced at us, then politely turned away.

"Hello Phil," I said. "This is a sad day, show some respect." Dennison hates being challenged.

"You two are in way over your heads, poaching Sam Calhoon. What did you do, bribe him with a lifetime supply of Musigny Grand Cru?"

I'm not very tall, but neither is he. I stepped into his space. "Sam Calhoon left you and came to us of his own accord. Everyone knows that."

A sneer masquerading as a smile flicked across his lips. "With all due respect, Miss, um, Miss…"

He knew damn well who I was. I waited.

"…You're way out of your league. Your two-bit firm can't possibly service the needs of a client like CDC."

You want to play it hard, let's play it hard. I lowered my voice in mock concern. "I was so sorry to hear about poor Julianna Westerberg. And how she died on the sidewalk right outside your building. How's the investigation going? Not impacting client loyalty, is it?"

His face turned purple. His mouth popped open. Nothing came out. He pivoted and stalked away. Satisfied that I had riled him more than he had riled me, I continued searching for AJ and found him near the ornate wooden doors at the front of the chapel in quiet conversation with Sergeant Pritchard.

"My goodness, what are you doing here?" I asked.

Pritchard said he'd assigned an officer to stand outside the chapel to prevent any reporters from disrupting the service. Plausible, but I couldn't help wondering whether Pritchard had another motive. Was he checking the crowd to see who may have had a reason to kill Nick? No, that was ridiculous. I clung to the belief that Nick's killer was a nutcase, one of those lunatics who creeps out of the shadows to harass a public figure, only this time something went horribly wrong. The alternative was too frightening to contemplate.

By the time I got home my head was pounding. Quincy stretched and yawned when I came through the door. I stroked his ears and told him he was not getting a run today, I felt miserable and was going straight to bed. He sighed and slumped at the foot of my bed to wait patiently for Louisa to come home.

19

My useless umbrella fluttered like a trapped bird in my hand as I raced across the parking lot into the building. It took all of my strength to pry the front door open; by the time I stumbled into the reception area I looked like I'd rolled out of a ditch.

Bridget spread her arms across her desk to keep her papers from flying away. The sweet peas at the corner of her desk were long gone, replaced with a vase of purple asters. "You look like you just blew in from Kansas, via tornado… or is it hurricane…I can never remember."

"Tornado," I muttered attempting to pat my hair back into place. "Tornado, land. Hurricane, sea."

Bridget shook her head. "Nope, don't tell me, I always forget."

My cell rang as I hustled down the hall and tossed my sodden raincoat on the hook behind my door. *Sergeant Pritchard.* My stomach lurched. Did he have news? My voice cracked when I said hello.

"Evie?"

"Yes, hi, morning voice. Need to rev up the vocal cords." He said nothing, maybe he was smiling. "How can I help you, Sergeant Pritchard?" I sat down at my desk and pulled out a yellow lined writing pad. Why do lawyers use yellow pads? I've sent Bridget all over town in search of yellow pads when our usual supplier runs out.

"Can you stop by the station?" Pritchard asked. "I'd like to talk to you."

"Sure, about what?"

"Let's talk when you get here. Can you come this morning, say around nine-thirty?" I glanced at my calendar, yes, that would work.

I slipped back into my soggy raincoat and raced through the pelting rain to my car. My breath fogged up the front windshield. I cracked open the windows and the damp morning breeze whistled across the front seat. The fresh air would clear my head. Then I caught a glimpse of myself in the rear-view mirror. The humidity was curling my hair. I looked like a raving banshee.

"Pretty wet out there, eh?" Pritchard said as he led me into an interview room.

"You can say that again." I draped my raincoat over the back of a chair and sat down across from him.

Pritchard set a file folder down on the table and pulled out a few pages. "Evie, we're investigating a couple of lines of inquiry in Nicholas' death."

"A couple of lines of inquiry…?"

"Yes. It's unlikely Nicholas was killed by a stranger. We're looking into his personal life, his work at City Hall, and his work as Michiel's campaign manager..." He paused, waiting for me to fill in the dead air.

I maintained a neutral expression. If there's one

thing lawyers learn right out of the chute, it's to let the interrogator finish their question before blurting out an answer. Answering a question you haven't been asked is the quickest way to get into trouble.

"Right," Pritchard said, tidying the papers into a neat pile. "What can you tell me about what Nicholas was working on?"

"Working on? You mean at City Hall?" I tried not to fidget in my chair. "Surely his colleagues at work can help you with that."

"We've talked to them. They said he was working on a big project for Sam Calhoon and that your firm, you specifically, were his main contact." Pritchard folded his hands together on top of the file and looked at me with one blue eye and one brown eye.

I glanced out the window. There was an old misshapen birch outside, its trunk white and blotchy. The wind shuddered its branches and a couple of spindly twigs smacked the windowpane. How could I answer this question? Client confidentiality barred me from saying anything about the Pavilion project until it was approved by City Council.

"That's right," I said, "our firm represents CDC, Sam Calhoon, on a project. Nick, um, Nicholas, was our contact at the City, but I can't give you any more details, solicitor-client privilege, you know." I tried not to sound like a sanctimonious prig.

"I understand that," Pritchard said patiently. "I'm not asking for information about the deal itself, I'm looking for anything you can tell me about Nicholas' interactions with you and others in the weeks before he died. This is a murder investigation, Evie. Anything you can tell me, no matter how trivial, could be helpful."

Pritchard looked very sincere. I wanted to help him but passing along campaign gossip—O'Halloran was a jerk, Sarah Hamilton was running a very distant third, the rising tension in our own campaign—was hardly relevant. I shook my head slowly. "I'm sorry, Sergeant Pritchard, I really can't help you."

We locked eyes for a moment. A look of disappointment crossed Pritchard's face, followed by an expression I could not place, frustration, anger, it was hard to tell. He stood up and extended his hand. "Thank you for stopping by, Ms. Valentine. Let's stay in touch."

I said he could call me anytime if he had any more questions, but we both knew it was pointless because I couldn't tell him a thing.

I walked down the hall, through the door that separates the staff from the rowdies and out into the lobby. It seemed unusually quiet, but what did I know, the only other time I was here I was sitting in an interview room telling Pritchard how I found Nick's body.

20

Why is it taking so long?" I stared at the coffee pot, willing it to drip faster. Louisa ignored me. "I can't believe you let me do that." I cast a sleepy eye at Louisa, who was making Quincy's breakfast. They had just returned from their morning walk and she was racing around the kitchen like the Energizer Bunny.

"Do what?" She pulled a tin of dog food out of the pantry. "Would Quincy like liver?" He squirmed around her legs. "I'll take that as a yes."

"Stay up to binge watch *What/If.*"

She stroked Quincy's ears and said, "Auntie Evie is grumpy this morning." His tail whipped back and forth, tapping the kitchen cabinet. He didn't care who was grumpy as long as someone fed him.

The coffee emitted one last blurb and I filled two cups and set them down on the kitchen island. Louisa started the pancakes, our usual weekend breakfast, while I poured the orange juice and set two places with plates and cutlery. "You're not working today?" I asked.

"Nope; off until Tuesday. Jess and I are going to the Farmers' Market. Want to come?"

"Thanks, but I've got work to do. Are you taking Quincy with you on this little junket?"

"No, he's too rambunctious." She gazed down at him. He watched mesmerized as she lifted a forkful of pancake to her lips. "Do you really have to work? It's Saturday, the sun is shining, you don't want to be cooped up in an office all day."

"Ah, but that's the beauty of the internet. I'm working from home." After a short debate about who would get the front section of the newspaper we ate and read out bits of news stories the other might find interesting.

Louisa was gone by the time I finished my shower. So was the fine weather. Heavy storm clouds had rolled in from the west, in the distance thunder rumbled. So much for my original plan of sitting at the patio table reviewing files and watching the fly fishermen try their luck down by the river.

I was settled in the leather chair in the study, laptop propped open on my knees, when I heard a furtive scratching sound. Quincy was pawing at something behind the bookshelf.

"Whatcha got there, Quincy?" *Dear God, don't let it be a mouse.* I'm not afraid of mice, not really, I just don't like the way they skitter about and run up your pant leg for no reason.

He looked at me and wagged his tail expectantly. I got down on my hands and knees, pushing him aside so I could peer into the narrow space between the bookshelf and the wall. There was something back there all right, wedged between the baseboard and the bookshelf just beyond my reach. I retrieved a wooden spoon from the kitchen and tried to wiggle it free. This made Quincy crazy but whatever it was, it did not budge. I needed more leverage and got the broom. After a few minutes of prodding, a couple inches of cardboard tube protruded past the end of the bookshelf. I pulled it out. A red poster tube, the one AJ had given me just before our first meeting with Sam Calhoon.

The tube was covered with bite marks. "Did you do this, Quincy?" The dog quivered with excitement. Cardboard tubes, paper towel tubes, wrapping paper tubes, you name it, he shreds it in five seconds. He must have seen the poster tube on the corner of my desk and knocked it to the floor only to have it bounce behind the bookshelf.

The tube opened with a soft pop. A drawing slid out and unfurled on the carpet; pastel blue sky, concrete planters, and smack dab in the centre a ten-storey multi-use complex. Plan B.

Something small and hard bounced onto the carpet. Quincy scooped it up in a flash. A USB stick. *This was it.* This had to be what Moe was looking for when he attacked me on my doorstep and at the campaign office.

Quincy was going to crush it in his powerful jaws.

"Drop it," I said sternly to the dog. He looked at me and then looked at the poster tube in my hands. I bounced the tube on the floor. It made a hollow ringing sound.

"Drop it. Now. I mean it, Quincy." His mouth snapped open; the wet USB stick flipped out onto the carpet. He lunged for the tube. I scooped up the USB stick and snatched the poster tube out of his mouth.

"Does Quincy want a treat?" The dog hesitated, then raced around like a demented creature while I carried everything back into the kitchen.

I gave him the stinkiest dog treat I could find and went

down to the basement to hide the poster tube inside a roll of Christmas paper. The drawing and the USB stick would be safe there until I could figure out what made Plan B so bloody important.

21

LATE SEPTEMBER 2 weeks to Election Day

I was desperate to be done with Michiel's campaign and return to my relatively sane life as a name partner at Lawson Valentine. Edgy and impatient, I paced the reception area waiting for Madeline to arrive and tell me what she'd learned from her visit with Bev in Quebec City.

"Are you solo pacing or can anybody join in?" AJ came alongside of me.

"You're in a good mood."

"That's because I've got fantastic news."

I stopped pacing. "Good, I could use the distraction."

"The City's lawyer just called. They're happy with the Memorandum of Understanding. They expect City Council to rubber stamp it at next week's council meeting."

"AJ, that's excellent news. And well within Calhoon's

deadline."

He beamed and then grew pensive. "Nick did a fantastic job of getting the bureaucrats on board. All the lawyers had to do was dot the T's and cross the I's."

"It's the other way around—cross the T's, dot the I's." He rolled his eyes just as Madeline sauntered through the front door.

"Welcome home," I said as I propelled her into my office. "Sit, sit." I waved her into a visitor's chair. "You look like the cat that's swallowed the proverbial canary. How did it go?"

She took her time settling into the chair, flipping her auburn hair off her shoulders and smiling sweetly before embarking on a detailed description of her tedious flight to Quebec City, which was made even more unbearable by an annoying child whinging in the seat behind her.

"Yes, Madeline, I've got all that, long, miserable flight, whiney child. Get to the good part."

"My goodness, aren't you impatient."

I raised my eyebrows and she moved to the heart of her story. After she checked into the Château Frontenac she phoned Bev to invite her to afternoon tea at a toney restaurant overlooking the Saint Lawrence. Bev was busy that afternoon but free later that evening so Madeline invited her for cocktails at the hotel bar instead.

"Turns out Bev likes her booze," Madeline said.

"That makes two of you," I said.

"Yes, but only one of us can hold our liquor. Bev was pie-eyed after two whiskey sours."

Poor Bev. She didn't stand a chance. Madeline is thin and small boned but she can drink a linebacker under the table if the situation calls for it.

"Did you learn anything or was she too blotto to string two words together?"

"Oh, I learned plenty." Madeline's voice dropped to a conspiratorial whisper. "Bev has no use for Sam Calhoon. She says he's nothing like his dad—Bev worked for Calhoon Sr. for fifteen years. She worshipped the ground he walked on, but Sam, well let's just put it this way: Sam is *not* a chip off the old block."

"So why did she stay?" I asked.

"Loyalty to the dad, loyalty to the firm. Something like that, but it wasn't easy." Madeline frowned. "Sam made it abundantly clear to his employees that unlike his father, he would not tolerate projects that ran over budget or fell behind schedule. He didn't care why a project was delayed, he wanted it back on track, get 'er done or get the hell out. Bev thought Sam was going to have a stroke when his first big project ran into permitting problems. Sam stormed into the project manager's office screaming that if the man was too stupid to fix it, he was fired and Sam would do it himself. Then he stomped over to Bev's desk and demanded she book a meeting with City Hall. From that day forward only a handful of projects were held up by permitting delays, and even those weren't delayed for long."

"What? Did he have compromising photos of the building inspectors?" A few years ago social media was flooded with photos of a building inspector snoring in his truck when he was supposed to be at a jobsite. To say that it torpedoed the City's reputation would be an understatement.

"Not quite, but the wheels of commerce always roll smoother when they're greased with cash," she said.

"I'm not following you."

"This is where the red box company comes in." Madeline

placed Nick's business card on my desk.

"Whenever Sam got word that the bureaucrats at City Hall were unhappy with a project, he instructed Bev to deposit a cheque in the red box company's bank account. Since the red box company is a private company, its accounts aren't public record."

My stomach lurched. "How big a cheque?"

"At first the cheques were smallish, maybe $50,000 or so, but over time—remember Sam's been running CDC since 1983—they ran to hundreds of thousands of dollars. The biggest cheque Bev can remember was for $420,000."

I whistled under my breath. "What happens to the money?"

"That's where it gets a little vague," Madeline said. "Bev isn't sure, all she did was deposit the cheques into the red box company's bank account. She doesn't know what happened to the money after it got there."

"Someone is funnelling money out of the red box company to a bureaucrat at City Hall. They're taking bribes to make Calhoon's permitting problems disappear."

"Oh, and another thing," she said, crossing her arms. "The red box company is the only subsidiary still getting payments in the form of handwritten cheques. The money going in and out of the other subs goes by way of electronic bank transfers."

"Something is terribly wrong with this picture, Madeline."

She rolled her eyes. "You think?"

We were silent for a moment as the realization sank in: our client was a crook.

"By this point in the evening Bev and I were bosom buddies, united against unreasonable bosses."

"Yeah, yeah…" I made a motion urging Madeline to move along.

"Bev wants to stay in touch. I get the impression hanging out with the grandchildren isn't as fulfilling as she thought it would be."

"So why did she leave?"

"Calhoon said he needed someone younger, more proficient with modern technology…oh, and he offered her a big buyout package. She'd have been a fool not to take it."

I reached across my desk and took her hands. "Madeline, you did great!"

She blushed, then stood up and said, "I'd like to do a deeper dive on the red box company's historical records to get the names of its directors and its five largest shareholders."

I gave her a thumbs up and went off in search of Keith. He was talking to AJ about an upcoming wind farm application when I barged through the door. "Guys, we need to talk."

By the time I outlined what Bev had told Madeline, Keith's face was haggard, completely drained of colour.

He said, "Calhoon is funnelling bribes to city officials through the red box company so they'll approve his projects?"

"It's beginning to look that way. Calhoon's projects sail through the approval process, that saves him hundreds of thousands of dollars in project financing, to say nothing of getting his properties on the market quickly to recoup his investment sooner."

AJ rose from his chair and leaned against the window ledge, silhouetted in the bright morning sunlight. "Let's stop right there for a minute. Before we do something that will blow up peoples' lives, remember Sam is presumed innocent until proven guilty. There's nothing to connect the money Bev says she put into the red box company on Sam's behalf with a corrupt bureaucrat at City Hall."

"Right." I nodded at AJ. "From what I've seen of Bev, her story would fall apart like wet tissue paper under aggressive cross-examination. But if what she says is true, then our client has been bribing City Hall since 1983. We need more evidence."

"How are we going to find more evidence?" Keith's face was etched with worry. And for good reason. Calhoon was an extremely powerful man with friends in high places. If word got out that we suspected him of corruption without concrete evidence to back it up, he'd sue us to hell and back. We'd lose our clients, we'd lose the firm. We'd never practice law again.

Keith is by nature methodical and cautious, I'm more of a risk taker. He needed to know I wasn't about to kick over the CDC empire and bury our firm in the process. "We're not running off half-cocked here. Madeline is conducting a second level search on the red box company's directors and shareholders, going back to 1983. Once we have that information, we can regroup, assess our position, and decide on next steps."

Keith nodded slowly and the tension around his eyes relaxed. AJ glanced from Keith to me and said, "That means it's business as usual until we have more information, right?"

"That's right," I said.

"All righty then, back to this wind farm application." AJ has a way of lightening the mood. His comment made Keith smile.

It wasn't until I'd returned to my office that I realized we might be able to smoke out who Calhoon was bribing at City Hall, but we still couldn't explain how the red box company's registry number ended up on the back of Nick's business card.

22

Later that week I was sitting at Dineen's, the newest addition to the city's café scene, waiting for my breakfast bagel and coffee when someone called my name.

"It's Evie, isn't it? Evie Valentine?" I tore my eyes away from a fluffy little dog trying to jump into the lap of the elderly woman sitting on the park bench outside, and looked up into the face of an earnest young man. "Do you mind if I join you?"

My first impulse was to say, yes, I do mind. I was in the zone, thinking about nothing, just letting the clatter and chatter of frenetic activity wash over me. The young man smiled tentatively and extended his hand. His face looked familiar.

"Paul Barry…" he said. "I'm Julianna Westerberg's husband, well, er…" He petered out.

Ah, that's it, the man with the laughing eyes in the newspaper photo with Julianna. Paul hovered until I invited him to join me. A server placed my bagel and coffee on the small table. "Are you having anything, Paul?" I asked as he slid his computer bag under his chair.

"No, just finished," he said. There was a long pause while I took a sip of coffee and waited to see where this conversation would go.

Paul said, "When I saw you staring out the window, I knew I had to come over and introduce myself." He coloured slightly. "I hope that doesn't sound too weird."

"I'm so sorry about Julianna." Now it was my turn to feel uncomfortable. I'd never met the woman, all I knew about her was what I'd read in the papers.

"She had a lot of respect for you," he said.

"Me? Really?"

"Yeah, according to Julianna you were a Gates legend, on track for an early partnership, then you pulled the plug and took Keith Lawson with you. Dennison and the executive committee were royally pissed." I bit my lip. My departure from Gates came on the heels of an internal investigation that, but for Dennison's stature in the firm, should have resulted in his ouster. But he didn't escape unscathed, the firm paid me a six-figure settlement in return for my silence. Dennison wasn't just pissed when I left, he was incandescent with rage.

A small shiver raced down my spine. I pushed the memories aside. "Julianna was a fourth-year associate, right?"

His eyes shone with pride. "Yeah, she was. She worked day and night. Not like me, I'm just an IT guy at the university, nine to five, no evenings, no weekends. But Julianna, well, she had a real career, already pulling down the big bucks." He picked up my serviette and started tearing it into confetti. "She loved Gates, that firm was her first choice for articles, you know, and she was very good at her job. She wanted to beat the guys at their own game."

I remembered how clubby Gates was. The young guys joined the firm's hockey team and went for drinks and cigars with the partners, forging relationships that would help them when the executive committee met to decide who would stay and who would be shown the door. Female lawyers were not welcome in the club and worked twice as hard as the men to get noticed by a senior partner who might put in a good word for them on decision day. The glass ceiling is set in concrete at Gates, Case and White.

Paul gazed out the window. "Some people said Julianna was too aggressive, but she was working at one of the Big Five law firms, she had to be aggressive to survive." He turned to me and sighed. "She said if she played her cards right, everything we'd ever wanted would be ours for the taking."

That's what all the junior associates tell their families when they're forced to miss another birthday party or cut a holiday short because they're urgently needed at the office.

"What kind of law did Julianna practice?" If Julianna was like most lawyers, she would have talked Paul's ear off with the arcane details of whatever file she was working on.

"Banking, corporate law. She supported the mergers and acquisitions group as well as commercial real estate. They gave her complex files, lots of responsibility—way more than is typical for an associate at her level."

I didn't know if this was true, but clearly Julianna saw it that way.

"Was anything troubling her?" I asked. "Was she overloaded, working too hard—?"

"Hell, no!" His eyes darkened. "She thrived on the stress and the fast pace." He glanced at the shredded serviette laying on the table in front of him, swept the bits up into his palm, then looked around for somewhere to deposit them. I pushed my plate closer to him. "I don't know who's spreading these lies about Julianna crumbling under pressure. That woman was strong, resilient. Nothing was too much for her." He blinked rapidly, as if daring me to argue.

"I'm sorry, I didn't mean—"

"I know what you meant," he blustered. "That crap about her screwing up a file…or our marriage being in trouble. That's all bullshit."

"Paul," I said softly, "I didn't mean anything by it, really I didn't."

He looked at me out of the corner of his eye, his head down. "Sorry, I didn't mean to bite your head off." Outside, the fluffy little dog was sitting in the old woman's lap, she patted it gently with a gnarled hand.

"It's been a tough few weeks," his voice caught in his throat. "I don't know what I'm going to do without her. We were happy, she didn't mind I was just an IT guy."

There was another long pause. I glanced at my watch. I had to be on my way to the campaign office. I urged him to take care of himself. If I had known him better, I would have suggested he talk to a professional. Losing Julianna so suddenly and in such strange circumstances was clearly taking a toll.

~

Angry voices bounced off the concrete walls as I stepped off the elevator at Campaign HQ. Not the best first impression. Lisbeth stormed out of the war room as I hurried around the corner of the elevator bank. I barely recognized her. Her eyes were bloodshot and her complexion was blotchy.

"For God's sake, Lisbeth, what's going on?" She shook her head. I put my arm around her shoulders and led her into the coffee room. She sat down at the kitchen table which was covered with cookie crumbs and I plugged in the kettle to make some tea.

"Lisbeth," I said gently, "is this about Nicholas?" She pawed at the pockets of her chinos and came up empty-handed. I handed her a napkin.

"No, not Nicholas," she mumbled. "Well, not directly…" I poured boiling water into her mug, waiting for her to continue. "Michiel wants Wendy to be his new campaign manager, to replace Nicholas in the final week of the campaign."

"Really? I didn't know Wendy had any experience running political campaigns."

Lisbeth scoffed. "I've got more experience running campaigns than she does." She blew her nose. "Clint and I said we could share the campaign manager duties—Clint, Wendy, and me—but Michiel says he needs me full time running the volunteers and Clint has to stay focused on the media."

"What about Wendy's social media work?"

Lisbeth's voice tightened. "She says she's perfectly capable of wearing two hats, social media strategist and campaign manager."

"If Michiel's made up his mind, what are they arguing about?"

"He's letting Clint make his points, but it's clear he wants Wendy." I saw a spark of outrage, then her face became expressionless. "This is typical. Michiel hates conflict, he says it's better when people work out their differences between themselves."

I grabbed a blue box off the shelf and handed her a cookie. A few more crumbs on the table wouldn't hurt.

"Lisbeth," I said, "Michiel's ahead in the polls, we've got a week to go before election day, nothing can hurt his chances now."

"I wouldn't be so sure about that," she said. "Michiel can be overly confident. He thinks he can skate by on his charm." Her mood flashed from misery to anger. "He can't throw away this election. We're so close. I won't let him!" She stood up suddenly and turned toward the war room.

I had no idea what she was talking about anymore, but I was convinced that if she returned to the fray in her infuriated state it would end in disaster.

"Lisbeth, wait." Surprisingly, she stopped, allowing me to catch up. "Let's give things a day or so to settle down. Michiel is smart, he'll sort this out. We have to trust his judgment, okay?"

She hesitated, mulling it over, then her anger evaporated as quickly as it had arisen. She bobbed her head and returned to her desk. I sat down next to her for a few minutes to ensure she stayed there. The war room door opened and Michiel emerged. "All sorted," he said with a satisfied smile. Lisbeth turned to the window, hiding her puffy eyes. Clint said a few words to Wendy in a clipped tone and left the room.

All sorted? Who does he think he's kidding?

23

I was running on autopilot, mornings at Campaign HQ, afternoons and evenings at the law firm. The next time I walk into a bake shop and a politician and his coterie ambush me I'm going to turn around and march right back out again.

A gust of wind had blown over the *Re-elect Michiel* sandwich board. I dragged it inside and propped it up against the wall. Remarkably it was the only thing in the lobby that shouldn't be there. Maybe the police told the construction company to clean up its mess after the EMTs had to pick their way through construction debris to get Nick's body out the door. And maybe the construction company actually listened for a change.

Lisbeth was rifling through some papers on her desk and didn't see me until I was almost on top of her.

"Jesus—" She jumped when I said her name.

"Sorry, I didn't mean to startle you."

Her face relaxed when she recognized me.

"What are you working on?" I waved vaguely at the papers on her desk. Lisbeth placed a delicate hand on a small stack of receipts. "Not much, just sorting through the bills so the accountant can update his files." No one wants the accountant's job. Campaign finance rules are notoriously easy to screw up if you don't know what you're doing.

"Are you going to the debate tonight?" she asked.

"I thought there wasn't going to be a live audience."

"No live audience, but the candidates can bring along a few members of their team." She tucked her dark hair behind her ears. Her gold earrings glinted in the rainy light. "Michiel asked me to come," she said with pride. "You should come too."

I assured her I wouldn't miss it for the world.

~

It was chilly inside the TV studio. Lisbeth, Wendy and I were huddled on hard plastic chairs facing the stage which was little more than a raised platform bathed in soft yellow light. Clint and Jamal sat behind us. O'Halloran's team mirrored us on the other side of the room. Sarah Hamilton, the third candidate, brought just one supporter, her teenaged daughter, who sat between us and O'Halloran's team.

The candidates were not yet on stage, in all likelihood they were trapped in a tiny room with the makeup person. The moderator, a local news anchor named Meagan Fellows, was off to one side chatting with two cameramen. Tall and sleek, her hair nicely shellacked into place, she looked like every other female news presenter on TV these days.

We were whispering amongst ourselves trying to figure out which of the bland young men in O'Halloran's group was his campaign manager when a door banged open to the right of the stage and the candidates filed in. They were heavily made up. Lisbeth whispered that Michiel looked too pale but at least they hadn't touched his hair and given him an Elvis-style pompadour.

The candidates gathered around Meagan who explained that as the incumbent Michiel had been assigned the middle lectern, the other two would flank him. This was good because it subliminally signalled to the audience that Michiel was still the man in charge, but also bad because O'Halloran and Sarah could fire shots at him from both sides. If they did it well, he could come across like a tired old bear besieged by a pack of wolves.

Michiel glanced around the studio, searching for us in the dark. He flashed an easy smile when he spotted us. We grinned and waved; Jamal whooped and gave him two thumbs up.

O'Halloran joined his supporters who hopped out of their chairs, murmuring and patting his arms and back as if he were competing in the Westminster Dog Show. Sarah blew her daughter a kiss and took her place on the podium. Michiel and O'Halloran quickly followed her up on stage.

Meagan explained how the evening would unfold: they would get five minutes for their opening—first Michiel, then O'Halloran, then Sarah—then Meagan would move to Q and A, they'd have two minutes to respond, then they'd wrap up with closing statements, three minutes please and not a second more. There would be no commercial breaks. Did they understand? Of course they understood, they'd received an email saying precisely the same thing several days ago.

It was a strange set, three silver lecterns arranged side by side in front of a dark blue backdrop. It looked like the deck of the Starship Enterprise. Meagan sat at a small table facing the candidates. Behind us the back of the studio was hidden behind a wide black curtain. It was as cluttered with junk as the lobby at Campaign HQ.

Meagan fixed her eyes on us, sternly reminding us to turn off our phones and remain silent throughout the program, no cheering, no applause, nothing. She'd barely finished her lecture when someone threw a switch, plunging the studio into darkness. The candidates squinted as the spotlights came up.

An assistant ran a final sound check, all systems go. The cameraman next to Meagan held out his fingers, counting down to the start of the program. The air filled with urgent choppy music meant to convey that something newsworthy was about to happen and the other cameraman rolled his camera into position.

We could see Meagan on a tiny screen mounted on the side wall. Her eyes were grave as she welcomed the audience to the most important event in the campaign. Apparently the only events that matter are the ones covered by the media. She asked the candidates to outline their political platforms. This was the easy part of the debate. Michiel's opening and closing remarks were tightly scripted. He could recite them under anesthesia if he had to.

Michiel highlighted his accomplishments and quickly shifted to his major campaign promise: he would revitalize the downtown core by attracting residential developers to build in the inner city. He ended on a personal note, saying he was profoundly saddened by the death of his chief of staff and dear friend Nicholas Silva.

The camera shifted to O'Halloran who stared into the camera and said absolutely nothing for a full five seconds—it felt like an eternity on air—before glancing dismissively at Michiel and asking Meagan, “Are you going to let him gaslight the entire city?”

Michiel looked at Meagan who appeared to be preoccupied by a piece of paper on her desk. Clearly, she was not going to intervene. O’Halloran’s attack right out of the chute was exactly the kind of pyrotechnics that would boost her ratings.

O’Halloran shifted his gaze from Meagan back to the camera. “Now that I have your attention, folks, let’s talk facts, not rainbows and unicorns.”

He accused Michiel of being short-sighted, of believing the oil boom would last forever, of blowing pots of money in the good times, saving ‘not one thin dime’ for the bad times. Now the city’s coffers were empty and we couldn’t pay for basic services like police, fire, and roads, because Michiel squandered this bounty on fripperies like bicycle paths and public art.

I caught Wendy’s eye and mouthed *fripperies*? She shrugged.

O’Halloran blasted Michiel for not cutting the budget and ‘living within our means.’

Michiel tried to interject but O’Halloran plowed ahead with the steady determination of a bulldozer. “Folks,” he said, “developers won’t pay sky-high taxes in the downtown core. So how is the City going to pay for basic services?” O’Halloran pointed into the camera. “I’ll tell you how. By taxing people struggling to get by. People like you.” He paused briefly before hammering home his campaign slogan. “It’s time for courage, folks, courage to elect a mayor who’ll help us live within our means.”

Two red spots appeared high on Michiel’s cheekbones. He lashed out, saying O’Halloran was a carpetbagger who hadn't the slightest idea of what a mayor does or how City Hall operates, then he rattled off some examples of what he had accomplished over his last term. This immediately backfired.

"That was yesterday," O'Halloran snapped. "I'm talking about today." Phrases like 'rats abandoning a sinking ship' and 'hocus pocus financing' filled the air. Michiel was shouting to be heard but O'Halloran waved him off.

"—Gentlemen, please!" Sarah Hamilton's cool voice sliced through the studio, stopping both men in mid rant. "This is a PG-rated program, but I have a ruler handy if you want to measure who's the manlier man." She held up a six-inch ruler. Someone tittered.

Sarah stepped into the stunned silence and glanced at the moderator. "I believe it's my turn."

Meagan Fellows bobbed her head. Sarah explained she was running for Mayor for the same reason she ran for City Council—she wanted to create a better future for her daughter and for all children—a better future for children meant a better future for everyone. Sadly, her joy at being elected to City Council evaporated when she discovered how dysfunctional it had become under Michiel's leadership. Petty spats, vote trading, that was no way to serve the people. She promised to lay out her vision for 'a better future' over the course of the evening.

Michiel frowned when she criticized his leadership but did not interrupt. Sarah was a small middle-aged woman; a harsh rebuttal could make him look like a bully.

Sarah glanced at Meagan. "Isn't this the part where you lead us through the Q and A?" She sounded like a schoolteacher gently nudging a wayward student back on track.

Meagan asked predictable questions, the candidates gave predictable answers, but the acrimony of the first fifteen minutes hung over the stage like woodsmoke.

I shot a sideways glance at Wendy and Lisbeth. Wendy was as still as a statue, her face giving away nothing. Lisbeth clutched the collar of her oversized sweater with both hands as if she were about to pull it over her head. Someone, either Clint or Jamal, was breathing heavily behind me.

Michiel did a credible job in his closing statement which he had adjusted on the fly to rebut O'Halloran's gaslighting accusation.

But was it enough?

Meagan closed the debate by urging viewers to vote on election day or at one of the advance polls which opened tomorrow. Perfect, I thought, a voter casting his ballot tomorrow will start the day with a steaming cup of coffee and newspaper headlines shrieking *O'Halloran Wins Debate.*

The studio lights dimmed and the urgent music blared while the candidates shook each others' hands and wished each other well. O'Halloran's team swarmed him with jubilant high-fives and hearty thumps on the back. Sarah's daughter gave her mother a warm hug. Michiel smiled and said he'd be out right after he removed his makeup. Wendy told him we'd meet him in the lobby. Silently we trouped down the corridor and returned our ID badges to the woman at the front desk.

Wendy gathered us together by the window wall as far away from the front desk as possible. If we could have squeezed behind the philodendron we would have. We had a few minutes to regroup before Michiel appeared, Wendy wanted to ensure we were all on the same page. We were to downplay the seriousness of O'Halloran's attack and praise Michiel's rebuttal. Tomorrow we'd regroup at Campaign HQ and turn this debacle into a 'Michiel wins debate' story.

Michiel and Meagan were laughing when they emerged from the corridor. Michiel shook her hand and turned to us with open arms. "Let's go for a drink," he said. He was cheerful and relaxed throughout the evening which unfolded exactly as we'd planned.

24

The pigeons were unusually raucous when I awoke the next day; at least that's what I thought until I opened one eye and realized a hangover was amplifying the sound of their crooning and scratchy feet.

Louisa, bless her heart, put the coffee on before she left for work. I popped a bagel into the toaster and brought in the morning newspapers. Quincy butted my leg hoping for some table scraps as I settled at the island and slid the papers out of their plastic sleeves.

"You're outta luck, bud." He slumped at my feet with a heavy sigh.

"Quincy, I was wrong." The dog cocked his head. The papers did not run with the headline *O'Halloran Wins Debate.* They led with Michiel the gaslighter and Sarah's condemnation of both men in the 'manly man' department. Neither storyline helped Michiel's image.

I texted Bridget to confirm I was going to the campaign office before heading to the law firm. She responded immediately:

That was brutal!

I know. See you at noon.

A bubble with three little dots appeared, but she didn't send anything further. I suppose the word 'brutal' summed it up quite nicely.

Lisbeth was pacing back and forth in front of the elevators in the main lobby when I arrived. "You look nice," she said absently. "Is that a new jacket?" It wasn't, but we were just killing time waiting for the elevator to arrive. Women talk about clothes and hair cuts when they're trying to avoid a serious conversation, men talk about sports.

The elevator door whooshed open and we stepped inside. Lisbeth said, "If I'd known you were going to be here early, I'd have brought you a coffee." She looked down at the two cups in her hands.

"No problem," I said. "Who's getting 'my' cup?"

"Michiel."

"He's here already?"

"Yeah, we stayed behind after you guys left the pub last night. He's pretty shaken up."

Before I could reply, the elevator door slid open. Michiel emerged from the coffee room, looking like he had stepped off the cover of a men's fashion magazine. He was carrying a bag of chips. "That's not much of a breakfast," Lisbeth said. He snorted and told her to hand over his coffee.

I raised an eyebrow at Lisbeth and said, "He doesn't look too broken up to me." We followed Michiel into the war room and joined Wendy and Clint who were gathered around the phone. Bernie was on the line, Jamal was off somewhere doing something.

Michiel started by saying he was disappointed in his performance. Nicholas had pressed him to schedule more time for debate prep, but Michiel had refused. Clearly that was a mistake, he said. "I'm just glad Nicholas isn't here to say, 'I told you so.'"

I'm just glad Nicholas isn't here to say, 'I told you so'? Nick had been brutally murdered; his killer was still at large—was I the only one who thought Michiel's comment was flippant and heartless? I glanced around at all the placid faces. Apparently so.

Wendy and Clint tag-teamed the meeting. While last night's performance had not gone as well as expected (no kidding!) we still had time to 'change the channel.' Michiel needed a narrative to counter O'Halloran's gaslighter accusation. Sarah was trailing in the polls so her 'manly man' crack was not worth worrying about. Wendy outlined a new communications strategy to convince voters Michiel had anticipated the latest economic downturn and had laid the foundation for a more diversified economy in the future.

I was skeptical. "'A more diversified economy in the future' simply parrots Sarah's position and fails to rebut O'Halloran's assertion that Michiel's plan to lure developers into the downtown core is a non-starter. Surely we can do better than that."

The room became so quiet I could hear the Bobcat beeping four floors below. The others scrutinized their notepads or poked at their cell phones. Michiel looked at me as if I'd yelled an obscenity in church, then said he liked Wendy's plan and was sure she could massage the message to make it sound fresh and achievable. With that, my concerns were dismissed.

Wendy tilted her pixie head and said Michiel would unveil a series of incentives for the tech and finance sectors. She told Lisbeth she needed solid examples of such incentives together with meaty quotes from top executives saying Michiel's plan would create jobs and diversify the economy.

Lisbeth, who had been dutifully taking notes up to this point, raised her head. The perplexed look on her face indicated she knew as much about transforming the city into a beacon for tech and finance entrepreneurs as I did, which was nothing.

"Um, okay," she stammered. "I can dig around. Maybe the acting chief of staff, or—"

That's when Michiel lost his temper. "Damn it, Lisbeth. I don't care *how* you do it, just bloody well do it." Lisbeth shrank back in her chair, eyes wide with shock. Michiel's expression immediately shifted from anger to something bordering pity. He touched her hand lightly and apologized. She bent her head, her raven hair falling forward, hiding her face, and resumed scribbling in her notebook. Wendy made a production out of pulling her phone out of her bag and rattling off the details of the new media plan. Clint shifted uneasily in his seat. Michiel folded his arms across his chest. His dark eyes darted from Wendy to Lisbeth, finally coming to rest on me. There was no warmth in his gaze, just cool, calculating ambition.

At that moment I knew everything I needed to know about Michiel Van Dijk. He was just another razzle dazzle politician whose sole objective was to win. If he had to steal from Sarah Hamilton to bury O'Halloran, so be it. The sense of betrayal bubbled up in my throat. I had to leave, now, before I said something I would regret.

As I made my excuses Lisbeth rose to leave as well. She hesitated in the doorway, wondering what she should tell the volunteers about the debate.

Wendy replied, "Tell them O'Halloran was extremely unprofessional, no surprise there, he's new to politics and doesn't know the rules, so Michiel had to put him in his place, and Sarah, well Sarah was unladylike, and Michiel is too much of a gentleman to comment on her behaviour."

Michiel nodded in approval. When someone points out your mistakes, attack their character. Spin bad news like cotton candy; the voters will never know the difference.

~

By the time I pulled into the Lawson Valentine parking lot, the sun was high in the sky and the squirrels were chittering loudly. I shuddered. I don't like squirrels, especially when they parkour off my car leaving random footprints on the windshield.

Madeline and Bridget looked up when I entered. They were having a heated debate about whether it was appropriate for Sarah Hamilton to allude to the candidates' genitals (Bridget called them 'man bits') on live television. "Evie," she demanded, "you were there, what did you think?"

Madeline's eyes narrowed as she waited for my response. She may be fifteen years older than Bridget but of the two of them, Madeline is the free spirit, Bridget is the prude.

Politics demands loyalty to your candidate. Fealty above all. But loyalty has its limits and this morning I had discovered mine.

"From where I was sitting—and I mean this in the metaphorical sense as well as the physical sense—Michiel and O'Halloran both had it coming."

Bridget was scandalized. "But the language— "

"All the candidates knew the order of speaking: Michiel first, O'Halloran next, Sarah last. O'Halloran attacked

Michiel. Michiel retaliated and stepped all over Sarah's speaking time. It smacks of male privilege and they both deserved to be called on it in the harshest way possible."

Madeline looked at Bridget, an *I told you so* look on her face. "See! What did I tell you?" Bridget didn't bother to respond, she scooted her chair up closer to her computer and began typing at great speed.

25

One week to Election Day

Bridget was scolding Madeline when I arrived at Lawson Valentine. "Will you please stop flitting in and out of my workspace, you're ruining my concentration."

Madeline scowled and was about to speak when she spotted me in the doorway. Her expression was uncharacteristically bleak. "Evie, we need—"

Just then AJ burst out of his office. "Evie!" He loped down the hall and swung me around like a rag doll.

"Hey, hey, decorum…" I protested.

"Oops, sorry." His face flushed right up to his eyebrows.

"What brought this on?" I smoothed my linen jacket. "Did you win the lottery?"

"Not quite. City Council rubber stamped Calhoon's MOU today."

I felt no joy, just irritation. Calhoon's name evoked dull

pain, like a sliver buried too deep to dig out. "Have you told Calhoon yet?"

"Hell, yeah. Keith and I were on the phone to Sam the minute we heard. Sam's delighted—" he bit his lip "—sorry, should we have waited for you?"

"Absolutely not, better that the client gets the good news from us than his cronies at City Hall." I wrinkled my nose. "Perhaps 'cronies' isn't the right word under the circumstances."

"Evie…" Madeline's tone became more urgent. "We *really* need to talk."

I glanced at AJ, he shrugged and I followed Madeline down the corridor into her office. Madeline's office faces the parking lot which is nestled at the base of a low hill covered in evergreens and deciduous trees. The woods are packed with birds, squirrels, and assorted wildlife. Although she'll never admit it, Madeline starts each day at the edge of the parking lot throwing birdseed and stale bread into the bushes for her feathered and furry friends. Usually she finds it relaxing, but not today. She hustled me into her office and pulled a bulky file off the top of her filing cabinet before coming around her desk to sit beside me.

"What's this?" I asked.

"The results of my second CORES search."

"And…did you find anything interesting?"

"Uh-huh."

Her voice was flat, emotionless. I was mystified. "Are you going to tell me, or do I have to drag it out of you one word at a time?"

Madeline's eyes met mine, then darted away. She placed the heavy file in front of me and flipped it open. "I'm going to walk you through this first, then we'll take it to Keith."

"What did you find, Madeline?"

She took a deep breath. "To recap, the only time Bev had anything to do with the red box company was when Calhoon told her to deposit a cheque in the company's bank account, but we don't know how the money went out, or to whom—"

"Why didn't someone in CDC's finance department issue the cheque?"

"I'll get to that in a moment. I ran a historical search on the company's directors and shareholders from 1983 when Sam took over to the present day. The company—I'm calling it 'Red Box' because all these numbered companies can be a little confusing—Red Box has two shareholders: Sam Calhoon and a numbered company that changes over the years. Red Box has two directors, Sam and Bev. Poor Bev is a lovely woman but knows nothing about corporate law, she'd sign anything Sam put in front of her." Madeline paused. "I'm convinced Sam kept her on because she was clueless and didn't ask too many questions."

"And now he's got that Brock woman—" I said.

"He found himself another Bev."

Madeline slipped a sheet of paper out of the file and placed it in front of me. On it were some numbers:

1983 – 1999 266245 Ltd.

1999 – 2004 796051 Ltd.

2004 – 2008

2008 – 2016 1338442 Ltd.

2016 – present 1817245 Ltd.

"What's this?" I asked.

She pointed to the numbers at the top of the page. "From 1983 to 1999 Red Box was owned by Calhoon and the numbered company 266245 Ltd. From 1999 to 2004 Red

Box was owned by Calhoon and 796051 Ltd. This pattern repeats itself all the way down to the present day, except for the years 2004 to 2008 where there's no numbered company on record."

"Don't tell me. The numbered companies are owned by the crooked city official, right?"

She nodded. "Sam tells Bev to deposit money into Red Box's account. Some time later Red Box pays a dividend to its shareholder who happens to be the crooked city official."

"Madeline, we have to find out who owns the numbered companies on your list. This is the paper trail connecting Calhoon with the bureaucrat taking bribes."

Her eyes were grave. "I've already done that."

That's when she slipped another piece of paper out of her file and lay it gently down on the top of the pile.

"Oh shit," I said.

~

It took Madeline and me two hours to round up Keith and AJ who picked this day of all days to be out of the office at client meetings. I thought I'd go mad waiting for them to return. Finally we were assembled in the conference room. Bridget was under strict instructions to hold all our calls, no one would be put through unless they were a family member en route to the hospital.

"What's going on?" Keith shot a nervous glance at Madeline and then me.

"Madeline's got the results of the CORES searches. It's not good."

Madeline slid open a mahogany panel inset in the back wall, revealing a large whiteboard. Her black marker squeaked as she scribbled down the list of years and across from them, the company identifier numbers she'd shown me a couple of hours ago. She explained that Sam Calhoon used Red Box to funnel money to the shareholders who owned the numbered companies.

Keith interrupted her. "Whoa, back up. How does the money get into Red Box in the first place? CDC's auditors would notice large amounts of money disappearing out of CDC's bank accounts. They can't *all* be crooks."

"Oh yes, I meant to go into that. From what Bev told me after her second whiskey sour it isn't CDC's money, it comes straight out of Sam Calhoon's personal bank account."

AJ was incredulous. "Calhoon gave Bev access to his personal bank accounts?"

"Well, to one of them at least."

"Why would he do that?"

Madeline smiled. "Dear boy, Bev was the perfect office wife. She did whatever it took to keep Calhoon happy, be it paying off his personal credit card bills or buying gifts for his kids."

AJ cast a wistful glance toward the reception area. I looked at him and shook my head.

Keith drummed his fingers on the conference table. "I still don't get it. If Calhoon is prepared to break the law by paying bribes to city officials, why run it through Red Box, why not just slip a wad of bills into a plain brown envelope and hand it to the bureaucrat on a quiet park bench somewhere?"

"I've been thinking about that," I said. "Calhoon is an aggressive man who's willing to take big risks. He's creating a paper trail in case the bureaucrat balks when a really contentious development comes along. Funnelling the cash through Red Box to a bureaucrat on record as a shareholder is rock solid proof that the bureaucrat is taking bribes."

"Yeah," AJ said, "but that cuts both ways. Calhoon's threat 'do as I say or I'll go public,' proves Calhoon is corrupt, too. It hurts Calhoon as much as it hurts the bureaucrat."

I nodded. "Sure. It's mutually assured destruction, but look at it from the bureaucrat's perspective, he can continue to get rich by taking bribes, or he can be exposed as a crook, lose his job, and go to jail. In order to call Calhoon's bluff he has to risk annihilation." I looked around the table. "Calhoon is a calculating bastard. The minute the bureaucrat accepts the first bribe, they're cooked."

No one spoke. Madeline's black marker tap, tap, tapped on the whiteboard's eraser ledge. I gave her a nod to proceed.

Madeline said the CORES search revealed the shareholders' names, the officials taking bribes. Her marker flew across the whiteboard. Four names appeared in chronological order. At the top of the list was the man who was mayor from 1983 to 1999...and at the bottom of the list was Michiel Van Dijk.

The air in the room thinned, everything became still. All I could hear was Keith's clock on the credenza ticking like a metronome. Madeline sat down next to me, her chair bumping along the carpet. Keith rubbed his hand across his forehead and stared at the whiteboard in disbelief. "Sam Calhoon is bribing Michiel Van Dijk? He's bribed every mayor we've had since 1983? *Jesus*."

"Not *every* mayor," Madeline said firmly. "There is no numbered company for the years Gordie Brown was mayor. It looks like he wouldn't play ball—"

"Hold on." AJ stood up and began to pace. "Public officials have to declare their interests in private companies, otherwise it could be a conflict of interest."

"AJ," I said patiently, "the law may require them to declare their interests but if they're breaking the law by accepting bribes, they're hardly going to come clean on who's bribing them and how."

AJ stopped pacing and sat down again. "Oh...of course..." I understood his confusion. I'd had two hours to come to terms with this discovery and was still vacillating between anger and disbelief.

"Keith." It took him a moment to drag his eyes away from the whiteboard when I said his name. "It was bad enough when we thought Calhoon was pulling a bait-and-switch, but this, corruption and bribery, this is criminal. We have to report it to the police." As I said it something niggled at me, but in the intensity of the moment I didn't stop to consider it.

"I agree," Keith glanced at his watch. "Give me fifteen minutes, I need to make a quick phone call, then I'll meet you back in your office." I asked Madeline to join us.

I knew how the rest of the afternoon would unfold: slowly. Keith is a methodical and thorough lawyer. He would need a couple of hours to sift through the evidence to be absolutely certain it supported the accusation we were about to make. Then he would want to discuss which of us, him or me, should inform the police, and finally when he was satisfied, we would proceed. In my mind I'd already reached the end point: we had all the evidence we needed to support the accusation, this was my file so I should be the one to file the complaint, but I was his partner and I had to respect his need to proceed with caution. I wondered whether I should send out for pizza.

AJ closed his file folder, picked up his water glass and said, "On the bright side…"

"There's a bright side?" I asked, incredulous.

"It's not every day a law firm uncovers a corruption scheme that's been hidden in plain sight for decades." A mischievous grin crossed his lips. "We'll be famous."

Everyone groaned.

We'd be famous all right. Not for our excellent legal work but for being the firm that brought down a sleazy developer and a string of dishonest politicians...or, if the charges failed to stick, we'd be known as the firm that blew itself up..

Madeline returned to her office to duplicate her file while I went into mine to wait for Keith. I was too agitated to work. I pivoted in my chair and swung my feet up onto the window ledge in what Mom would have said was an unladylike position. I tilted back and stared out the window. The river was shaving chunks off its banks in the late afternoon light; the longer it flows, the wider it becomes.

I knew we were doing the right thing but I felt like I'd stepped into an elevator and the brake cable just snapped. My thoughts turned to AJ. This morning City Council approved the Pavilion deal, this afternoon everything turned to ash. I wandered down to his office. AJ had his back to me, slouched in his chair with his feet up on the window ledge.

"That's not a ladylike position, you know."

He jerked his feet off the sill and spun around to face me. "What?"

"Just something my mom would have said. How are you doing?"

"Okay, I guess."

I sat down across from him, resting my arms along the edge of his desk. "AJ, is there any reason Calhoon would have had to bribe Michiel to get the Pavilion project approved?"

"No." AJ was adamant. "Calhoon caved on all the touchy issues right from the outset. He had no reason to bribe anyone, he gave the City exactly what they wanted."

My eyes drifted over to the window. AJ's view of the river was peaceful, like mine, not that he noticed. "It's just those stupid Plan B drawings. Calhoon turned to ice when he discovered we had them, and he's never explained why they existed in the first place." I rubbed my temples and sighed. "It's been a grueling day." I heard Keith tell his wife he'd be home late tonight. "Got to figure out what we're telling the police."

The little voice in my head added: *and what we're going to do to protect ourselves from Sam Calhoon.*

26

When I wheeled into the Lawson Valentine parking lot the next morning, I found Madeline standing at the edge of the lot, facing the woods that rise gently to the west. She slipped a plastic bag into her purse and waited for me to catch up to her.

"What did the police say?" she asked.

"I haven't called them yet."

Madeline looked shocked. She'd stayed late last night to walk Keith and me through CDC's corporate structure. We're regulatory lawyers, more than a little rusty on the mechanics of corporate law. Just when I thought we were finished, Keith asked Madeline to explain how the CORES system worked. This was completely irrelevant but typical of Keith. After Madeline finally left we discussed who should call the police. Eventually he agreed (as I knew he would) that I should report our suspicions to Pritchard. When I dialed Pritchard's number and discovered he'd left for the day I almost lost it. Exasperated, I told Keith I'd call Pritchard in the morning.

On my drive home I had to remind myself that our partnership was successful precisely because Keith and I work so differently. He's the kind of guy who slowly lowers himself into a swimming pool, whereas I dive in at the deep end and am doing laps before he pushes off. Normally this isn't an issue, but at times like these, it could be infuriating.

Madeline nodded as I gave her the abbreviated version. As we approached the double glass doors, a magpie landed at our feet. It strutted toward Madeline with a belligerent eye.

"I think he wants what's in your bag," I said.

"Well he's not getting it." She flapped her hand at the bird. It sashayed closer, undaunted.

Two more magpies swooped down from the sky, forming a scrum directly in front of us. "We'd better get inside before they take matters into their own…er, talons," I said, waving my briefcase at them.

"They're getting more aggressive every day," Madeline said as she opened the door.

Bridget looked up from her desk and snorted. "That's because you feed them all the time."

Madeline pretended not to hear her.

I told Bridget to hold my calls—we'll have to fill her in soon or the poor woman will think she's getting fired—and punched Pritchard's number into the phone.

Pritchard was mumbling to someone when he picked up his phone. "Good morning, Ms. Valentine. What can I do for you?"

I spoke calmly, forcing myself to slow down. "Sergeant Pritchard, I'd like to meet with you as soon as possible. I, well actually Lawson Valentine, would like to report suspicious activity that may be of a criminal nature."

Pritchard paused for two beats before replying. "Can you give me some idea what this is about?" When I said I preferred to speak to him in person he asked me to drop by in an hour.

I stepped out of my office, almost bowling over Madeline in the process. She thrust a slim file into my hands. "I've cleaned up the org charts to make them easier for a non-lawyer to understand. And I made extra copies for you to leave with Pritchard. Call me if he has any questions."

"Thanks. I'm sure he'll have questions. This meeting is just to get the ball rolling." *Ball rolling? More like a millstone that will crush everything in its path.*

~

An hour later I was sitting in the waiting room of the District 2 police station. Cops and civilians breezed by, chatting with each other; someone escorted a bewildered-looking man down a pokey corridor. No one looked in my direction. I could have a full-blown coronary right here in my chair and no one would notice.

I was restless and pulled out my phone, searching for Michiel's Twitter account. Who knows why, it would only make me edgier. I was about to click on a gif when Pritchard rounded the corner and invited me to follow him into a small room, just big enough for a square table and two chairs. The walls were beige and covered with scuff marks. A long narrow window high up on the wall provided a view of the dingy stucco building next door.

"What? No two-way mirrors on the walls?"

He smiled. "How can I help you, Evie?"

I took a deep breath and started from the beginning

when Calhoon hired our firm to shepherd the Pavilion project through the City's development process. I placed Madeline's file on the table and walked him through the corporate structure, describing how we'd discovered the true purpose of the Red Box company. Pritchard listened patiently. When I was done, he whistled through his teeth. "This is big. Real big."

"No kidding."

Pritchard put his hand on the file. "Can I keep this? I'd like to pass it along to the fraudulent crimes group."

"Absolutely, that's your copy. It includes our contact information." I felt relieved now that I had told Pritchard everything…well, not exactly everything …

"Can I have that back for a moment?" Pritchard slid the file back across the table. I extracted Madeline's chart of the corporate family. "See this company…?"

"The Red Box company? Yep."

"It's owned by Calhoon and a numbered company, 1817245 Ltd."

Pritchard said, "Right, and the numbered company is owned by Michiel Van Dijk."

"So, when I was at Nick's—Nicholas Silva's—place the night he died, I found one of his business cards on the floor. This number, 1817245, is on the back of his card."

Pritchard levelled his eyes at me. "And you didn't think to mention this sooner?"

I looked out the narrow window. "The number didn't mean anything to me sooner." That sounded weak, even to me.

"This is a murder investigation, Evie," he said pointedly. "This card connects Nicholas Silva to Sam Calhoon, it ties the two investigations together." Before I could ask what he was implying he pushed his chair back and stood up. The metallic sound of screeching chair legs filled the tiny room. The interview was over.

"Do you still have the business card?"

"I do, but not with me. It's at home on my dresser."

"Bring it in the first chance you get." He held the door open for me. "Evie," his voice sounded firm but soft. "When you're dealing with Michiel, or Calhoon for that matter, it's business as usual, you got that? We can't afford to spook these guys."

Right. Business as usual with two of the most powerful men in the city, who just happen to be up to their eyeballs in fraud and corruption. No problem.

~

The barista, a two-time world champion finalist coffee brewer according to the plaque on the wall, brought a coffee and a chocolate cupcake to my table which was tucked up against the brick wall in the corner. The coffee foam was shaped like a palm tree. I told her it was the best foam art I'd seen, she grinned and said she would do Saturn amongst the stars for me the next time.

Keith would be roaming the office waiting for my call. I'd promised to update him after my meeting with Pritchard. Keith sounded relieved when I reported the meeting went exactly as we'd expected, and Pritchard was transferring the file to fraudulent crimes. "They'll contact us if they need more information. In any event, until charges are laid, it's business as usual."

"Well, in keeping with the 'business as usual' theme, Calhoon's secretary called. Calhoon wants to take us out for a victory dinner. I don't think we have any choice but to accept." I groaned so loudly the people at the next table turned and stared.

"Who's us?"

"You, me, and AJ—us. Calhoon says he likes to strike while the iron is hot, and thank his amazing legal team while they're still basking in the glow of victory."

If it were anyone but Calhoon I would applaud the gesture. I don't know how many closing dinners I'd attended at Gates, Case and White that took place months after the deal had closed. By then even the most egotistical lawyer had run out of self-aggrandizing stories about how they'd saved the deal at a critical juncture; the conversation would flag and we would quickly resort to the time-honoured tradition of getting plastered on the client's dime.

Keith and AJ were available Thursday evening, was I? Yes, damn it, I was.

"Right, I'll tell Calhoon we're on. Seven-thirty, Banco's."

Banco's is one of the primo restaurants in town. It takes weeks to get a reservation. I wondered which City luminary would be shuffled off to the table next to the kitchen to make room for Calhoon's party.

27

Music I couldn't identify…house? garage? basement?... banged off the porcelain sinks and shiny mirrors of the empty salon. Whatever it was, it was loud, really, really loud, especially at seven in the morning. Luka, my hair stylist, said it was exactly what he needed to jump start his day. I texted him last night, begging him to squeeze me in before his first client; I may not want to go to dinner with Sam Calhoon, but at least I would look presentable once I got there. Luka agreed to come in early just for me, so I really wasn't in any position to question his taste in music.

"What's the name of the band?" I don't know why I do that, he tells me and I instantly forget. He said something that sounded like 'arms.' It went in one ear and out the other and not just because my head was in the sink. He put an apricot concoction on my hair and massaged my scalp.

"That's exactly what I need," I murmured.

"Your neck muscles are tight as a drum."

"If I were a cat I'd be purring right about now."

Luka gave me his *you always say that* smile. I've

been Luka's client for seven years. We had an awkward relationship at first. I found him a little intimidating; young, fit, clear blue eyes and a short beard that makes him look like a brooding poet. He found me, the lady lawyer, intimidating as well. Later we joked about people's misconceptions. I told him everyone thinks female lawyers are bitches, but we're not…well, not all the time. He replied, try being a male hairdresser, everyone thinks you're gay. I said, you *are* gay, and he said, yeah but I might not be. It was hard to argue with his logic.

Luka rinsed my hair and led me back to his station. "You're working on Michiel's campaign, right? Think he'll win?" In hairdressing, unlike other forms of customer service, nothing is off limits, not even religion and politics. What I know about Luka's love life would fill a book.

"Michiel's doing okay," I said cautiously. After Madeline's devastating revelations I decided to compartmentalize my feelings about Michiel. It was the only way I would survive the next few days. Michiel the corrupt mayor accepting bribes would go into a box labelled 'bury him,' Michiel the mayoral candidate would go into another box labelled 'go through the motions, then bury him.'

"Luka," I said to his reflection in the mirror, "who do you think is going to win?" Luka moves in circles very different than mine; I was genuinely interested in his opinion.

He dragged a comb through my wet hair. "An inch off, right?"

"Yes." I've worn my hair in a wavy chin length style for ages. Dad said my bob reminded him of the flapper girls who flaunted the social conventions of the 1920s. The comparison pleased me.

Luka pulled a section of hair through his fingers and

started to cut. "I liked Michiel in the last election and thought I'd stick with him this time around, but halfway through I started paying attention to O'Halloran, and now I'm leaning toward Sarah Hamilton."

"Sarah? Why?" I could understand business-minded voters—Luka owned this salon—considering O'Halloran, but Sarah? Her image was more soccer mom than a cost cutting, hard-nosed politician.

"She clobbered them in the debate. She gave real answers, Michiel and O'Halloran were so busy beating on each other I have no idea what they stand for." His eyes met mine in the mirror and he grinned. "And that ruler comment, priceless!"

Soccer mom appeals to cool hair stylist? "What about your friends, do they like her?"

"You know how it is, they're not into politics, but they follow social media and Sarah is killing it."

"Sarah is killing it on Twitter? Facebook—?"

"—and Instagram. Totes."

"Really?"

"Yeah, look at this." He stopped cutting and pulled his phone out of a drawer under the mirror. He smiled as he thumbed through the posts. "Here she is at Pride." He showed me a video of Sarah laughing and dancing at the front of the parade, she was wearing a rainbow-coloured tank top with a pink feather boa slung around her neck. Her blonde hair was flying all over the place.

"And the Stampede Midway." Sarah was dressed in tight jeans, cowboy boots, and a black cowboy hat. She was doing the Texas Two Step better than the pros. "Oh, and remember when her daughter dared her to go on the Zipper and they streamed the whole thing? The kid said you could hear her mom screaming clear across the park." Luka tucked his phone back in the drawer. "She's a real person, not a politician."

"What about Michiel, is he real?" *As if I didn't know the answer.*

Luka pulled up a stool and spun my chair around to face him. His face was eight inches from mine, eyes narrowed in concentration.

He tilted my head up a bit. "Is Michiel a real person?" *Snip, snip.* "In the beginning Michiel was just Michiel. You could stop him in the street and talk to him about whatever was bothering you." *Snip, snip.* "But he's changed…you never see him around anymore…not unless you fork over a wad of cash to go to a fundraiser or something." Luka trailed off, he looked worried, had he said too much? "I mean, I'm sure he's a good guy and all." *Snip, snip.* "But times are tough, and things are getting worse, not better. Maybe it's time for a change." Luka unclipped a blow dryer from the side of his workstation and rummaged in the drawer for a round hairbrush. We'd be done in a couple of minutes.

"And don't get me started on property taxes!" he said. "They're going through the roof." Luka and his partner own a small house in the Warehouse district. If anyone would know about skyrocketing property taxes in the inner city, they would. "Then there's this place!" He waved the blow dryer in the direction of the front desk. "The business taxes on this place are ridiculous. If something doesn't change soon, we're moving to a cheaper location." My first thought was a selfish one: God, not again. I've moved with Luka twice; I really didn't want to follow him to a strip mall in the suburbs.

"So why Sarah and not O'Halloran? He says he's going

to cut taxes."

Luka snorted. "Oh, he'll cut taxes all right, by slashing the budget to the bone. He'll take care of his friends, the rich will get richer and the rest of us will get stuck with crappy transit service and broken-down sewage treatment plants."

"And you think Sarah will be better?"

He tipped my chin down. "Sure. She's not confrontational, not so much 'my way or the highway.' She doesn't have to prove she's the smartest person in the room. She'll pull City Council together; they'll get more done if they're not at each other's throats all the time."

Luka turned off the blow dryer and turned my chair around to face the mirror. My gloomy reflection stared back at us.

"Uh-oh," he said. "Don't you like it?"

I pasted a smile on my face. "Oh Luka, sorry, I was just thinking. It's perfect. My hair is perfect." I smiled to assure him the compliment was sincere. But Luka was right. The old Michiel was gone. Maybe he never existed in the first place.

~

I couldn't stop thinking about Luka's comments after I left the salon. They echoed a conversation I'd had with an Uber driver a few weeks ago. I was returning from an evening fundraiser. The crowd was enthusiastic and generous. When Michiel said their support would give him the momentum he needed to sweep back into the mayor's office they cheered the house down.

I had just settled into the back seat of the Uber when the driver spotted the *#VoteMichiel* button pinned to my jacket.

"So, you think Michiel's gonna win the election?" He eyed me in the rear-view mirror.

"He's got a healthy lead," I said. "What do you think?"

The driver hit the brakes hard at a stop sign and I lurched forward into my seat belt. "I got my eye on O'Halloran," he said. "He's picking up support."

"Not in the polls."

"Polls, schmolls, I'm talking about social media. O'Halloran's Twitter's exploding." He accelerated hard and soon we were careening in and out of traffic. "Same on Facebook."

"Maybe they're bots." *What do I know about bots?*

He shrugged. "Don't know, but O'Halloran's posts are great. Him trying to catch that greased pig, genius." He pulled his eyes away from the rear-view mirror and focused on the road ahead, it was dusk and getting harder to see the pedestrians darting across the street.

A greased pig...?

I was about to ask him what he liked about O'Halloran, other than his social media, when he screeched to a stop in front of my house. "There you go, ma'am. Home sweet home."

Luka's admiration for Sarah Hamilton, together with the Uber driver's praise for O'Halloran…random comments, sure, but something had shifted. Something Wendy had not brought to the attention of the inner circle in our morning conference calls. Michiel could be in trouble.

The only question facing me was whether I should raise this with Wendy or not. I revisited my Michiel boxes: This was a campaign issue. Go through the motions, then bury him. I pulled off the road and reluctantly called Wendy who agreed to meet me at Mars Diner in twenty minutes.

I found her in a dark, wooden booth at the back of the restaurant. She was wearing a form-fitting sweater dress with suede boots. Her hair was spikier than ever. A server appeared and took our orders: coffee for me, Coke for herself and coffee for Clint.

"Clint's coming?"

She nodded. "I told him you've been hearing things about O'Halloran and Sarah. He's running some analytics."

We didn't have long to wait before Clint rolled in the door on a puff of wind. I was reminded of when I was a child and got stuck in a tumbleweed on my way home from school. It chased me down the street and latched on to my leg, I thought I was going to die. Mom raced out of the house when she heard me screaming. She pulled it off and snapped it into tiny bits to show me there was nothing to be afraid of.

Wendy pulled up O'Halloran's Twitter feed as Clint made his way to our booth. A tiny smile crossed her lips. "The greased pig is cute. More than a thousand retweets."

"Greased pig?" Clint said as he slid into the booth next to Wendy. He grunted appreciatively when she said she had ordered for him.

"I've been tracking Michiel's enthusiasm gap," he said.

The server arrived with our orders. Clint decided he wanted toast and the server returned with water and cutlery. We waited while he placed the silverware just so.

Clint explained political campaigns track how eager their supporters are to vote. Michiel started strong, but his supporters' enthusiasm was waning. If O'Halloran's supporters' enthusiasm picked up and Michiel's continued to flag, Michiel could lose the election.

The server returned with our drinks and four thick slabs

of hot toast for Clint. It smelled delicious.

"I still don't understand," I said. "Who cares if the voters are enthusiastic or...or…blasé, as long as they vote?"

He stuffed a piece of toast into his mouth and washed it down with coffee. "That's just it. Enthusiastic voters vote. Blasé voters stay home."

Wendy chimed in. "It's not that Michiel's voters switch to O'Halloran, it's that they won't vote at all."

Clint made a muffled sound. Wendy reached across to his plate, tore the corner off his toast and delicately placed it in her mouth. He raised an eyebrow as she continued. "It looks like Michiel's message isn't resonating with the voters."

"And O'Halloran's is?" The more I'm around politicians, the less I know. "He's all about slash and burn. That's a promise of pain, not hope. How can that possibly resonate with anyone?"

Clint signalled the server for more coffee. "Ah, but that's the genius of it. O'Halloran says Michiel is the devil incarnate who created the economic disaster while he, O'Halloran, is the hero who's going to lead us to paradise."

"How? He hasn't told us how."

Clint said, "He doesn't have to. He's making an emotional appeal, not a rational one."

Wendy frowned. "I should have seen this coming, but with, well, running the campaign, I kinda lost focus." She looked at Clint out of the corner of her eye. He had been dead set against her taking on the campaign manager role for precisely this reason. "I'm really sorry." To Clint's credit he didn't say I told you so.

She fidgeted with her phone while Clint stared hard out the window. Finally I broke the silence. "What's Michiel been putting into the ether lately?"

Wendy reddened. Her flushed face looked strange against her blue hair. "Until we get a couple of CEOs to endorse Michiel's new pitch we're stuck with the usual short policy clips, revitalizing the downtown core, affordable housing, that kind of thing."

I signalled the server and ordered a plate of scrambled eggs. Wendy ordered a bran muffin and another Coke. Clint asked for more toast. I was deep in the box labelled 'go through the motions, then bury him.' I felt like a first-class hypocrite.

28

A gentle breeze whispered through the trees and fluttered the candles on patio tables jammed with people grabbing a drink on their way home. Even with the economic downturn the restaurants and bars were packed.

I found a tiny parking spot a couple of blocks south of Banco's. It took me three tries to get the Mini close enough to the curb that I could step out of the car with my head held high.

Keith, Calhoon, and Garry Johnston were already seated when I arrived. AJ strolled in right behind me. Calhoon, ever the gentleman, stood up when I reached the table and with a grand sweep of his arm invited me to sit next to him on the blue velvet banquette. AJ pulled out the chair between Keith and Johnston on the other side of the table.

Banco's is in a historic building that used to be a bank, hence its name which alludes to the bank as well as baccarat; what better place to blow a ridiculous amount of money on upscale food and drink. Its lofty ceilings, mahogany fixtures, and French doors opening on to a flagstone patio give it a dignified, old-world feel. Our table was nestled in a corner, hidden behind a massive marble column and a heavy iron screen that served as a room divider.

Calhoon said I looked lovely and handed me the wine list. The leatherbound menu weighed half a kilo. The blurb said the original bank vaults in the basement housed more than ten thousand bottles of wine. “I’m not really a wine connoisseur,” I said, searching the menu for a white wine, any white wine, so he wouldn’t order for me. “I’ll have the Pinot Grigio.”

He nodded and turned to Keith and AJ who were engaged in a spirited debate with Garry Johnston about the relative merits of a certain red wine. Keith winked at me, wine snobbery is alive and well at Calhoon Developments Corporation. Their conversation reminded me of when I was an articling student at Gates. I was tucked away in the law library when a senior partner burst through the doors. He rounded up every articling student he could find, shouting, ‘The Beaujolais is in, get to a wine shop and purchase every bottle you can find.’ I said I was researching a memo for a senior litigation partner and he replied, ‘Priorities, sweetheart, priorities.’ I didn’t know which was more offensive, being told to drop everything so the partners could stock up on their precious wine or being called ‘sweetheart.’

Dinner lasted for hours; appetizers (I skipped the baby octopus), main course, desserts, artisanal cheese, all of it punctuated by bottle after bottle of wine selected by Calhoon to perfectly complement our meal. The sommelier fawned all over him, congratulating him for yet another inspired choice. At these prices any choice should be an excellent choice.

Calhoon asked us to raise our glasses and gave an

eloquent little speech praising our brilliance and legal acumen. Johnston's mouth twitched like a cat stalking a sparrow when Calhoon said that with Michiel in our corner, the future for CDC, and by extension, Lawson Valentine, looked bright.

Keith, AJ, and I said all the right things: we were pleased to work with such a professional team, we knew the Pavilion project would be a testament to what CDC could accomplish in the downtown core, and so on. The entire experience was surreal.

There was a lull in the conversation while we waited for the bill. Johnston cast his pale eyes over me and said, "What a shame Nicholas isn't here to see this." It sounded like a taunt. Not an expression of sorrow.

I leaned my elbows on the pristine tablecloth, fingers interlaced. "Yes, it's an awful shame," I said. "But Nicholas' killer will be brought to justice soon, you can bank on it." He continued to stare at me, silent. Just then the waiter materialized with the bill and we watched Calhoon fuss with the credit card machine.

29

ELECTION DAY

The sweet aroma of chocolate chip cookies filled the air. I had been baking since dawn, well maybe not dawn, but early nevertheless. Two sheets of cookies were cooling on a rack on the kitchen island, another batch was in the oven. Quincy peered up at me, begging for a crumb.

"You're fat, no cookies for you." He continued to watch me with soulful eyes, not an easy thing to pull off for a bull terrier.

Louisa bounced into the kitchen wearing her running gear. "A fit of domesticity? What brought this on?"

"I volunteered our place for a home base, remember? You're supposed to take Quincy to puppy daycare so he doesn't kill the volunteers when they come in the front door."

Louisa's eyes widened. "Right." She popped a cookie in her mouth, grabbed Quincy's leash and led him to the door. He followed her reluctantly, convinced that wherever he was going, it would not be as nice as cookie heaven.

I put a fresh pot of coffee on and cleared everything off the dining room table to make room for the campaign paraphernalia Gordon McLeod would be bringing over in less than thirty minutes. Gord was the home base commander for our ward. Lisbeth asked me and a dozen other volunteers across the city to turn our houses into home bases. She assigned volunteers to each house and tagged experienced volunteers like Gord to organize them for one final day of door knocking. The volunteers would return to their respective home bases between shifts to eat, rest and get fresh assignments. It was my job to feed and water them. Lisbeth insisted I provide healthy snacks—not just junk food!—but by this point in the campaign everyone was running on adrenalin and the ratio of Cheezies and potato chips to cauliflower and snap peas on my kitchen table was three to one.

After today I was done. There would be no more volunteering on Michiel's campaign, no more compartmentalizing Michiel the political candidate and Michiel the crook. I was done. I was more than done.

I was putting the finishing touches on a sign that said 'MICHIEL VOLUNTEERS, COME IN, DOOR'S OPEN' when the doorbell rang. Gord stood on the doorstep, a big smile on his face, a bulging computer bag slung over his shoulder and a cardboard box in his arms. I grabbed the box which was heavier than I expected and lugged it into the dining room. He dropped his computer bag in the hall and ran back to his car which was parked at the curb, trunk wide open. He staggered back up the stairs with two more cardboard boxes and followed me into the dining room.

"Thanks again for doing this," he panted.

"No problem. The dining room is all yours."

"Wow, you've got a fantastic view of the river." He stood at the French doors leading out on to the balcony that runs the full length of the house connecting the dining room, the living room, and my study. I opened the door and we stepped outside. The morning air was crisp, the sound of traffic shimmered across the river.

"It's going to be cooler today," he said. "Better for the volunteers, they'll be hoofing it." He was right; the city looks flat when you fly over it, but this part of town is quite hilly. I left Gord sticking maps to the walls with painter's tape and went back to baking.

"Nice sign." Louisa was back from dropping Quincy off at puppy daycare. "What if they're not Michiel supporters but Duffy O'Halloran's spies?"

"Then we draw and quarter them and hide their bodies in the basement." Louisa gave me a deadpan stare. I laughed. "Gord's got a list of who's coming. If they're not on the list, they don't get in." She said hi to Gord and reached for a cookie; I slapped her wrist. "Nope, first you bake, then you eat."

An hour later the kitchen and dining room were jammed with volunteers eating and gossiping about how big Michiel's win was going to be. No one expected him to crush it, but they were confident he would sweep back into office with a sizable majority.

Gord interrupted the speculation by calling everyone into the dining room and giving them their assignments. Ten minutes later they were gone and the house was quiet except for Louisa and me murmuring in the kitchen.

By noon we had baked eight dozen cookies. The

#VoteMichiel Twitter feed was flooded with photos of me in my *Bazinga*! apron. My face was red, my hair was a mess, and I had gone viral.

Gord ordered six large pizzas timed to arrive when the volunteers returned for lunch. I lay the pizza boxes on the kitchen island and opened the lids. Volunteers crowded around me, reaching over each other to pick their favourite slices. Chattering like magpies, they settled into chairs and on the floor.

"Evie! Your fame as the cookie queen surpasses your fame as a lawyer." Michiel materialized by my side. I almost jumped out of my skin.

"Hey, Michiel, I didn't hear you come in." I forced a small grin. "How are you?"

"Good!" He was wearing a light cashmere sweater and chinos and carrying a slim black leather folder. "My speech," he said, glancing at the leather folder. "Just putting on the finishing touches."

"I presume it's a victory speech, not a gracious loser speech, none of that 'the people have spoken, and they're always right' stuff?"

He laughed his charming laugh. "No," he said, "not this time." Some of the volunteers heard his voice and came over to talk. He shook their hands, telling them they were doing an outstanding job, then looked back at me. "Where's Gord?" I pointed in the direction of the dining room. Gord updated him on what the volunteers were hearing at the doors. Michiel looked very pleased when he returned to the food table.

He was fishing around in a bowl of jellybeans when his phone rang. "It's Lisbeth," he said, "is there somewhere I can take this?"

I led him upstairs to my bedroom. He walked over to the tall windows facing the river and started talking to Lisbeth in a low voice. Louisa was chatting with Gord when I returned to the kitchen. She held up a slice of pizza. "Evie, you've got to try the Ambrosia, it's got artichoke."

"No," Gord interrupted, "don't eat anything. We've got to get these people back out into the street where they belong. They're getting too comfortable." We shooed the volunteers out the door, reminding them it was election day, do or die time. Ten minutes later the last of the stragglers were gone, leaving pizza crusts, crumpled napkins, and half-empty pop cans in their wake.

I was debating with Louisa about making another batch of cookies when I heard Michiel come down the stairs. "Have you got time to eat?" I waved a hand in the direction of the pizza boxes which looked like they'd been ravaged by a pack of hyenas.

He looked blank for a moment, as if he had forgotten where he was, then shook his head. "Ah, no, I've got to visit a few more home bases and then return to campaign headquarters." He looked around the kitchen. "Have you seen Lidia?"

Lidia was his driver. She was chatting with Gord in the dining room and called out, saying she was ready to leave anytime. Michiel was halfway out the door before he realized he had not said goodbye. He returned to the kitchen and gave me a distracted hug and pumped Louisa's hand before heading back to the foyer. He glanced back at me once more before closing the door.

Louisa thrust a slice of pizza in my hand and I took a bite. It was cold.

"Did Michiel look spacey to you?" I asked. "He looked

spacey to me."

She laughed. "I'd look spacey too if my fate rested in the hands of 'the people.'" She crunched on a carrot. "Yesterday I asked the nurses on my shift when they were going to vote. Two of them didn't even know there was an election on. Can you believe it?"

Yes, I could believe it. In some countries people die for the right to vote, here they sleep through the whole thing.

After we cleared away the pizza boxes we baked one last batch of cookies for the late afternoon crowd. I was washing a measuring cup for the millionth time when my phone rang. It was Lisbeth.

"What's up?" I asked.

"Did Michiel leave his speech at your place?"

"I don't think so, he had his leather folder with him when he left."

"I know that." She sounded irritable. "He's got the folder, the speech isn't in it."

"I'll check, but isn't it on your computer?"

She sighed loudly. I could picture her massaging the bridge of her nose with her fingertips. "Yes, it's on the computer, but he made notes on his copy and he wants it back."

"Right. I'll look around."

She hung up without saying goodbye.

I found Louisa in the dining room talking to Gord and told her we had to find Michiel's speech.

Louisa said, "God, I hope I didn't throw it in a garbage bag with the pizza boxes. There's all kinds of gunk in there."

"Check the obvious places first." We tore the kitchen, dining room and living room apart. Nothing. Then we put on rubber gloves, dragged the two big green garbage bags sitting in the corner of the kitchen out on to the patio and pawed through them. Lots of gunk, no speech.

"Wait," Louisa said, "didn't Michiel go upstairs?" She was right. He went upstairs to take Lisbeth's call. With any luck I would find the speech in my bedroom.

I sprinted upstairs and retraced Michiel's steps: he had walked across the room and stood in front of the tall window facing the river while talking to Lisbeth on his phone. As I turned and scanned the room my eyes lit on the highboy dresser. I hate clutter. Louisa says I'm tidy to a fault. The only thing on top of the highboy was Dad's Art Deco clock—that is, until a couple of days ago when I had carefully propped Nick's business card up against the clock face. The card was gone.

My heart started pounding in my chest.

Frantic, I looked around the room. There was a dent in the puffy white duvet. I make my bed every day, fluffing up the duvet until it looks like a soft marshmallow. No one, not even Quincy, would dare lie on my bed. Michiel's speech lay on the deflated duvet. The pages were covered in double-spaced typing and pink highlighter. It is right there. How could he forget it?

I sat down where Michiel had been sitting and scanned the room. There, tucked under the clear glass base of my bedside lamp was Nick's business card. Michiel must have sat down to examine it.

I picked up Michiel's speech. He'd made notes in the margins. *Spice this up...humour? Economic downturn started 2014, not 2015. Need empathy, we're all in this together.*

The pages shook in my hands. The number *1* in *2014* and *2015* had a tail like the number *1* in the sequence of numbers written on the back of Nick's business card.

I raced back downstairs, taking the steps two at a time, to retrieve my phone. I had to take a photo of Michiel's handwriting before I returned his speech to Lisbeth.

"Good Lord, that took you long enough," Louisa said as I rushed past her. "Did you find it?"

"Yep, be right back." I scooped my phone off the kitchen counter and sprinted back upstairs. I lay Nick's business card on the duvet next to the marked-up page of the speech and took a couple of deep breaths to steady my hands before I could take the shot.

Now to call Lisbeth. She sounded cross when she picked up.

"Did you find it?"

"Yes, it's here."

"Good, bring it right over." No, that wasn't going to happen. One look at my face and Michiel would know I had made the connection between him, Nick, and the Red Box.

In my best uncooperative lawyer tone I informed Lisbeth that I couldn't possibly leave the house, too many volunteers traipsing in and out, but I would leave the speech in an envelope on the hall table and she could send someone over to pick it up. Reluctantly, she agreed.

My next call was to Pritchard. I could barely hear him over the sound of traffic and I wondered where he was. I apologized for not bringing Nick's card to him sooner and explained I'd had a chance to compare the handwriting on the card with Michiel's handwritten notes on his speech and to my untrained eye it looked like a match.

"I have photos, I'm sending them to you now." I fiddled with the phone.

"Got it," he said, "but I still want that card. And the

speech. Do you still have it?"

"I have to give the speech back. They're coming to pick it up right now." I remembered Michiel. He was distracted, almost puzzled, when he left. "Sergeant Pritchard, I think Michiel suspects I know something."

He was silent; if it wasn't for the traffic noise, I'd have sworn I lost him.

"Look," he finally said, "this case is really heating up—"

"—Which one? Calhoon bribing Michiel or Nick's murder?"

"Evie, I need that card." I told him Lisbeth was expecting me at Campaign HQ this afternoon before we joined the rest of the volunteers at Max Hall to celebrate Michiel's victory.

"Will Michiel be at campaign headquarters?" Pritchard asked.

"Not after the polls close. The candidates are sequestered with their closest advisors and watch the returns in private. I think it's to make sure they don't have a meltdown in public if they're trounced."

"Yeah, but Michiel's going to win, right?"

"I know, but that's how it's done; win or lose, the candidates don't show their faces until the end of the evening."

"Look, don't bring the card to the station if you're pressed for time. Are you at home? I can meet you at that coffee shop near your place." We agreed to meet at Campana's in thirty minutes.

When I returned to the kitchen, I found Louisa arguing with an old guy who insisted politics was nastier now than it was in his day—the young people ruined it with this Facebook webby thing. Louisa said John A. Macdonald accepted bribes from the railways. No, he said, I'm talking about today, not ancient history. She mentioned the politician who'd recently been caught with two lists on his computer: voters who wanted their bribes in cash and those who preferred government contracts and committee appointments. The old man glared at her, then said it was time to leave. I thanked him for his help and offered him some cookies for the drive home. He gruffly accepted my peace offering and made a point of ignoring Louisa on his way out the door.

"I can't leave you alone for a minute, can I?"

She chuckled.

"Listen, I have to go out. Can you stick around until someone from the campaign office picks up the envelope on the hall table?"

"No problem," she said.

"And try not to pick fights with the volunteers, okay?"

"You can count on me."

I harrumphed and grabbed my jacket and keys.

~

Campana's Café is tucked between a three-storey walk-up apartment building and a dance studio. It is only a block and a half from my place. I hoped the walk through the quiet leafy streets would clear my head, but I kept returning to one question: does Michiel know I know and has he said anything to Lisbeth? I touched Nick's business card, now safe in the pocket of my jeans, as if it were a talisman. Not that it did Nick any good. *Focus on Michiel.* He could not say anything to Lisbeth without revealing he had accepted bribes from Calhoon. Lisbeth worships him. He would never do anything to violate her trust. No, Michiel will stay quiet and hope I failed to understand the significance of the numbers he'd scribbled on the back of Nick's card.

The faded green door to Campana's was stuck again. It made a loud creak when I banged it open with my hip, a few customers looked up from their laptops and cell phones, Pritchard was not among them. I waved at Mitch, the owner, and asked for my regular camomile tea. He nodded and put the kettle on.

Campana's looks like it is frozen in time, the 1970s I think. The wooden tables and mismatched chairs are wobbly and packed with customers in the morning. It is much quieter in the late afternoon. Mitch called my name and I went to the counter to pick up my tea. I placed it carefully on the table and scanned the titles of the used paperbacks sitting on the bookshelves lining the wall behind me. The only time I feel the urge to pick up a potboiler is when I'm at Campana's.

Creak! The stuck door announced Pritchard's arrival. He spotted me in the corner and sat down; his knee bumped the table leg and my tea slopped down the side of the cup.

"Sorry," he said.

"Don't worry, it happens all the time." I mopped up the mess with a serviette. "Are you having anything?"

"No more coffee for me or I'll be up all night."

"You're rationing your caffeine? I thought you guys lived on coffee and donuts."

"Don't start." His tone was firm, but his eyes smiled.

I pulled my chair closer and passed him Nick's card. He compared the handwriting on the card with the photo I had sent him of Michiel's notes on his speech. I edged closer and bumped against the table, my tea splashed over the rim of the cup again.

"See the tail on the number *1* on Michiel's speech?" I asked. He spread his fingers across the screen, enlarging the photo. "My mom used to do her *1*s like that, it's a European thing."

He peered at the screen and the card. "I thought Michiel was born here."

"He was, but his parents were born in the Netherlands, maybe that's how he first learned to write, or maybe it's just an affectation."

He nodded slowly but didn't say anything as he examined the photo.

"Sergeant Pritchard—" He looked up at me. I pushed my chair back, I was practically sitting in his lap. "Are you any closer to finding Nick's killer?" I had not allowed myself to think about Nick's murder for a while now. It wasn't the image of him in death that stopped me, it was my growing suspicion that Nick was as corrupt as Michiel. How else could he afford that stylish condo, the expensive clothes, the original artwork? A civil servant's salary is chump change compared to what he pulled down in private practice.

Pritchard glanced over at Mitch who was noisily unloading the dishwasher. A muscle twitched in Pritchard's jaw. "The case is coming along." He stopped, eyeing me carefully. "I'm going to tell you something that wasn't disclosed to the public."

I think I stopped breathing.

"You saw his eye. There was a small puncture wound in his eye socket. It destroyed his eye, but it was the skull fracture in the stairwell that killed him."

"Someone stabbed him in the eye and threw him into the stairwell…?" I was horrified. "Dear God, why?"

Pritchard shook his head. "We know how he died; we're

trying to work out why."

"But I—"

"—Enough, Evie. We're working the case, hard. That's all you need to know." He glanced at his watch. "I've got to push off."

The Kit-Cat clock on the wall said it was almost six. I had to get back home, freshen up, and then return to the campaign office. Pritchard touched my arm. He told me to be patient and, most importantly, to be careful. It would be over soon. I assured him I would let the police do their job.

My mind was blank as I walked home. The trees rustled, a harvest moon caught in their branches.

When I got home the envelope was gone.

30

The mood at Campaign HQ was one of pent-up anticipation. The few volunteers who trickled in to drop off campaign materials did not linger long, anxious to join their friends at the victory celebration at Max Hall.

Lisbeth was fiddling with a flat screen television perched precariously on a metal stand just outside the war room. "Will that hold?" I asked as she stuffed a rolled up *#VoteMichiel* T-shirt under one corner of the set.

"It better." She flicked a lock of hair off her face. Her dark blue midi dress complemented her pale complexion and glossy black hair; she looked elegant but also tired.

I put my hands on her shoulders, forcing her to look at me. "There's nothing more you can do now, Lisbeth, it's over." I steered her toward the coffee room but she slipped away.

"Not yet, I'm tallying the unofficial results, you can help."

I didn't have to be at Max Hall right away so I grabbed a handful of corn chips and joined her in the war room.

She waved at a large whiteboard attached to the back wall. “The scrutineers will start calling in soon, I’ll give you the numbers, you post them on the whiteboard.”

The exhaustion in her face gave way to pride. She said, “This time we’re going to do it right.”

“How do you mean?”

“Last time we were caught off guard, none of us thought Michiel would actually win. And when he started to rise in the polls it was too late to book a decent conference hall. We had our victory celebration in that crummy little campaign office.” She made a face in disgust. “People showed up with food and booze and the party spilled out into the streets. It’s a wonder we weren’t arrested.” She had a dreamy smile. “This time we’re doing it right.”

A volunteer popped into the room asking where he should put a stack of pamphlets. Lisbeth directed him to leave the materials on the long work table and proceed to Max Hall.

“Where was I? Oh yeah, that grotty little hellhole of a campaign office. This time, the victory party will be spectacular. I booked Max Hall months before Michiel confirmed he would run again, why he hesitated in making that decision I’ll never know, he *had* to run again, there’s so much left to do.”

She radiated energy; talking about Michiel’s victory and next term revitalized her.

“Evie, Max Hall has the biggest conference room in the city. It has the highest ceiling. I need the height to accommodate the confetti cannons and the balloon drop.”

“Confetti cannons and balloon drop?”

“Michiel said the whole thing was way over the top, but stopped fighting me on it when I said it was balloons and confetti or a ticker tape parade." She chuckled to herself.

Then her phone rang. "Scrutineer," she whispered. I picked up a marker and waited for her to reel off the numbers. The polls closed thirty minutes ago. Michiel's scrutineers from the smaller polling stations were already feeding us the preliminary results. They meant nothing of course, being too insignificant to predict the outcome. But as the evening progressed we'd get a sense of how well Michiel had done and whether his margin of victory came close to what he'd achieved in the previous election. Lisbeth would call him throughout the evening to pass along the updated results so there would be no surprises when he took the stage to deliver his victory speech.

"Oh look," I nodded in the direction of Lisbeth's TV. "It's Meagan Fellows, our favourite debate moderator."

"You mean non-moderator," she grumbled.

I went over to the TV and was fiddling with the volume button on the remote when someone stepped on my heel.

"Sorry!" It was Gord McLeod, my home base commander. He was so focused on the screen he walked right into me.

"No problem," I said, looking back at the TV. "Ward 8, that's my ward."

"I'm surprised," he said as the preliminary poll results scrolled across the bottom of the screen.

"By how well Sarah is doing?"

"Yeah, based on what our canvassers said Sarah had good support, but the majority of Ward 8 voters were supporting Michiel."

I glanced back at the TV. "It's less than half the polls, too soon to tell."

"Yeah, but Ward 8, it's one of the canary wards…"

"What's a canary ward?"

He pulled his eyes away from the TV to focus on me. "Canary, like 'canary in a coal mine.'"

"I'm not following you."

"It's like Pennsylvania. A presidential candidate has to win Pennsylvania to take the White House. Ward 8 is our version of Pennsylvania. Michiel has to win Ward 8 and a couple of other wards to win this election." He gave his head an impatient shake. "Never mind. Like you said, it's way too early in the game to be making predictions." I could not tell whether he was trying to convince me or himself. Then his phone buzzed. He smiled apologetically and walked away to take the call.

My phone buzzed too. It was a text from AJ.

Where are you?

I typed back: **Campaign HQ. You?**

Office. Was going to Max Hall. You going?

In about 1 hr.

Want a lift?

Sure. Text when you get here.

He sent a thumbs up.

Lisbeth was on the phone when I returned to the war room. She frowned and pushed a piece of paper across the table to me. The scrutineers from the remaining polling stations in Ward 8 had reported in. I scanned the numbers: Michiel took Ward 8 but not by much. I glanced at Lisbeth. She was nodding and making "hmmm" noises into the phone. She grimaced as she pulled the scrap of paper back from me.

"Yes," she said. "That's right. You won Ward 8…" She pulled a notebook out of her leather tote bag. "…Just a sec, I've got the numbers here." She held the phone between her shoulder and her ear while she flipped through her notebook. "Okay, last time you took Ward 8 with a margin of 6,000 votes...yes, yes, I'm getting to that..." She glanced back at the slip of paper. "This time it looks more like 1,800 votes."

Michiel's voice squawked through her cell. Lisbeth nodded, mumbled something, and hung up.

"Michiel?" I asked.

"Yeah. He's antsy. The scrutineers are reporting numbers much lower than the last time around."

"But we haven't seen all the polls yet," I protested.

"Maybe not *all* the polls, but enough to see O'Halloran and even Sarah are doing way better than we expected." Lisbeth pivoted in her chair to stare at the whiteboard. It was covered with multi-coloured scrawls. Most of the polling stations in Ward 8 and a big ward in the northeast were labelled 'Michiel' but many in the northwest were labelled 'O'Halloran.' The polling stations south of the river were showing Sarah running slightly ahead of Michiel and O'Halloran. Frown lines appeared between Lisbeth's eyes. "It's turning into a three-way race."

"How's Michiel taking it?" I asked.

"You heard him. Not great. When we started this campaign he wanted to crush O'Halloran. We warned him it wasn't going to happen—" I was pretty sure that 'we' was Lisbeth and Nick "—and look at the board." She flicked her hand at the whiteboard. "At this rate he'll win, but not by much."

"A win is a win," I said, realizing how inane that sounded under the circumstances.

"Yeah, but it's not much of a mandate, is it."

I came around the table and squeezed her shoulder. "It will be all right, Lisbeth."

She patted my hand. "I know. I just wanted better for him." She glanced at the whiteboard and sighed. "Evie, why don't you head out to Max Hall? I'll meet you there."

"You're sure…?" She nodded and picked up her phone. Another scrutineer reporting back. She shooed me out of the office just as my phone buzzed. AJ was double-parked in front of the building.

31

Disco balls traced rainbows across the ceiling, laser lights sliced through the air, the music throbbed, and the crowd swirled in and out of the spotlights.

The final outcome would not be known for at least another hour but that did not stop Michiel's supporters from celebrating as if he had already been anointed king. AJ and I elbowed our way toward the dais, searching for a good spot from which to watch Michiel's triumphant return to power, fleeting though it may be.

"How are things at Lawson Valentine, AJ?" I yelled in his ear as the noise level cranked up another decibel. We were engulfed by a wave of volunteers yelling and flinging their arms around each other.

"Fine, no new developments on our favourite file." I could barely make out his words over the din. Someone slipped an arm around my waist. I smiled at the volunteer and turned to introduce her to AJ but by the time I turned back, she'd melted into the crowd.

I said, "It's weird being here, isn't it? I don't know what

to feel anymore."

AJ's smile faded a watt or two. "Yeah, you do, that's why it's so weird." He pointed at the stage. "All this is an illusion, bought and paid for by—"

Suddenly the crowd erupted in a chorus of jeers and catcalls. I looked over my shoulder at an oversized TV screen. The volunteers were outraged by the news that Sarah Hamilton had pulled ahead of Michiel and O'Halloran in Ward 10.

Meagan Fellows appeared on the screen. The room became even more raucous. Meagan's face was solemn, her lips were moving, but she could have been speaking from the moon for all the difference it made to the unruly mob.

"What do you think she's saying?" AJ yelled.

"Probably talking about Sarah's stellar performance in the debate." I paused. "Sorry, that sounded sarcastic. She did an incredible job, holding her own against two formidable opponents. She deserves all the credit she can get."

An intense white light blinded me momentarily. A CTV cameraman was setting up a live feed a couple of metres in front of us. "AJ, let's move." The last thing I wanted was to be caught on tape blathering on about Michiel's outstanding campaign only to have it replayed as a counterpoint to the story of his spectacular downfall. AJ tilted his head toward a dim corner near the back wall and we zigzagged through the heaving crowd.

The TV screen on my left flickered. The reporter was talking to Clint. No one could hear what Clint was saying but his sound bite would be perfect for the folks at home. The camera switched back to Meagan who was now very animated. A chyron crawled across the bottom of the screen: CTV was ready to call the election. My phone buzzed. A text from Lisbeth. **He won! They're calling it!** She would know, she had spent the evening tabulating the scrutineers' numbers. I sent her a thumbs up.

The music died in the speakers as Meagan's voice filled the hall. Michiel Van Dijk would be returning as mayor, he had won the election with a respectable margin; Sarah Hamilton came in a surprising second and Duffy O'Halloran, third.

The room exploded, people shrieked and embraced each other with manic joy. They didn't care whether Michiel won by a landslide or inched his way across the finish line; a win is a win and that was all that mattered.

I touched AJ's arm to attract his attention and shouted in his ear. He shook his head; he couldn't hear me. A map setting out all the City wards flashed up on the screen. Sarah Hamilton did much better than anyone expected, picking up wards the pollsters predicted would go to Michiel or O'Halloran. The pundits would turn themselves inside out trying to explain this topsy turvy outcome.

My phone buzzed. A text from Lisbeth. She'd be here in 20 minutes. She was bringing Michiel in through the back entrance to give him time to settle before he stepped up onto the dais.

I became aware of AJ talking to me.

"What now?" He asked, for the second time.

"Now we get the victory speech. Lisbeth is coming with Michiel. They'll be here in…" I glanced at my watch "… fifteen minutes."

"Want to get closer to the stage?" he asked. People surged toward the front of the room. The music was even louder than before. Suddenly I was overcome with dread. I did not want to be anywhere near the stage. In fact I didn't want to be here at all. But I was trapped. A member of the inner circle can't just slink out the side door. *Paste on a cheery smile, it will be over soon.*

My phone buzzed. A text. Lisbeth. They had arrived. She told me to go to a little room at the back behind the dais and join the ten or so volunteers who would act as wallpaper for Michiel's victory speech. The 'wallpaper' is the row of people who stand behind the candidate, smiling and clapping when the candidate says they're humbled to be the people's choice and very much looking forward to an exciting four years; the usual political blather.

"I don't want to be wallpaper."

"What?" AJ looked at me.

"Lisbeth wants me to join her and Michiel on the dais."

"Right, let's go." AJ is much taller than I am, he surveyed the crowd searching for a path forward. I stood stock-still. "No, wait, we won't get through in time."

AJ gave me a skeptical look. "You sure?"

I nodded and replied to Lisbeth: **Crowd too thick. Can't get through. See you on TV.**

The other two candidates materialized on the TV screens. Duffy O'Halloran's glittering conference room was packed with supporters screaming and waving signs. O'Halloran was standing next to a reporter. The camera closed in for a tight shot. No one could hear what he said, no doubt some variation of good race, the people have spoken, when what he really wanted to say was the people were imbeciles who'd missed an opportunity to elect the smartest guy in the room. The reporter, an earnest young man, nodded as O'Halloran spoke and then looked blankly into the camera, waiting for the feed from Sarah's campaign headquarters.

Then Sarah's face filled the screen. She looked calm as

she waited for the reporter to ask the same question: how are you feeling right now? *She lost. How do you think she's feeling*?

Sarah's reporter was also young—why are they so young, they have no history, no relevant experience—and a chyron ribboned across the bottom of the screen: Michiel's victory speech was coming up soon. O'Halloran and Sarah dissolved and were replaced by the mob in Max Hall.

The crowd, bathed in swirling rainbow light, whooped and waved their signs when they saw themselves on the screen. "Four more years, four more years!" They chanted.

Just as they reached fever pitch, a cloud of multi-coloured balloons and sparkling confetti filled the air. The crowd exploded, screaming "Mich-iel! Mich-iel! Mich-iel!"

The wallpaper volunteers filed up onto the dais, squinting in the bright lights. They were squashed together like tinned sardines.

The music picked up pace and volume. Freddie Mercury and Queen erupted from the speakers and the mob stomped their feet in time to the beat. What if the racket brings down a structural beam, I wondered, who will be liable?

Then the glitterballs stopped turning and the speakers were silent.

Michiel materialized at centre stage in the reverberating silence. He stood alone in a golden halo of light, sparkling bits of confetti twinkled in his hair, a few stray balloons bobbed at his feet. He wore an immaculate grey suit and pushed his dark hair back with one hand. Then he flashed an impish grin and the mob went mad, screaming, crying, and waving signs. Someone blew a vuvuzela. Then silence.

Michiel laughed his magical laugh and asked, "How are you feeling?"

They cheered.

"Amazing night, eh?"

They cheered even louder.

He held up a hand. "Bear with me, I want to take a selfie." They laughed as he turned his back on them and held his phone high to capture as many of them as possible in the shot. "Say Michiel!" he instructed. They yelled his name so loudly the disco balls rattled in the rafters. He slipped his phone back into his pocket and raised his hands to quiet them, then he began to speak.

His words were like icicles melting in the sun. Pretty but insubstantial.

I scanned the wallpaper volunteers: Wendy and Lisbeth claimed the coveted spots to Michiel's left and right, sending the right diversity message. Behind Lisbeth, that horrible man, Sal something, the guy who had dumped his senile father-in-law on us, was pressing up behind her, trying to nudge her aside. Lisbeth wore a radiant smile but her elbows were up. No one would muscle her out of the spotlight tonight.

"—only regret…" Michiel's brilliant smile faded "… is my dear friend Nicholas Silva isn't here to share this moment with me." The crowd murmured sympathetically.

I held my breath, listening.

Michiel's voice dropped to a whisper, the mic picked up every syllable. "I've known Nicholas since law school. We were dreamers, the two of us, nothing was impossible in our world, nothing." He extended his arms to the crowd. "Nicholas, my friend, this victory is yours as much as it is mine."

The music swelled. Rapturous applause. Tears rolled down the cheeks of the woman beside me. Michiel waved to the mob. His speech was over. The wallpaper volunteers streamed off the podium, glistening with sweat. Lisbeth embraced Michiel, then Wendy touched her arm and the two of them left the stage.

Michiel plunged into the crowd, laughing and shaking hands as he plowed forward in search of the CTV reporter. That wretched Sal fellow muscled past some volunteers, determined to catch up to Michiel. Clint and the acting chief of staff, Mark Patterson, cut him off. Sal gestured at Michiel, babbling urgently in Mark's ear. He pressed something, a business card likely, into Mark's hand. Mark accepted it graciously. It would be the first of many such cards foisted upon him tonight.

"Let's blow this popsicle stand," I said to AJ. He didn't hear me. He was focused on the far corner of the room.

"Look over there," he yelled.

"Where?"

"There, under the TV screen closest to the door." He positioned me in front of him so I could follow his line of sight: Sam Calhoon and Garry Johnston. Calhoon was laughing, Johnston's shoulders were hunched. "Wonder what that's all about," AJ said.

"Let's go find out." I forged across the room. Calhoon spotted us and waved. He took Johnston's elbow, turning him slightly to face us. Johnston grimaced. A small group of volunteers flitted by, temporarily blocking him from view. By they time they passed Johnston was smiling. "Well, will you look at that," I yelled to AJ, "they're happy to see us."

"They should be," he grumbled, "we got them their Pavilion."

Calhoon reached out and grabbed my hand, shaking it vigorously. "What a great night!"

I nodded toward Michiel who was still talking to the earnest young reporter. “It’s a great night for Michiel, isn’t it?”

Calhoon said, “Evie, you were closer to the campaign than the rest of us, was there ever a moment when you thought O’Halloran might win?”

“Not really.” I glanced at Michiel again. “O’Halloran made some inroads with his gaslighting comments, but it wasn’t enough to deter Michiel’s base.” I could feel Johnston’s pale eyes upon me. “My bigger concern was Sarah. When she started to rise in the polls, it was conceivable that she and Michiel would split the vote and O’Halloran would come up through the middle to win.”

Calhoon smacked Johnston on the arm. “That’s exactly what I told this guy, he didn’t believe me.” A shadow flickered across Johnston’s face, he didn’t like being made to look like a fool, then he laughed.

“Evie! AJ! You made it!” Michiel came steadily toward us, shaking hands with everyone he met along the way. Calhoon and Johnston congratulated him on a great race and said they were looking forward to working with him for another four years. He gave them a self-deprecating grin and uttered one word. “Likewise.”

He grabbed both of my hands and said he could not have done it without me. We both knew this wasn’t remotely true. He clapped AJ on the shoulder and asked if this was his first victory party. AJ said it was and I was reminded that most people aren’t political junkies like me. Who can blame them? Politicians are crooks.

Wendy appeared at Michiel’s side, she cupped her hands over his ear, his head bobbed. He said something along the lines of ‘duty calls’ and melted back into the crowd.

"Yes, duty calls." I caught AJ's eye, he confirmed that we did indeed have to get going, busy day at the office tomorrow. We shook hands with Calhoon and Johnston and snaked our way out through the mob.

"You look knackered," AJ said as I slipped into the front seat of his car.

"Knackered?" I laughed. "Is that something your granddaddy used to say down on the farm?"

He chuckled as he eased the car in gear and explained the old English roots of the word, something to do with harnesses and slaughtering horses.

32

One day after the election

"You look terrible," Madeline said. Well, of course I look terrible: yesterday I'd spent a solid fifteen hours hosting a home base, secretly meeting with Pritchard in a coffee shop, pretending to sympathize with Lisbeth over Michiel's slim margin of victory, and faking joy with Calhoon at Michiel's victory party. That much subterfuge would take a toll on anybody.

Bridget came to my defense. "You look wonderful," there was a slight pause, "just a little tired." She thrust a box wrapped in glittery gold paper into my hands. "From all of us."

"Presents?" I ripped the wrapping paper off a box of Rogers' Chocolates dessert truffles. "Thank you!" I love chocolate, truth be told I'd eat a cotton ball if it were dipped in chocolate.

Bridget laughed. "It's your welcome-back-to-full-time-practice present."

"Trust me, full time practice anywhere, even a big firm, would be heaven after this campaign." I passed the box to Madeline while Bridget threw her arms around me and hugged me so hard my back cracked.

Madeline said, "Right, now that the mushy stuff is out of the way, come with me." She marched down the hall to Keith's office.

I set the chocolates down on the corner of Bridget's desk. "Don't eat them all before I get back!"

"Howdy stranger," Keith said with a big grin. "Madeline shared some interesting news with me this morning." He looked over at Madeline who was leaning against the wall. In her '50s sheath dress she looked rather dramatic.

"Not 'news' exactly," her voice dropped to a stage whisper, "more like a rumour from a highly placed source." She arched an eyebrow.

"Out with it, Madeline," Keith said.

She eased off the wall and slipped into the chair next to me. "I have it on very good authority that a very important city official will be receiving a visit from the police soon."

"'A very important city official'? Michiel?" My heart leapt. "Is it Michiel? Who told you? What did they say?"

Madeline pursed her lips and said "Mmmmm." My mind rifled through who her source might be. The police chief? A judge? No, wait, a member of the police commission, yes. "It's Duffy O'Halloran, isn't it! He told you. What exactly did he say?"

She blinked at me slowly like a cat. "My source, who shall remain nameless, says the police are investigating a high-ranking city official who may have gotten a little too cozy with the developers, one developer in particular." She tried to look blasé but she couldn't keep the excitement out of her voice. "Apparently, they're very close to making an arrest."

"It's Duffy. Why are you still seeing Duffy?" I said, hoping to goad her into confirming her source but she wouldn't take the bait. "When are they coming for him?"

"I don't know, but I get the impression it will be soon."

Keith watched me thoughtfully, then said, "Evie, stay out of it, let the police do their jobs." I swear that man can read my mind. I was rapidly turning over the pros and cons of calling Pritchard to confirm Madeline's story and had come to the same conclusion, it was a bad idea.

"I know, I know." A shiver ran down my spine. "It's such a weird feeling, isn't it? Like someone just issued a tornado warning but we don't know where to hide."

On my way back to my office I scooped up a handful of truffles. I had one in my mouth when my cell rang. I almost choked when I saw the caller ID. *Michiel.* He thanked me again for all my help with his campaign and asked whether I might be free for a late lunch sometime today.

"Today? Are you sure? You must have a billion things to do."

He insisted. Just a quick bite in the dining room at the Mac Jones House.

The sting of memory flooded back. Nick and I hunched over his laptop watching a campaign video of Michiel outlining a policy in front of the large Victorian mansion. That was the day Nick shared his fears that Michiel was becoming more erratic and uncooperative.

"I know it's short notice," Michiel said, "but I'd really like to talk to you." Pritchard's warning came back to me.

It's business as usual until the fraud squad is ready to lay charges. I agreed to meet him at 1:30 p.m.

The fall garden overflowed with violet monkshood, purple cone flowers and pink turtleheads. If I hadn't been running late I'd have stopped to take a photo for Louisa. As it was I'd be lucky to arrive before Michiel. The hostess took me through the great hall to the dining room. I was surprised to see Michiel already seated at a small table by a mullioned window overlooking the vegetable garden.

He half rose in his chair to greet me and asked whether I'd eaten here before. "It's a fine restaurant," he said. "They grow as much of their produce as they can."

He looked weary, the strain of the last few days showing around his mouth and eyes. I said this was my first visit and scanned the menu, eager to get the fuss of ordering out of the way. We made small talk until our salads arrived and the server disappeared down the hall.

Michiel picked at his heirloom tomatoes while I waited for him to get to the point. Eventually he said he was looking forward to progressing his agenda. "You must be pleased Calhoon is pushing ahead with the Pavilion project."

I wasn't sure how to respond. Then he pushed his plate aside, put his elbows on the table, and clasped his hands together under his chin. "As you no doubt know, Evie, sometimes applications don't proceed as originally planned."

I stopped pretending I was eating. "In my experience with the energy regulator, applications go exactly as planned. The only uncertainty is whether my case is strong enough for the regulator to grant the application."

He inhaled deeply. "Things are a little different with

rezoning applications. Sometimes things happen, the original application is scrapped and something else takes its place."

I glanced around the empty dining room. At this hour of the day we were the only ones left. "What do you mean, Michiel?"

He pressed his lips together. "All I'm saying is developers often have alternative plans for sites they're developing."

There was movement on the other side of the window. Someone was in the vegetable garden pulling up handfuls of radishes and parsnips and putting them into a large basket. I looked down at the uneaten radish sitting on my plate, then said, "Really, like a plan A and a plan B?"

Something sparked in his eyes. "That's exactly what I mean—hypothetically speaking." Then he unclasped his hands and took a deep gulp of water. "It's best not to get too focused on the original application when plans change."

All this dancing around was driving me mad. "So, hypothetically speaking, let's say City Council approved a plan A that would, say for the sake of argument, restore a heritage building. How would a developer get rid of the heritage building and switch to a plan B? A change of that magnitude would require a public hearing. The heritage people would fight it tooth and nail."

Michiel's eyes narrowed. For a second I thought our conversation was over. Then he said, "Sometimes heritage buildings burn down, squatters get in, light a fire...these things happen."

"Are you talking about *arson*?"

"Keep your voice down!" Michiel hissed, glancing around the room. "I'm simply saying developers have millions of dollars riding on projects. There's so much money at risk, they're bound and determined, shall we say, to get their way." He pushed a lock of hair off his forehead. "It's not a good idea to get in their way…or—Evie, are you listening to me—to hold onto things that belong to them that could make them look bad, if say, something untoward were to happen."

My hand flew to my throat. "Oh Michiel, no!"

"Look," he said, "I'm just trying to protect you and the firm."

I stood up, bumping into the edge of the table. His water glass tipped forward. By the time he'd caught it I was striding past the polished mahogany staircase, crossing the black and white tiled foyer, and running down the sandstone steps into the street.

It's not a good idea to hold onto things that don't belong to you.

This was about the USB stick hidden in my basement.

33

"Where did you disappear to yesterday afternoon?" Keith asked. After my lunch with Michiel I told Bridget to cancel all my appointments, I'd be out for the rest of the day.

"I'll fill you in as soon as I find AJ," I said. AJ popped into the hallway when he heard his name and I asked them to join me in the conference room. I tilted the blinds to soften the glare of the morning sun. It was strangely appropriate that this conversation take place in the shadows.

"Did you hear back from Pritchard?" Keith asked.

"No, this isn't about the Red Box scheme," I said. "Yesterday I had lunch with Michiel. He gave me what amounts to a warning."

"What?" Keith said with a puzzled frown. "Why? Did he get wind of the bribery investigation?"

"No, no, Michiel has no idea he's under investigation for bribery. He took me to lunch to tell me not to fuss about Plan B."

AJ interrupted. "How does Michiel know about Plan B?"

"How do you think? Calhoon. Michiel said a lot in his own cryptic fashion and I connected the dots to figure out the rest." Keith and AJ looked as if they were waiting for a horror movie to start, a look that conveyed anticipation and dread.

"Calhoon knew the City was desperate for cash and made a lowball offer for Glen Park. The only way he could convince the City to release the park from land reserve and rezone it to residential was to promise to restore the pavilion and build a cute little nine-unit townhouse development."

"Plan A," Keith said.

"Once Calhoon owned the property and got the rezoning he wanted, he was going to pull a bait-and-switch to Plan B, the ten-storey mixed use residential and commercial tower."

"Wait," AJ raised both hands. "Even with the rezoning in place, the development permit has to go to a public hearing. The heritage people would go nuts."

"Yes, but what if the pavilion burns to the ground? Calhoon already owns the land, he's got the rezoning, he can build whatever he wants. The heritage people can't save a building that no longer exists."

"*Christ*!" Keith smacked the palm of his hand down on the conference table. AJ and I both jumped. "Calhoon is an arsonist? Are you fucking kidding me?" I could count the number of times I've heard Keith swear on one hand.

"It's beginning to look that way." I turned to AJ. "That's why Calhoon acquiesced to all of the City's demands. He knew he'd never be held to any of them. All he really wanted was to close the deal fast, time is money. The minute the pavilion is torched, his crew will be on the site pouring the foundation for the ten-storey monstrosity that will take its place."

"What *exactly* did Michiel say?" Keith asked quietly.

"Michiel insinuated it would not be wise for me, for any of us, to stand in Calhoon's way. And that Calhoon wants the USB stick back."

"What USB stick?" Keith asked.

AJ said, "The one Bev sent me at the very beginning of this file, that showed Plan A and Plan B."

I added, "When Calhoon realized we had it, he didn't ask for it back. He didn't want to draw attention to it. Instead he hired those two idiots, Moe and Curly, to retrieve it."

"Hence the attacks on you at your house and the campaign office," Keith said.

"And the potential break-in here," AJ reminded us. "When Bridget blasted us for leaving the window in the coffee room open."

"Right," I continued, "I stashed it in my basement and will deliver it to Pritchard this morning."

Keith shook his head. "Wait, what's the USB doing in your basement?"

I explained I'd taken the poster tube home not realizing it contained the USB stick and the dog knocked it behind a bookshelf. By the time I found it Nick had been murdered and we'd discovered Calhoon's bribery scheme. "It was the least of our worries."

Keith closed his eyes and rubbed the bridge of his nose. "One of us should go with you."

"Don't be silly. I'm perfectly capable of dropping a USB stick off with the police." I gave them a reassuring smile.

~

The Mini flew up the streets and across the avenues. At

this rate, I'd get a speeding ticket before I reached the police station. Did Nick know about Calhoon's arson scheme? Is that why he was murdered? The sooner I got the USB stick into Pritchard's hands, the better. The poster tube rolled under the passenger seat as I careened into the parking lot, showering gravel over the dead junipers next to the entry. It took a few minutes to wiggle it free.

Pritchard met me at reception. "That was quite an entrance." I muttered something banal and he took me to a meeting room at the back of the station. A tiny window looked out across an empty field. A train snaked across the horizon in the distance.

"You don't want any coffee, right?" I shook my head. We sat down at a small table and I placed the poster tube between us.

"What's this?" he asked. I slid the USB stick and the Plan B drawing out of the poster tube and explained that Michiel, likely on Calhoon's behalf, intimated it would be in Lawson Valentine's best interest, my best interest, to keep our mouths shut if the pavilion burned to the ground under suspicious circumstances.

"Michiel delivered a warning? Calhoon is going to torch the building and you guys will get hurt if you come forward after the fact?"

"Not in so many words, but the message was clear. Calhoon wants this USB stick back. It and the drawing are the only pieces of physical evidence showing he intended to build a high-rise tower on the site from the very beginning."

"That's conspiracy to commit arson," Pritchard said thoughtfully. "It's not easy to get a conviction on conspiracy charges. We'd have to identify and track down whoever Calhoon hired to torch the place—"

"Moe and Curly?"

"Those two mutts, would Calhoon trust them with something this tricky?"

"He trusted them to attack me in my home and at the campaign office. Someone pawed through Lisbeth's stuff and we're now wondering whether those two broke into our law firm. Who knows? Maybe Sam is getting desperate."

~

By the time I pulled up in front of my house, the neighbourhood was shrouded in velvety blackness. I almost tripped over Quincy when I sank into the sofa, his brindle body blended into the pattern of the Persian rug. He cocked his head and thumped his tail vigorously and I told him to go bug Louisa.

"He's happy you're home," Louisa called from the kitchen. She was making crepes. "We missed you."

I swung my legs off the sofa and scratched Quincy's chin. "I missed you too," I crooned into his beady little eyes and followed him into the kitchen.

"So I guess I can tell you now," Louisa said as she swirled crepe batter around in a large skillet. "Oh, could you stir that?" She nodded in the direction of the vegetables sizzling in a frying pan.

"Tell me what?" I stirred the mushrooms and shallots and turned down the heat before grating some Gruyère. Quincy eyed me pathetically, pleading for a crumb.

"I didn't vote for Michiel." She sounded defiant and a little sheepish.

I laughed out loud. "Neither did I."

"You're joking! Why not?" She tipped the crepe onto a

warm plate, I filled it with savoury vegetables and folded it into a cone.

I evaded her question. “Please tell me you didn’t vote for O’Halloran.”

She rolled her eyes, “God no,” and poured the batter for another crepe into the hot pan. “Sarah Hamilton.”

“Why Sarah?” I poured white wine into two large glasses.

“I met her at a coffee party. Evie, she’s smart and genuine. She said it’s time to focus on the future and stop clinging to the past. The world is changing at lightning speed, if we don’t act quickly, it’ll be our children, not us, who bear the brunt of our stupid decisions. Oops—” the crepe flopped up the side of the skillet; she eased it off with a spatula.

“Have you seen Sarah with her daughter?” Louisa continued. “She’s a lovely girl. They have a wonderful relationship. You can tell a lot about someone by watching how they interact with their kids.”

“Birds of a feather, you mean?” I filled the second crepe and dished up mounds of green salad. We made ourselves comfortable at the kitchen island and started to eat.

“No, not birds of a feather, that means that you surround yourself with people like you. Good people surround themselves with good people. Bad people surround themselves with bad people.”

“True.”

“More like soulmates. Sarah and her daughter are polar opposites. Sarah is extroverted and outspoken. Her daughter is shy and quiet, but they share the same values…and the same sense of humour. They get each other’s jokes—”

“Like you and me?”

She laughed. “Yeah, exactly like you and me.”

"Louisa, remember when you asked Mom why the mountains move?" Louisa smiled slowly. We could see the mountains from our bedroom and Louisa asked Mom why they were closer in the daytime and far away at night.

"Oh yeah," she laughed, "and Mom said the mountains tiptoe in to greet the day and tiptoe out at bedtime."

"Right, and we decided to test Mom's theory on that road trip through the Rockies."

"The one where she said train tunnels were made by giant mountain worms and forest rangers used avalanche cannons to keep them at bay." Louisa shuddered. "I spent that entire trip with my nose pressed against the car window."

"You were convinced you'd seen Mount Rundle shrug."

After dinner we watched a Spanish heist movie and scrolled through our social media feeds showing each other cute animal posts. Just as I crawled into bed I remembered my conversation with Pritchard. *Maybe Calhoon is getting desperate.* I shuddered. In my experience, desperate men can be dangerous.

34

Three days after the election

A sound like tiny bells tinkled in the forecourt of the Calhoon Tower, the silvery birds in the giant bird sculpture shivered in the breeze. It was early morning. I was here to stop Calhoon from carrying out his plan to burn the pavilion to the ground.

One of the two young women in matching blue CDC uniforms glanced up from behind the long reception desk as I strode past them toward the elevators.

"Excuse me, Miss," she cried out, "you need to check in."

I gave her a jaunty wave and darted into the elevator. The doors whooshed shut as I pressed the button for the thirty-sixth floor. There was no point in checking in. I didn't have an appointment.

The elevator bell dinged and I stepped out into the hushed lobby. With an air of purpose, *yes, I have every right to be here*, I marched past the brutal Soviet era artwork and headed down the glass walled corridor to the C-suite.

Calhoon's new executive assistant, Brock, was chatting to someone on the telephone. She glanced up when she saw me. I cocked my head and mouthed *is he in*? She nodded and I sailed right past her. Madeline was right, Brock really was a pitiful assistant.

Calhoon was at his desk with his phone pressed to his ear. He twirled his pen, a Montblanc, between his fingers. The door clicked shut behind me. He looked up and said, 'I'll call you back,' before setting the phone down and glancing behind me at the door as if to confirm I'd come alone. "I don't believe we have an appointment," he said.

I strolled across the expensive carpets laid on imported stone tiles and sat down across from him in one of his ergonomically designed chairs. "This will only take a minute. I was in the neighbourhood and decided to drop by to tell you Lawson Valentine can no longer represent you."

He leaned back in his chair and crossed his arms. "Is that so? Well, you're wasting your time. I told my secretary to call your office and tell your people to send the Pavilion file back to Gates, Case and White."

"Of course. Just so you know, I delivered part of the file to the police yesterday, a USB stick containing a drawing labelled Plan B." I gestured toward the antique walnut map cabinet. "Not that you need it. I'm sure you've got plenty more at your fingertips."

"Good for you," Calhoon's lips stretched in a thin smile. "Now get the fuck out of my office before I have security throw you out."

I settled deeper in my chair and brought my hands together, fingers steepled under my chin. "I had a nice chat with Michiel over lunch the other day." Calhoon's eyes became hooded. "Michiel explained, no, hinted at, the significance of Plan B and how it would come into play if for some inexplicable reason the pavilion went up in flames. I passed that information along to the police as well."

"Michiel?" He snorted. "That man won't say anything, not on the record at any rate."

"Perhaps not, but I will."

There was a sharp rap at the door. Garry Johnston hesitated for a fraction of a second before entering. "What's she doing here?"

"Have a seat, Garry." Calhoon gestured to the chair next to me and waited while Johnston sat down and made himself comfortable, slinging one ankle casually over one knee. Calhoon sat back, mirroring Johnston's position. He tilted his chin at me and said, "Ms. Valentine here is spouting some bullshit theory about the supposed significance of Plan B." His eyes were calm as he met Johnston's gaze. "Apparently she delivered the USB stick to the police this morning."

Johnston's mouth twitched as if he were suppressing a smile. "I see—a tiny little USB stick is safely tucked away in an evidence locker somewhere, *secure* in police custody, is that it?" I wondered just how many cops, prosecutors, and judges Calhoon had on his payroll.

Johnston turned his pale eyes toward Calhoon and frowned as if mystified. "Sam, what is it with these *lady* lawyers? Always sticking their noses in where they don't belong."

I raised my eyebrows. "Now, now, gentlemen, not all female lawyers are the same."

Calhoon's face hardened. "Ms. Valentine, the world is

a dangerous place. You really think a USB stick *safe* in police custody is going to implicate me or my company in anything, let alone protect you and your firm from… whatever fate might have in store for you?"

"Mr. Calhoon, you underestimate me. I know how to protect myself and my people."

They watched as I lifted my leather purse off the floor and placed it in my lap. "I know we're not working together anymore but I brought you a memento. It's a cute new gadget, part of our marketing campaign."

I reached into my purse and pulled out my keys. They jingled softly on my keychain. Calhoon spotted it first.

"Do you like it, Sam?" I asked. "It's called a swivel drive." I unclipped the flash drive from my keychain. It gleamed like a ruby in the palm of my hand. "It's a promotional trinket. All we had to do was pick a colour and emboss the firm's name on this swively piece right here." I opened and closed the metal clip. "Pretty slick, eh? I didn't think they'd be such a big hit, but you'd be surprised how versatile these little babies are. You can use them to copy and store tons of information, drawings, narratives explaining the purpose of those drawings, whatever you like." I placed the red USB stick in the centre of Calhoon's leather blotter. "Our office is littered with them. If something happens to anyone in my firm or the pavilion, we'll be forced to release these to whoever might be interested, the Crown prosecutor, the banks, the insurance companies, the Heritage Society, the media." I gave him a cold smile. "This one's yours."

Calhoon swept the swivel drive off his desk. It landed in his metal trashcan and rattled to the bottom of the bin. "I don't know what you think you're playing at, but when I ask for my file I expect you to return it, and everything,

everything, in it."

"Well, of course, Sam." I glanced at the USB stick in his trashcan. "If you didn't like the colour, I've got plenty more. They come in every shade of the rainbow."

Johnston rose slowly out of his chair to loom over me. "You have a legal obligation to your client. You can't hold back any of our information when we ask for it."

I stood up to face him, temper rising. "Don't you dare quote the law to me!"

There was a light knock at the door. "Not now!" Calhoon barked, but Brock was already in the door. She had Calhoon's lawyer on the line, he said it was urgent. She stopped mid-sentence, bewildered at the sight of the three of us glowering at each other.

"It's okay, Brock," I said. "I was just leaving." The thick carpet muffled the sound of my footsteps as I closed the door silently behind me.

~

It was almost two o'clock by the time I returned to Lawson Valentine. Keith was leaning against the hood of his car in the parking lot, staring absentmindedly into the thick underbrush at the base of the hill. First Madeline, now Keith, what is the attraction of this little patch of woods? I pulled up next to his car and noticed he was holding something in his right hand.

"Are you smoking?" I said, a little more sternly than I had intended.

"Smoking? God no, I haven't smoked in fifteen years."

"Then what's that in your hand?"

He looked down. "A cigarette." He held it up. "Note, it's

not lit."

"Where did you get it?"

"Glove compartment."

"If you haven't smoked in fifteen years what are you doing with cigarettes in your glove compartment?"

"Cigarettes help me think." He coloured slightly. "I never light up. This is as far as I get."

I stood next him and we both gazed into the shrubbery for a little while. I was content to kill time; I wasn't quite ready to tell him about my visit with Calhoon. "So, what's going on, Keith? Are you retiring to the Okanagan to open a vineyard?"

He shot me a rueful grin. "I wish." Then his face became more serious. "Walk with me?" We headed out to the main road. A cool breeze rustled through the trees; curly yellow leaves floated gently to the ground. "I had lunch with Curtis Chan today."

"Your nemesis at Gates?"

"Yeah, he's referring a client to us, a renewable energy company. Gates can't act, conflict with another client."

"And…?"

We stopped in the middle of a long bridge that spans the river separating the commercial district from the residential district and leaned against the parapet. Someone had placed five small stones in a neat row along the top of the parapet. A reddish leaf was pinned under the stone in the middle. Keith picked it up and dropped it over the side. It caught the breeze and wafted over our heads back into the street.

"Curtis told me something he probably shouldn't have."

Lawyers are notorious gossips. When it comes to who is doing what to whom, they simply can't keep their mouths shut, especially over a convivial lunch with their old buddies.

Keith flicked one of the small stones into the river. It landed with a soft kerplunk.

I nudged him with my shoulder. "You know you want to tell me."

He frowned.

"And you know I'll get it out of you sooner or later."

His eyes crinkled into a smile and he started to talk. After they'd finished discussing business, Keith asked Curtis how the police investigation into Julianna Westerberg's death was going. Curtis almost fell out of his chair, how did you find out, he asked. Keith said he hadn't heard a thing. For a minute Curtis agonized about saying anything more, then he blurted it out: the police had paid Phil Dennison a visit that morning and it had not gone well.

"Curtis says it's become painfully obvious the cops are focusing their investigation on one of Julianna's clients. They combed through her computer and discovered she had a meeting booked with Sam Calhoon the day she died. Dennison said he knew nothing about the file—"

"—Keith, today I—"

Keith held up a hand, he didn't want me to interrupt, and continued. "CDC is Dennison's biggest client, there's no way Dennison's not running the file and racking up the hours. This morning the cops showed up with a warrant to check the firm's IT system and, guess what, Dennison was lying."

"Well of course he's lying. He's been CDC's lawyer for decades." Right then I realized what had been niggling at me since we'd unearthed the Red Box companies.

Keith said, "They pulled Dennison out of a client meeting and started asking questions. Dennison blew a gasket and demanded to see his lawyer. The cops said he could call one from the police station."

The thought of Dennison being escorted out of the building under police guard, or better yet in handcuffs, delighted me. I flicked one of the little stones off the parapet into the river. It landed on a rock and bounced away into the underbrush.

"If the cops think Julianna met with Calhoon the day she died, why didn't he show up on the CCTV footage for that day?"

"Curtis says the footage has some dead patches. The cops are trying to reconstruct it."

A small line appeared between Keith's eyes. "You know, Evie, that building is a CDC building. They'd know everything there is to know about the security system. They could have disabled it. But that would mean Calhoon went there specifically to kill Julianna, or at least was open to the idea of killing her if he thought she knew too much."

"I have no doubt that Calhoon and Johnston killed Julianna."

"What?"

"This morning I went to Calhoon's office to tell him I'd delivered the USB stick with Plan B to the police—"

"Jesus, Evie, you can't go barging into Calhoon's office after we've accused him of corruption—"

"He doesn't know that yet."

"Yeah, well he'll know soon enough."

"Okay, but listen." I told Keith about Johnston's sneering comment that 'lady lawyers' who poke around in CDC's business will get hurt.

Keith's face went grey. "That sounds like a threat to me."

I dismissed his comment. "Something's been bothering me ever since we discovered Red Box. It's a complex scheme, not something a non-lawyer could orchestrate. How much do you want to bet Dennison dreamed up the whole thing? We both know Dennison has no backbone. If the cops charge him with obstruction of justice or, better yet, being an accessory, he'll crack in no time."

Keith refused to be side-tracked. He took my elbow so I would face him. "Julianna got herself killed trying to outsmart these guys. They don't play by the same rules we do."

Okay, we've finally reached the tough part of this conversation.

"Tell me about it! Calhoon and Johnston practically laughed in my face when I said I'd delivered the USB stick to the police. If Calhoon torches the pavilion—he could do it today if he wanted to—I'm convinced the USB stick supposedly safe in police custody will disappear. And poof, the only piece of physical evidence showing why the building was torched is gone."

"Right, which is exactly why you shouldn't be anywhere near him."

"So we just let them get away with it? We're the lawyers who got them the pavilion, who must have known what Calhoon was up to, who helped him commit arson. Is that what you want?"

He didn't speak for a moment.

"I've worked too hard to protect my reputation after—" I stumbled, I hated to think about it, let alone say it out loud "—the incident at Gates. I refuse to go from being the 'victim' to being 'corrupt'. I just won't do it, Keith. I won't."

A series of emotions flashed across his face, first recollection, then empathy. He'd stood by me throughout the entire ghastly experience four years ago.

My voice softened. "All we have in law is our reputations. I went to Calhoon's office to tell him he wasn't going to get away with it."

I slipped my hand into my pocket, pulled out an orange swivel drive and dropped it into Keith's palm.

He looked at it as if he'd never seen a USB stick before. "What's this?"

"A copy of the USB stick I gave to Pritchard. I gave one to Calhoon. He didn't like it, by the way, he tossed it in the trash. Calhoon understands if something happens to the pavilion, or to us for that matter, a copy of the USB stick will be released to the Crown, the banks, the insurance companies, the media. His company will be mired in so much litigation it will go under. He won't take the risk."

Keith frowned and I wondered whether he was going to toss it in the river.

"Two can play this game, Keith. There are ten copies, yours, mine, Calhoon's, plus seven more in my safe deposit box with a letter setting out where they should be sent in case…well, in case something happens to me."

A muscle in his jaw jumped. "All this to save an old building?"

"All this to stop a rich and powerful man from doing something illegal and immoral."

He rolled the USB stick around in his hand as if testing its weight. "You should have told me, Evie. There are two names on the letterhead, *Lawson* and Valentine. Maybe together we could have found another way."

"There was no other way. Michiel's message was 'back off or get hurt.' How could we live with ourselves if Calhoon committed arson? What if someone was killed in the blaze? Could we turn a blind eye? A famous Supreme Court justice once said the rule of law is not enough, sometimes we need the rule of justice. This is one of those times."

He stared out across the river. A puff of wind rustled through the poplars along the riverbank, making a shushing sound like waves washing up on the beach. Either he'd support me or our partnership was over.

Finally he curled his fingers around the USB stick and slipped it into his pocket. "You're probably right. But for God's sake, Evie, we're partners. Promise me you won't do something like this again, not without talking to me first."

Relieved, I agreed to forewarn him if a similar situation arose in the future, but I knew my promise carried a caveat. As much as I valued our partnership, sometimes Keith moved too slowly to get in front of a dangerous situation.

So I smiled and said, "I'll have that cigarette now."

He was flabbergasted. "You're joking, right?"

"Yes, I'm joking." I patted his arm. He'd had enough shocks for the day.

He relaxed and flicked another stone into the river. It went sideways into the trees.

"You're going to have to work on your aim," I said.

He shook his head ruefully. "I've got the same problem with golf."

When we got back to the office Keith said he'd put an extra cigarette in the glove compartment for me.

35

Four days after the election

The river tumbled over the rocks like quicksilver, shiny and metallic in the crisp morning light. The windowpane was cold. Soon the view from my office would fade to a monochromatic vista of snow on the ground, snow in the trees, and snow on the ice creeping from one side of the riverbank to the other.

"What are you daydreaming about?" Bridget appeared in my doorway and passed me a handful of legal education pamphlets. I tossed them in the recycle bin.

"Nothing, actually." I shivered and slipped my jacket back on over my turtleneck. "Just thinking about September and how quickly it's flown by."

"You can say that again." Bridget lingered in front of my desk. "I've got a bumper crop of zucchini this year…" She looked at me expectantly. Bridget has a tiny house and a massive garden; she's always bringing her bounty to the office which is nice but there's only so much zucchini a human can eat.

"I'll take one," I said. She looked crestfallen. "Okay, I'll take two but only if they're small." She grinned and left me alone to catch up on my files. I looked up when AJ came in and parked himself in a visitor's chair.

"Have you seen it yet?" he asked.

"Seen what?"

"The letter from Sam Calhoon. We're fired."

"Again? He fired me two days ago right after I fired him."

"And no one bothered to tell me?"

I laughed. "Long story. Don't worry about it."

Bridget swept back into my office carrying two of the biggest zucchinis I had ever seen. She probably has a trunkful in her car. I started to protest but she insisted so I thanked her and said I'd give one to AJ. His eyes grew very round but he had the good sense not to argue and she returned to her desk secure in the knowledge her zucchinis were going to a good home.

"What were we talking about before the invasion of the pod people?" AJ asked.

"Calhoon," I said, rolling a zucchini in his direction.

"Right. Any word on Michiel's precarious status?" he asked.

"Nothing yet, but based on Madeline's intel something will break soon."

He frowned. "This is nerve wracking, like winding up a jack-in-the-box and waiting for it to pop."

I crossed my arms and looked at him. "A jack-in-the-box…"

"Yeah, you know, you wind and you wind and you wind, and bam! It flies up in your face."

I laughed. "Don't tell me, you're afraid of clowns." AJ sputtered and went back to his office.

By mid afternoon I was immersed in the tedium of drafting responses to information requests for a solar energy company that wanted to build a solar farm next to a country residential estate. I needed to describe the company's promise to create a well-treed buffer zone without making the residents wonder what they needed to be buffered from.

My phone buzzed with a text. Lisbeth asking whether we were still on for tonight.

Bloody hell. I'd forgotten that she'd asked me to help her close up the campaign office. I wanted to be free of this campaign so badly my teeth hurt but the thought of her alone in that concrete box picking through the detritus of Michiel's campaign was pitiful.

Sure, be there around 7 pm.

She sent me a thumbs up and a winking smiley emoji.

~

The sun had set by the time I left the office. Moths and dust swirled under the orange streetlamp in the alley. The oversized garbage bins were pushed tight against the building and for once I didn't have to zigzag the Mini between the bins on one side and the concrete barriers haphazardly dropped on the other.

The parkade door slowly clanked open. The garage was deserted but for Lisbeth's car and a beat-up truck parked at the far end. It hadn't moved for weeks. I pulled in next to Lisbeth's car and headed for the stairs, my heels tapping on the concrete floor.

The main lobby was quiet, the construction crew long gone. The flotsam of construction debris had migrated out of the lobby into the large glass-enclosed space opposite the elevators. One day this transparent box would be a high-end restaurant, but tonight it was packed with ladders, twisted bits of metal and shredded batts of pink insulation that loomed in and out of view in the glare of the headlights washing across the glass walls.

I rode the elevator to the fourth floor for the very last time and stepped out into eerie silence. No more chattering volunteers or people dropping off donations. Everything was gone, including most of the furniture.

Lisbeth was rummaging in the bottom drawer of a filing cabinet. Her glossy hair obscured her face. She was wearing a black jersey jumpsuit with Burberry loafers. Lord, this woman has an outfit for every occasion. She was deep in thought and had not heard me arrive.

"Lisbeth," I called her name softly. Her head whipped up in alarm, then her face relaxed into a smile.

"Evie, you're here." She sounded grateful.

"Well, of course I'm here." I set my jacket and purse on top of the filing cabinet. "Wow, this place is creepy without the furniture."

"They're coming for the rest of this stuff tomorrow, the filing cabinets, signs, swag, all of it." Lisbeth's voice echoed in the hollow space. "I've gone through my files. If you could sort through yours and pull out any outstanding bills, that would be great."

It didn't take me long to finish the job but I didn't want to leave her here alone, not after my nasty encounter with Moe and Curly, who were still on the loose as far as I knew, so I started bundling up the swag to make it easier to cart away. I piled the *#VoteMichiel* T-shirts into boxes and scooped the *#VoteMichiel* buttons into plastic Tupperware containers. Then I started on the lawn signs, sorting them by size so they'd be easier to secure with binder twine.

Lisbeth's phone rang, a gentle sound like windchimes floating across the empty room. She said Michiel's name. Her voice was soft, then hardened.

I was twisting a small lawn sign out of its metal frame when it slipped and the sharp end of one of the stakes pricked my thumb. A bead of blood. I popped my thumb into my mouth and looked at it again. I don't get queasy at the sight of blood but the hole in my thumb was deep and bleeding heavily—a puncture wound.

The pieces clicked, tumbling into place. Pritchard's voice, *there's a small puncture wound in his eye socket*, Nick's frustration, *what has Michiel accomplished*, and Lisbeth, dear Lisbeth, who worked late into the night doing whatever she had to do to ensure Michiel's victory. Nick came here to meet Lisbeth the night he died.

A grunt behind me, Lisbeth's pale face contorted with rage. She slammed into me, I pitched over a pile of lawn signs and crashed to the floor, twisting to avoid smashing my face on the concrete.

"Lisbeth, stop!" I staggered to my feet.

"You sanctimonious bitch!" she screamed. She grabbed a plastic container of campaign buttons and hurled it at my head. The button box exploded when it hit the floor, scattering metal buttons everywhere.

"For God's sake, Lisbeth, stop! It's over!"

"You couldn't leave it alone, could you. You had to be a hero like that fucking Nicholas!"

She lunged. I pivoted. Too late. We crashed to the floor. I landed on top of her. She moaned, gasping for air. I rolled off, struggling to my knees. She grabbed my sweater, red-tipped nails tearing through soft cashmere. I broke free, clutching at the swag rack for balance. It tipped forward and everything on the shelves, pens, magnets, metal water bottles, clattered to the floor.

Lisbeth was on all fours. "Michiel's been arrested…your fault," she panted. That phone call. "What's wrong with you people? First Nicholas barging in here, ranting about Michiel. Then you get him arrested." She was standing now, swaying.

I shot a frantic glance toward the stairwell. She sprang forward, slipped on a campaign button and rammed into me. We went down again, this time she landed on my chest and wrapped her long thin fingers around my throat. The floor tilted. Tiny specks of light flickered all around me. I flailed, my hand touched something cold. A metal water bottle. My fingers curled around its neck. I smashed it across her temple. Her grip loosened. I raised the bottle again. "You killed him," I hissed. The bottle cracked against her skull and she crumpled, limp on top of me.

Voices. "Stop! Evie. Stop!"

Footsteps raced across the floor. The room steadied. Pritchard swam into view. Martinez appeared next to him. Lisbeth clung to me like a limpet; Martinez dragged her off. Pritchard knelt by my side. "You okay?" he asked.

"In a moment," I croaked, rolling onto my stomach and then up onto one knee. Pritchard held my arm as I stood up. The floor rocked under my feet, then the dizziness passed.

"Lisbeth…" I tipped my head toward Lisbeth who was standing beside Martinez a few metres away. Her eye was starting to swell.

"...She killed Nick." I was certain of it. I stared at her. She stared back, then tucked a lock of raven hair behind her ear and smoothed her jumpsuit. At first, I thought she would deny the whole thing, but she didn't.

"I'm glad he's dead." Her voice was flat, no remorse.

Pritchard locked eyes on her, she had his full attention.

"I'm glad Nicholas is dead," she repeated firmly. Once she started, she wouldn't stop. She said Nicholas appeared around nine-thirty that night. He was agitated, pacing the floor. He accused Michiel of accepting bribes from developers and demanded it stop immediately.

"At first I played dumb," she said, looking coyly at Pritchard. "I needed to know what he knew. But it was too late. Michiel, that idiot, told Nicholas everything. He said they'd get hefty 'bonuses' if they eased Calhoon's projects through the application process. Calhoon was going to rebuild the inner city." Her voice rose in pitch as she mimicked Nick's reply. "'City staff don't get bonuses.' Michiel told him to stop being so bloody naïve. 'We help them, they help us. They get their buildings, we get their money, and we stay in power to do the good work we were elected to do.'"

Lisbeth beamed as if Michiel had said something exceptionally clever. "I don't think Nicholas believed in his heart of hearts that Michiel took the money until Michiel told him to run a corporate search on one of Calhoon's companies. 'Check it out,' Michiel said. 'That's the way it is, that's the way it's always been.'"

I stared at Pritchard. That's why Michiel wrote the Red Box company's corporate identifier on the back of Nick's business card.

Lisbeth shook her head in disbelief. "Michiel offered Nicholas the chance of a lifetime, we were doing so much good, and he threw it back in Michiel's face." Her eyes darkened. "When I told him I knew all about it he said, he said, he was disappointed in me…disappointed. How dare he judge me? Mr. Top 40 Under 40, how dare he?"

She began to tremble. "He started yelling, saying Michiel wasn't fit to be mayor and he was going straight to the police. I couldn't let him do that, could I?" She looked from Pritchard to me. "That's not loyalty. Evie, you understand, I know you do. Michiel worked so hard to get out of Forest Hills. He's done so much for the city…" She faltered, staring past me toward the stairwell.

"How did he die?" Pritchard's voice was quiet, almost serene.

Lisbeth blinked. "Nicholas went for the elevator. I told him to stop. He said his mind was made up. I caught him by the stairwell." She looked down at her hands. "I was holding a lawn sign. He turned around suddenly, so suddenly, and the set-stake flew up into his face. I don't know how it happened, it just happened."

Her hands were shaking uncontrollably now. "He fell backwards against the fire door. It banged open and he cracked his head on the concrete."

I shuddered, remembering Nick sprawled across the stairwell, his eye destroyed, his hair matted with blood. Then I lunged at Lisbeth. I wanted to shake her so hard her eyes rattled out of her head, but Martinez stopped me. "Why didn't you call 9-1-1? Why didn't you help him?"

"It was too late," she said quietly. "He was already dead."

"So, you left him there in the stairwell, all night long, waiting for someone to find him in the morning so you could play the grief-stricken best friend?"

"But you must understand." She was pleading now. "I had to protect Michiel. None of this would have happened if Nicholas didn't suddenly decide to be one of the good guys."

"Lisbeth, Nick was always one of the good guys." As I said it I was overwhelmed with guilt. I should never have doubted him.

"What happened to the set-stake?" Pritchard asked.

She said, "I took the sign home and planted it in my front yard. The sign guys are picking it up tomorrow." Pritchard glanced at Martinez. That sign would be in police custody within the hour.

We gathered our things. Pritchard pressed the elevator button and we descended to the main lobby in silence. Martinez tucked Lisbeth into the back of the squad car; its red and blue lights flashed across the blank windows of the space destined to become a high-end restaurant. It looked like a glassed-in junkyard.

"Evie, you'll need to come down to the station to make a statement." Pritchard sounded almost apologetic.

"How did you know to come here?"

"You can thank Michiel for that."

"Michiel?"

"Yeah. We picked him up tonight. He called Lisbeth and told her to get him the best criminal defence lawyer in town. I guess the City lawyers won't represent a mayor on corruption charges."

"Nor should they." It was a moment before I realized he wasn't serious.

"When he told her he'd been arrested, she lost it. She said you and your 'good friend' Nicholas betrayed them.

He heard something in her voice and was afraid you'd get hurt."

"He certainly got that right." I flashed back to Lisbeth's blazing eyes. "If you two hadn't arrived when you did..." My knees buckled and I sat down awkwardly on the front steps.

Pritchard called dispatch for a patrol car to take us to the station, then sat down beside me to wait. "Are you sure you're okay?"

"If Michiel's been arrested, it's for accepting bribes. So Calhoon's under arrest too, right?"

"Oh yeah, and he wasn't too happy about the perp-walk to the curb in front of his neighbours. It's already all over the news." I pulled out my phone and tapped my news app. A short clip appeared. Calhoon, a scowl on his face but his head held high, walking with whatever dignity he could muster toward the police car, and his wife Marianne standing in the doorway of their magnificent home, one arm across her chest, the other casually holding a cocktail glass.

36

Five days after the election

Three newspapers, two local and one national, were spread across the table in the conference room. Breathless headlines, variations of *Mayor and Calhoon in Cahoots*, screamed across the front pages. Some columnists suggested they should both be lined up against the wall and shot.

"Well, that didn't take long to land." Keith bit the top off a hard-boiled egg. We were clustered around the conference table, poring over our laptops. Meagan Fellows' earnest voice chirped on Bridget's computer in the reception area. CTV was positioning Meagan as an expert on the Mayor's deepest, darkest secrets based on her limited exposure to him during the televised debate.

"Do they mention Lawson Valentine?" I asked.

Before anyone could respond Madeline flew into the conference room. "We did it!" She paused, noticing the bruises on my neck but stayed true to her train of thought. "We brought down the most powerful men in the City."

"And we lived to tell the tale," I muttered under my breath.

Madeline looked at me carefully. "Your throat...what happened?" I tried to downplay the savagery of Lisbeth's assault, but Madeline was not convinced. "She attacked you?" I nodded. "She *physically* attacked you?" Madeline repeated.

"Yep."

"And you survived? How?" The others laughed when I said I wasn't completely helpless, that I'd hit Lisbeth with a water bottle, slowing her down long enough for Pritchard to arrive.

"Pritchard, what was he doing there?" Keith asked. The chorus of questions grew louder and more persistent. I promised to tell them the whole story after I returned from the police station.

Bridget was valiantly fielding phone calls when I passed her in the reception area. The press had made the connection between Calhoon, Michiel, and Lawson Valentine. I mouthed *police station* at her. She nodded and continued to speak firmly into her headset. No, Mr. Lawson was not available. No, Ms. Valentine and Mr. Braxton were not available. No, she had no idea when they would be available. Yes, she was sorry, goodbye. It would take a Sherman tank to get past that woman.

I put the Mini in gear and joined the remnants of the morning rush hour. Classical music filled the car. I was lost in my thoughts and almost missed the turn into the police station. The brakes squealed as I pulled into a parking spot next to the front door. It was an ugly little building, squat, surrounded on three sides by an asphalt parking lot and backing onto a scruffy field. In the distance I could see railroad tracks. Did Lisbeth's cell look out on to the parking lot or the tracks?

I took a deep breath and entered the building. The clerk summoned Pritchard who led me into an interview room and offered me a coffee.

"So, how are you doing?" he asked.

"I'm not here to talk about my feelings, I'm here to review my statement." That sounded prickly, and I smiled an apology.

"Fair enough." He pushed a piece of paper across the table toward me and we went through it again.

We were just wrapping up when there was a knock at the door. A young police officer popped his head into the room and asked Pritchard if he could spare a moment. Pritchard glanced at me. I shrugged, it was fine with me. Two minutes later he returned and sat down.

"Michiel's been released on bail," he said.

"I'm not surprised, it's not like he murdered anyone. Speaking of murderers, how's Lisbeth?"

Prichard corrected me. "Could be manslaughter, not murder. Michiel got her one of the best criminal lawyers in town. The lawyer wants her to renounce her confession. Mentally unstable or something."

I snorted.

"Yeah, that was Lisbeth's reaction when he suggested it."

"Lisbeth is not going along with it?" Maybe she really is unhinged.

What did I care? I just wanted to sign my statement and

put the horrific experience behind me. The weekend was coming and as Dad would say, with enough rest and strong sweet tea I would be as right as rain.

37

One week after the election

Louisa hovered over me all weekend, urging me to rest and take it easy. I slept fitfully, startled awake by images of Lisbeth and Nick screaming at each other. I assured Louisa I would be fine once I got back into my regular routine.

The following Monday I dressed with care, drove just a little over the speed limit to Lawson Valentine and settled in behind my desk, determined to make progress on at least one of the files Bridget had stacked in a tidy pile on the corner of my desk.

By mid afternoon my eyes were half-shut and my head was drooping onto my chest. It wasn't until I slipped sideways in my chair that I snapped fully awake. I looked around furtively, hoping no one had seen me.

"I was just getting ready to catch you."

"Madeline, you're standing in the doorway. I would be

flat on the floor before you caught me."

She tilted her head. "I'm faster than I look."

"Not in those heels."

She smiled and passed me a piece of paper with a Post-it note stapled to it. "Michiel wants to talk to you."

"You're joking." I looked at the slip of paper. Michiel had left his private cell number.

She looked at me, her eyes softer than I'd ever seen them. "You've been through a lot, Evie. Go home." She took my raincoat off the hook on the back of the door and handed it to me. "I don't want to see you sitting here when I come back, got it?"

"Got it." I slipped into my coat and put a file in my briefcase in the vain hope I would work on it when I got home. When I told Bridget I'd be out for the rest of the day she said Madeline had instructed her to barricade the door if I tried to return. There was nothing left to do but leave.

And yet when I got into the car I hesitated, keenly aware of the slip of paper crumbled into a little ball inside my coat pocket. What could Michiel possibly want to say to me, other than thanks for ruining my life. I dialed his number. He picked up immediately.

"Hello?" He sounded wary.

"You called?"

He cleared his throat. "Uh, yes. Listen, Evie, is there somewhere we could talk?"

"You're kidding, right?" Silence hummed on the line. "Michiel, does your lawyer know you're talking to me?"

"He knows and he's not too happy about it."

I mulled this over.

Michiel spoke again. "Are you still there?"

"Yes, but I'm hanging up now."

"All I'm asking for is ten minutes." The richness in his voice had faded. "Just ten minutes, Evie." He sounded desperate…and sincere. If I didn't talk to him, I would always wonder what he'd wanted.

"Okay, let's talk. You go first," I said.

"No, not on the phone. This needs to be done face to face."

"Seriously, Michiel? Every time someone comes within three metres of you, something horrible happens."

He persisted. "We could meet at Sandy Park, at the firepits near your place."

The firepits aren't that close to my place, but Sandy Park *is* on my way home. I felt a stab of paranoia. Did Michiel know I was in the car and heading home for the day? My apprehension quickly gave way to curiosity.

"I'll be there. We'll talk for ten minutes max, then I'm gone."

"Thanks Evie," he sounded relieved.

"And Michiel, if anything spooks me, I'm gone, you got that?"

"Yes." He hung up.

I wondered if this was the stupidest thing I had ever done. I texted AJ so someone would know where I was going and why.

He immediately texted back: **Are you nuts?**

I responded: **All good, just wanted someone to know.**

Coming with you.

No. Call you. 30 min.

I glanced into the rear-view mirror as I nudged the car into traffic and was relieved to see AJ was not racing to the parking lot to save me from myself.

~

Sandy Park is a large inner-city park that runs along the river. Even now in the cooler, darker days of autumn, joggers clog the footpaths and people lose their dogs in the underbrush. I parked in the gravel lot and crunched down the path to the firepits.

I spotted Michiel before he saw me. He was sitting on a park bench, legs crossed at the ankle, arms slung across the back of the bench, staring at the river. A few metres away two teenage boys were tossing a Frisbee around. The wind was up, blowing the Frisbee off its trajectory. They shouted and cursed, trying to catch it before it sailed into the river.

Michiel started when he saw me. He was wearing a bespoke suit and a soft cashmere overcoat. No hiding under a hoodie and baseball cap for this man. The wind whipped his hair into his eyes, his smile was charming, but a little tentative.

"Why am I here, Michiel?" The wind carried my words away and I had to shuffle a little closer to him to hear what he had to say.

"Thank you so much for coming." Despite the natty clothes and the lovely smile he looked like he hadn't slept in a month. Blowing up your career will do that. "Evie, I want you to know I'm sorry about what happened."

"Which part, the killing Nick part or the bribery part?"

A vein pulsed in his temple and he looked away. "It's easy to stand on the sidelines and criticize, but once you're on the inside you quickly realize you have to play the game or nothing gets done. Especially in the poorer wards. You think anyone in their right mind wants to invest in places like Forest Hills? Politics is a series of trade-offs—"

"—Michiel, what you did was more than a trade-off. You accepted bribes. You crossed the line. You're a lawyer for God's sake."

He shook his head. "I'm not here to discuss the allegations made against me—"

"Good, because it's in the hands of the Public Prosecutor, it has nothing to do with me or the firm."

He put up his hand to silence me. "I want to talk about Lisbeth."

"Lisbeth? What about Lisbeth? That lunatic killed Nick and she almost killed me."

"She didn't mean to," he said.

"She damn well *did* mean to." I spat out the words. "She would have choked the life out of me if Pritchard hadn't stopped her." The thought I'd been suppressing flooded back to me. If Pritchard hadn't arrived when he did, I would have smashed that water bottle against her skull until she stopped moving.

"It's my fault." Michiel watched the boys playing with the Frisbee. One of them was poking a stick into the water. The Frisbee was in the river, stuck on a broken branch just beyond his reach.

"How so?"

He flipped his collar up against the wind and turned to face me. He described his close relationship with Nick in law school and how they'd drifted apart when Nick went to work at Gates, Case and White and Michiel joined a non-profit. Michiel's decision to run for political office revived their friendship and brought Lisbeth into the circle. The three of them saw themselves as the modern-day equivalent of Dumas' champions for justice; they planned to change the world, or at least their little part of it.

Nick and Lisbeth worked tirelessly to get Michiel elected the first time. After Michiel won, Nick left Gates to work as his chief of staff and Lisbeth resigned from a small non-profit to oversee his government relations group.

"That's when things went to hell in a handbasket," Michiel said quietly. "Lisbeth insisted she should report directly to me, not Nick. As far as she was concerned she and Nick were equals."

"That's ridiculous," I said. "Nick was your chief of staff, everyone in the mayor's office reports to the chief of staff, that's why it's called the *chief* of *staff*."

"That's not how Lisbeth saw it."

The sun slipped behind a cloud, easing our park bench into the shadows. Michiel rubbed his hands together to warm them. "I tried to reason with her, but it was hopeless. Lisbeth made it clear to everyone, including Nick, that she reported directly to me. It caused no end of confusion, but in the end I decided to leave well enough alone."

Why do people do that? They say they're leaving well enough alone when all they're doing is sweeping a mess under the rug where it will fester.

Someone yelled. We turned to see the boy lying spread-eagled in the shallow water at the river's edge, one hand gripping the Frisbee. The second boy was on his knees cursing that his pants were wet.

"Well, at least they saved the Frisbee," I muttered. A small smile crossed Michiel's lips.

"I wanted you to understand their relationship when they went into this campaign." Michiel bunched his hands into fists and slid them into his pockets. I found a pair of neon pink gloves in my purse and slipped them on.

"It doesn't matter what I understand about their

relationship," I said. "Nick is dead and Lisbeth confessed to causing his death."

Michiel's eyes met mine. "That's why I wanted to see you. You have to talk to her, tell her to change her plea to not criminally responsible."

"You're joking! You think she should plead insanity? Not a chance. She stabbed him in the eye with that set-stake, she made him fall through the stairwell door, and she left him there to die."

"Evie, she's young, she's bright, you don't understand her background. She clawed her way out of Forest Hills. She made something of herself. We both did. When Nick told her he was going to the police about Calhoon and the numbered company, something snapped."

"Right, let's talk about your numbered company—"

"—No," he said, irritation rising. "I am not going to talk about that. I'm here to talk about Lisbeth. My relationship with Calhoon has nothing to do with this."

That was true. The problem with Lisbeth wasn't Calhoon, it was Michiel who'd failed to understand that her devotion to him was not normal. Rather than address her need for a special place in his universe, he ignored it, hoping it would sort itself out.

My mind returned to the night she attacked me. She greeted me warmly when I arrived. It was only after Michiel called that she turned into a madwoman. The transformation was so fast I didn't realize she intended to kill me until I was on the floor with her hands wrapped around my throat.

I told him I'd consider it.

38

Eight days after the election

You took an unnecessary risk yesterday." AJ loomed in my doorway, standing shoulder to shoulder with Keith; they wore matching scowls.

"And a good morning to you too," I replied cheerfully.

"This is serious, Evie," Keith said. "You can't be pulling stupid stunts like that." I understood his frustration. He was still coming to grips with my decision to confront Calhoon.

"Guys, I know Michiel. He'd never hurt me, or anyone." *At least not intentionally.* They didn't look convinced and I continued. "So, do you want to know what we talked about or not?"

AJ flung himself into my visitor's chair. Keith entered my office more slowly, reluctant to forgive me quite yet.

AJ tipped back in his chair and shouted out the door to Bridget to hold our calls.

"She hates it when you yell down the hall like that," I said. He leaned back in his chair again and yelled out an apology. I shook my head at him. He almost looked contrite.

"To cut to the chase, Michiel wants me to tell Lisbeth to listen to her lawyer. To change her plea from guilty to 'not criminally responsible on account of a mental disorder.'"

AJ was flabbergasted. "An insanity plea? Are you even allowed to talk to Lisbeth? She tried to kill you."

"Her lawyer thinks it's worth a shot." I shrugged. "Obviously, I can't pressure her one way or another. Pleading 'not criminally responsible' isn't a free pass, you know. She'll be incarcerated at a psychiatric facility until the doctors decide she's fit to return to society. The stigma will haunt her for the rest of her life."

They agreed it was my call, which was nice. Neither of them offered to come with me to the police station, which was even nicer.

~

"You're becoming a fixture around here," Pritchard said as he led me to an interview room.

I glanced at him and said, "I have no idea how to respond to that, but I notice you didn't offer me a coffee when I got here."

"You don't like our coffee."

"True."

He stood just inside the door while I sat down on the far side of the table, then he asked, "You ready to see Lisbeth now?"

I nodded and spent five minutes staring out the window after he left. There was a train on the horizon. It looked like it was more than one hundred cars long. What was it hauling, crude oil, canola, wheat?

The door clicked opened and a young female officer appeared with Lisbeth in tow. The officer directed Lisbeth to sit in the chair facing me. Her hair was as smooth and glossy as ever, but the delicate skin around her left eye was mottled black, blue, and yellow. She tucked a strand of hair behind her ear; whenever she did that at Campaign HQ her silver bracelets jangled up her arm. There was no jingling sound today, her bracelets were gone.

"How are you?" Lord, was I starting to feel sorry for her?

"All right, I guess," she said. "Lots of visitors…" Her voice trailed off.

"I'm glad." There was an awkward silence as we eyed each other. She looked down at her hands, the red polish on one nail was chipped.

"Evie," she said, "I'm sorry about…well, you know."

I said I couldn't stay long, I just wanted to make sure she was talking to her lawyer and carefully considering his advice. "Lisbeth, he's one of the best criminal lawyers in the city. He'll have some really good ideas on how to get you back home as quickly as possible."

She hung her head. "I didn't mean to hurt anyone."

"I know you didn't." It shocked me when I realized I believed this to be true. Lisbeth worshipped Michiel. Whatever he did was right and good. She would not, could not, let anyone get in his way. It was as simple as that.

Her hands were loosely clasped on the table in front of her. I covered them with my own. "Lisbeth," I said softly, "promise me you'll talk to your lawyer and discuss his advice with—" I hesitated, did she have a family? "—with people you trust. Promise me you'll do the smart thing, Lisbeth?"

A tear rolled down her porcelain cheek. Then another.

I wanted to tell her Michiel didn't deserve her devotion. He was just like all the rest, an ambitious politician. He may have started with good intentions but quickly surrendered his ideals to stay in power. *We help them, they help us. They get their buildings, we get their money and stay in power to do the good work we were elected to do.* Michiel called it a trade-off. It wasn't a trade-off, it was a tidy rationalization for greed.

She put a hand to her face to brush away the tears. Nothing would be served by telling her the truth. I rose to my feet and said, "Take care of yourself, Lisbeth."

39

The moon sparkled on the river, bobbing up and down in the gentle current. Soft voices floated up to the balcony from the riverbank. The homeless guy was back. He'd set up a makeshift lean-to about fifty metres away from my place. It drove the neighbours crazy, but we couldn't see it from our houses and he wasn't bothering anyone.

"A penny for your thoughts," Louisa said as I drained my wine glass. She put a cheese board laden with brie, crackers, grapes, and olives on the patio table next to a flickering tea light.

"What, no Cheezies?" I asked. She laughed and poured me another glass.

We anchored our paper napkins with our wine glasses and assembled the food on our plates. Mine was heavy on the olives and light on everything else.

She raised her glass in a toast. "Here's to surviving another political campaign."

"I'll drink to that, and to the setting sun, and to the rising moon, and—" I caught the look on Louisa's face

"—I'm kidding!" Four years ago, a sexual predator was terrorizing professional women across the city. It turned out the monster was a lawyer a couple of years ahead of me at Gates. Despite all the warning signs Dennison allowed him to roam unchecked because 'boys will be boys.' This beast of a man almost killed me before he was caught. I began drinking heavily after 'the incident.' It wasn't until Louisa convinced me to see a therapist that I got my drinking under control. I still suffer from bursts of anger that register way too high on the Richter scale.

"Louisa," I said, "I know I put you through hell after… well…you know. Trust me, I'll go right back to Dr. Rose if I think I'm slipping."

She gave me a look, but let it drop. "It's been days since you talked with Lisbeth, any idea what she's going to do?"

"I do, actually." I popped an olive into my mouth. "Lisbeth is taking her lawyer's advice. She's going with the insanity plea, 'not criminally responsible.'"

"Do you think it will work?"

"Maybe. Her lawyer got that society woman off a charge of attempted murder a few years ago. He said her husband's abuse and infidelity drove her to alcohol and drugs and she wasn't in her right mind when she put six bullets in the guy and let him bleed half to death in their garage."

Louisa pursed her lips. "Yeah, well this wasn't attempted murder. Nick is dead. He didn't abuse Lisbeth, she attacked him when he threatened to expose Michiel." She took a sip of wine. "Would it bother you if she got off?"

"Not so much anymore. I'm beginning to think she really is unbalanced." I looked out across the river to the skyscrapers shining in the distance. "Louisa, what's really troubling me is the feeling that I could have done more to protect Nick."

"What on earth are you talking about? You had nothing to do with Nick's death."

"I'm not so sure. A few days after Michiel was arrested, Nick's mother invited me to tea." I paused, the memory of Mrs. Silva greeting me at her front door brought tears to my eyes.

Mrs. Silva had taken me to the pergola in the garden. Like all the estate homes in her neighbourhood, the lawn was a lush green carpet edged with sweeping banks of perennials and carefully trimmed shrubs. We settled under a mountain ash just starting to turn gold. Soon the cedar waxwings would be wobbling around on the flagstones, drunk on fermented berries.

She told me stories about Nick when he was a little boy. He'd always been a stickler for the rules. When he was a fourth-grade school patroller he tried to arrest his teacher for jaywalking.

Mrs. Silva said Nick wasn't going to stay with Michiel after the election. I asked if he was returning to private practice and she said no, he'd inherited some money from his father—Mr. Silva was a geologist who'd started an oil company and sold it to an international conglomerate during the boom—and Nick wanted to give back to the community. He was going to leave the mayor's office and run a foundation for underprivileged kids.

My breath caught in my throat as I remembered the look of pride on Mrs. Silva's face.

"We had such a pleasant visit," I said. "Mrs. Silva is all alone now. I promised I would come back soon, but I don't know if I can. I feel so guilty."

Louisa pushed the cheese board closer to me, refusing

to acknowledge the quaver in my voice. "Why? You have nothing to feel guilty about."

An animal crashed through the bushes beneath the balcony, I glanced at Quincy who raised his head but showed no interest in pursuing it. "Nick tried to talk to me the night he died. We sat on his balcony in the dusk. He said things I didn't understand then, but I understand now."

"What kinds of things?"

"He dismissed Michiel's campaign promise to build in the downtown core. He almost lost his temper when I said Michiel's ability to deliver on that promise depended on the developers' pocketbooks." *It always comes down to the developers' pocketbooks.* I looked down at my half-empty wine glass. "Maybe if I had listened, if I'd let him open up, he would still be alive..."

Louisa shook her head impatiently. "Evie, don't you dare blame yourself for Nick's death. It was Michiel, not you, who accepted the bribes. It was Michiel, not you, who tried to make Nick complicit in his corruption. Michiel knew Lisbeth was unstable, but still he used her on his campaign. She killed Nick and she tried to kill you. There is nothing you could have done to stop her. Nothing."

"I know, but still—"

"No, stop, we're not discussing this any longer." In classic Louisa fashion the matter was closed. But she was right. It was time to put it all behind me.

Louisa was in the middle of an animated story about an attractive new intern who'd joined the neuro group when my phone pinged with a text.

"Who is it?" she asked as I glanced at my phone.

"Sarah Hamilton." I rubbed Quincy's ear. He was plastered against my leg, praying something would drop off the table.

"What does she want?" She narrowed her eyes. "No, wait, don't tell me. She came close to winning against Michiel the last time, and she's going to run again in the race to replace him. She wants you on her team, right?"

"Perhaps..."

Louisa set her plate down and glared at me. "Please tell me you're not considering it."

Our eyes met over the top of my wine glass. "You said it yourself, Sarah is different from the rest."

"Oh for God's sake, Evie!" Louisa turned to Quincy, grabbed his head and stared directly into his eyes. "You are not allowed to leave Auntie Evie's side, *ever*, do you understand me?"

I laughed and tossed Quincy a cracker. ❧

ACKNOWLEDGMENTS

So many wonderfully talented people shared their time and talent in support of this book. I'd like to thank a few of them here.

Thank you to the CWC judges who read the manuscript and provided invaluable feedback, and Pip Wallace, my editor who improved the book immeasurably, and Joanna Vander Vlugt, my publisher, whose energy and creativity knows no bounds.

A special thank you to those who work in the legal profession, your dedication is inspiring, and to the volunteers who support political campaigns, you are truly fearless.

Thank you to colleagues in the writing business including the wonderfully welcoming people at Sisters in Crime and Crime Writers of Canada. It's true, writers really do help writers.

Gratitude to my dear friends for your support and encouragement over the years.

A special thanks to four of most important women in my life: my mother Mary Szasz, and my sisters Rose Marie MacKenzie-Kirkwood, Linda Maki and Joanna Vander Vlugt.

I've dedicated this book to my remarkable family, my husband Roy, the most wonderful man in the world, and my daughters Kelly and Eden, brave and funny, who would have clocked the villain long before Evie did.

Finally thank you to my readers, you bring the story to life.

About the Author

©Photo by Barbara Blakey
honeycreative.ca

Susan Jane Wright studied anthropology and architecture before settling on law. She worked as a litigator before moving in–house. Her career has taken her from the boardrooms of Calgary to the streets of Beijing.

She writes legal thrillers. *Box of Secrets* is her debut novel and the first in the Evie Valentine mystery series. It was a finalist in the 2021 Crime Writers of Canada Award of Excellence for Best Unpublished Manuscript.

When she's not writing she's travelling with her husband and two daughters. Her favourite vacation was a trip from Prague to London on the Orient Express.
https://susanjanewright.ca

www.ingramcontent.com/pod-product-compliance
Ingram Content Group UK Ltd.
Pitfield, Milton Keynes, MK11 3LW, UK
UKHW012251290726
14090UKWH00016B/593